Heretic's Daughter
Sarai's Journey, Book 1

By Michelle L. Levigne

 Zion Ridge Press LLC

Mt Zion Ridge Press LLC
295 Gum Springs Rd, NW
Georgetown, TN 37366

https://www.mtzionridgepress.com

Copyright © 2020 by Michelle L. Levigne
ISBN 13: 978-1-949564-79-2

Published in the United States of America
Publication Date: March 1, 2020

Editor-In-Chief: Michelle Levigne
Executive Editor: Tamera Lynn Kraft
Editor: Deborah Cullins Smith
Cover Art Copyright by Mt Zion Ridge Press LLC © 2020

Inn of the Healer
Sarai's Journey, Book 2

Coming April 2020

Author's Note:

This is entirely a work of fiction, a product of my imagination, sparked by long hours sitting backstage with the cast and crew of the Easter pageant my church produced for thirteen years in a row. We occasionally discussed other approaches to telling the story of Easter. One was the viewpoint of the people whose lives Jesus changed. I make no claim to any biblical/historical accuracy, when it comes to actual people and events beyond what is stated in the Bible. Church history most likely disagrees with me on the movements and fates of real people mentioned in this book and its sequel, **Inn of the Healer.** *My knowledge comes from Sunday school lessons, Bible trivia contests, and efforts to research Bible-era geography and terminology. An earlier, shorter version of this story was published with By Grace Publishing, under the title,* **The Price.**

Jesus' teachings are taken from the NIV and ESV translations of the Bible. The specific references are listed below. After all these years and revisions, there is no way to determine which translation originally provided which specific wording. NIV is copyright 1973, 1978, 1984 and 2011 by Biblica Inc. ESV is copyright 2001 by Crossway, a division of Good News Publishers.

Parable of the sower: Matthew 13, Mark 4, Luke 8
Parable of the Pearl of Great Price: Matthew 13
Parable of the Weeds in the Wheat: Matthew 13
Beatitudes/Sermon on the Mount: Matthew 5, 6, 7
Predicting the Weather: Matthew 16
Take Up Your Cross: Matthew 16
Man of Sorrows: Isaiah 53
Lord of the Sabbath/Healing on the Sabbath: Matthew 12
Final Judgment (did it not to the least of these): Matthew 25
Rocks Will Cry Out: Luke 19

Chapter One

"Life and death always arrive together," Midwife Huldah had taught Sarai early in their time together as teacher and pupil. "As you rejoice and sing over the new life in your arms, do not sing too loudly. Otherwise you will make death curious, and both joy and sorrow might enter the same house."

Years later, Sarai realized there were many kinds of death. The worst death was not physical, but in the heart and soul, and so the greatest pain. Sometimes, though, if El Shaddai was merciful, death led to life.

That morning, however, she didn't look for shadows of ill omen or sorrow on the path back to her father's home, in the cool, rosy light of dawn. Sarai hummed the song she had sung over Lydia's newborn son as she washed him, rubbed him with salt and oil, and swaddled him. Her father's steward, Enoch, walked beside her to frighten away shadows and beggars and any brutes who might threaten the only daughter of the wealthiest rabbi in Bethany.

When they reached the gates of the household, Enoch exchanged a smile with her. Their steps divided, he to the back portion and servants' quarters, and she to walk through the inner courtyard and up the stairs to her chambers. Sarai's sandal caught on one of the steps, but she barely noticed. Her mind was full of the memory of the sweet weight of the newborn. When would she hold her own child? Sometimes, it seemed that day would never come. Jude ben Boaz had returned eight days ago from his trading journey, all the way to exotic Britannia. He had yet to come visit. He had yet to formalize the understanding between their families that she would become his wife. She was a woman grown now. Why was Jude delaying?

Perhaps the understanding was only on her part? Maybe Jude had only pretended to want to marry her, as part of the rivalry with the other boys, back when he was her father's student.

Miriam, her nurse, was waiting when Sarai reached her room. She clucked and bustled about, hurrying Sarai to the curtained bathing area off the kitchen courtyard. A vat of rainwater and clean clothes and cleansing oil waited, for the ritual purification. Just once, couldn't that wait? Her belly ached emptily, but even more than breakfast, Sarai wanted to go to bed. Lydia's husband had come to fetch her before midnight, to assist Huldah. Miriam could not be dissuaded, however. Sarai needed to be purified from the ceremonial uncleanness attached to childbirth. Better to obey than irritate the faithful nurse so she spoke with Sarai's father. Enough people told Rabbi Eliakim ben Levi it was not seemly for his daughter to assist Huldah and pursue her healing studies. No need for Miriam to add her voice to the critics. The daughter of a wealthy, respected and renowned scholar had better things to do than serve as a healer and midwife. Or so the loudest, most critical voices claimed. Miriam was proud of Sarai's education, able to read and write and keep household records, but considered her studies of the healing arts from many cultures and countries frivolous. Something to keep Sarai busy until an appropriately wealthy and socially prominent man made her his wife.

Sarai thought sometimes only her father understood her need to learn healing after the inexplicable illness that had killed her mother. None of the girls she had been friends with understood her passion for more knowledge, or her satisfaction in finding brews and pastes of herbs that eased the suffering of the ill.

Miriam brought the soft-bristled brush to scrub Sarai all over and rub the sweet-smelling cleansing herbs into her skin. She closed her eyes and stretched out on the sheet spread on the tiles and drifted into a half-doze as her nurse scrubbed her. She didn't rouse very far when the elderly woman questioned her about the baby, and which member of the family the boy looked like. Miriam clucked sympathetically, when Sarai related how a messenger had come for Huldah before she finished the ritual cup of sweetened wine the family offered them. Old Zenobia, widow of the stonemason Hiram, had been bedridden for two months now, and her sons feared she would soon breathe her last.

"Next time, Huldah will take me with her," Sarai said. "It's time for me to learn the other part of a healer's duties. Serve Adonai in guiding new life into the world, and sing the songs of parting as they step once more into His presence."

"Time enough for you to taste that bitterness." Miriam grunted and stepped back.

Sarai heard the scraping of pottery on stone, all the warning she had before rainwater gushed over her, rinsing the cleansing oil away. Sputtering, she rolled over and sat up. A weary chuckle escaped her. She rubbed water from her eyes and reached for the drying sheet lying across the nearby bench.

Her raven hair was still wet as the call rang through the household for her father's students to assemble in the courtyard for breakfast. Sarai chose to take her breakfast on the roof, overlooking the inner courtyard, so she could sit in the sun and let her hair dry, and not have to fuss with combs and pins and veils. These boys studying the scriptures and Israel's history under her father had barely been with him a year. She wouldn't scandalize them by joining them for breakfast and the morning recitations and prayers. Lydia's husband had awakened everyone when he came to fetch Sarai in the middle of the night, so the entire household knew where she had gone. Some of the boys were the sons and grandsons of the strictest Pharisees. They would consider her unclean after attending a birth. The leading families in Jerusalem still trusted Rabbi Eliakim ben Levi to give their sons a solid foundation, despite the criticism of High Priest Annas.

Sarai's drowsy good mood faded as she spread honey on the warm bread and listened to her father take the boys through the passages he had given them to memorize yesterday. Gone were the days when she could listen to her father teach on the prophecies she found truly fascinating. The passages referring to the coming Messiah as the Suffering Servant of El Shaddai, or speaking of sacrifice and paying the debt of rebellion and sin incurred by the descendants of Israel. Something had gone out of her father when he agreed to Annas' orders, delivered through Caiaphas, that he leave such heretical thoughts for the young boys to discover on their own. He still had such discussions with some of his scholar friends, those few still brave enough to remain his friends despite the increasing condemnation from Annas and his ambitious son-in-law. Even greatly revered Gamaliel still came to speak with Rabbi Eliakim, though more time passed between each visit. Sarai wondered if his extremely ambitious, rigidly self-righteous student, Saul of Tarsus, was finally having an influence on the aging scholar.

Still, she had hope that perhaps tonight some friends would

come, and Sarai could listen to them discuss rumors and hints of fulfillment of prophecy. They might speak again of a new wandering rabbi who had become the talk of Judea. She thought perhaps three weeks had passed since the last moonlight discussion. Surely it was time for another?

She stayed on the roof after her father dismissed the boys to pair off and help each other memorize another column from the scroll of the prophet Jeremiah. Enoch came to speak with Rabbi Eliakim before the boys had finished filing out of the courtyard of whitewashed stones. Sarai thought Enoch didn't look worried. She couldn't see her father's face in the shadows of the high wall. He gestured for Enoch to lead the way, and the two men departed.

By the time she had found her veil and gathered up the tray with her breakfast and her brush, she heard the front gates opening. Her father was gone, most likely heading out to the vineyard or the wheat fields to oversee something. She blamed her need for rest for the sudden dropping sensation in her belly. There was no real reason to feel so upset that she hadn't wished her father good morning yet.

Dorcas met her at the bottom of the stairs with a little scroll Eliakim had purchased yesterday when he was in Jerusalem. He had planned to spend the morning break in lessons discussing it with her. Since he was called away, he didn't want her to wait for the treat. Sarai thanked the servant girl and hurried off to her rooms, studying the heavy cloth sleeve on the scroll. The markings indicated this was another healing text to add to her collection. Several symbols weren't quite familiar. She guessed it came from Phoenicia, or Greece. Sarai hurried to dress her hair properly for the day and returned to the rooftop, where she could study in peace and have privacy to lie down and nap when she needed to.

Inside the sleeve was a note from her father's merchant friend, the Nubian Ebed, begging his indulgence. Much of the scroll contained invocations to several minor Greek deities of healing, but it also held recipes and instructions for preparing healing potions, which he thought the rabbi and his scholarly daughter would find interesting. Sarai smiled, remembering her first encounter with the massive ebony-skinned man. She had been nine, and still prone to stuff her veil into her belt to get it out of her way. That day, her father had taken her with him to visit Ebed's shop. Sarai had been

4

proudly reading aloud the inscription on the tag attached to a Greek scroll when the big man came around the corner. He had been amused at such a small girl who could read, as he put it, "such enormous, scholarly words." He had also been kind, and ever since made efforts to find something of interest for her, when he sought out scholarly writings for Rabbi Eliakim's library. When Sarai accompanied her father into Jerusalem, Ebed always had exotic treats to share with her. He teased her that if she was not careful, she would be swept up and away, to grace an emperor's palace, her education and intelligence treated as a great curiosity.

"How are you ever going to find a husband if you waste your time reading?" Her brother, Joseph paused at the top of the stairs and peered at her. His eyes looked bloodshot even from the far side of the roof. He braced himself on the half-wall and raked a hand through his tangled brown hair.

His wrinkled clothes were the ones he wore yesterday. Sarai guessed he had been out all night and had just returned. That had become a bad habit for Joseph. She felt a flicker of sympathy for Abner, her friend Norah's persistent suitor. Malachi, Norah's father, didn't like Abner because his association with the Zealots had brought them to meet in his inn. No good would come of their activities or their presence, he kept insisting. Joseph also worked with the Zealots. Their father regularly scolded Joseph for his risky choices in friends and activities. He warned that the day was approaching when he would have to bar his only son from his house, if he didn't mend his ways.

"I don't need to find a husband," Sarai said, after considering other responses. None sounded pleasant. "Father has that task well in hand."

"That is a matter of opinion." He winked and dropped down on the stool on the other side of the low table where she had spread the scroll. "It seems to me you have several suitors, and Father hasn't managed to send any of them away."

"Several?" Sarai's recent thoughts about Jude returned. To her irritation, she also thought of Simon, another of her father's former students.

Jude, Simon, and four other young men had been students together, growing up in her father's household. All six had declared at one time or another that when they were grown, they would marry their teacher's pretty daughter. Jude was the only one Sarai had wanted to encourage, and she knew better than to give him anything more encouraging than smiles.

The rivalry had prompted the other four students to be cruel to Simon. His father barely had enough funds to give his son the education he needed to become a scholar or scribe. Rumors and gossip said that a half-brother had persuaded several unethical lawgivers and a judge to side with him, so he received the entire estate when their father died. Simon had worked in Rabbi Eliakim's orchards and vineyard to help pay the cost of his education, and only Jude had refused to mock him for it.

None of the other students had lived up to their boasts that they would be successful enough to win Sarai as bride. Jude's wealth from his merchant father made him more than acceptable as a suitor. Simon would be a success someday. Just not now. He was an assistant to Rabbi Nicodemus, a prominent and respected member of the Sanhedrin. His future looked bright, but only time would tell if his intelligence and wit would ensure him a position of prominence and wealth. He lived in Rabbi Nicodemus' home, and had little income to speak of. He still wore the clothes he had when he lived in Rabbi Eliakim's home, because he spent most of his coins on scrolls or other equipment for his position as scholar and scribe. When Simon came every few months to pursue his suit before Rabbi Eliakim, Sarai tried to avoid him. She thought she was kind when she refused the small gifts he made for her. She wasn't sure what her father said, but she knew he refused Simon each time.

Simon couldn't seem to understand that it wasn't his lack of wealth that made him unacceptable. Rabbi Eliakim ben Levi refused Simon for Sarai because of his position on the teachings about the Messiah. Simon consistently echoed everything taught by Annas and Caiaphas. He was barely apologetic, though always respectful, when he told his former teacher that he was wrong, Messiah would never come in humble state and suffer before restoring Israel.

"Here, what's wrong?" Joseph said, yanking Sarai from her musings. He reached across the table and caught her chin with his bent finger, to make her tip her head up.

"You were out with the Zealots again, weren't you?" she said, instead of confessing the twinges of guilt she felt toward Simon, and the worry that Jude had changed his mind.

"So what if I was? There's work that needs doing. Our leaders certainly aren't resisting the evil of Rome."

"Are you at least careful?"

"Don't worry." He smiled and twisted his hand to cup her cheek for a moment before getting up to leave. "Adonai smiles on the righteous and guides their paths."

Sarai watched him go down the stairs, their father's words catching in her throat so she couldn't speak them: there was a vast difference between the righteousness of Adonai, and the righteousness that men claimed to justify cruel or selfish actions.

She was still reading on the roof when her father returned to the house. She nearly called down to him, but the sight of his bowed shoulders and shuffling steps halted her. Lately, her father looked so weary and concerned. Sometimes, his skin was nearly as gray as his hair, as if the same illness that killed her mother had come to claim him now. Sarai waited until Rabbi Eliakim went into the house, then rolled up her scroll, slid it back into the protective sleeve, and crept down the stairs. She was halfway across the inner courtyard when Caleb appeared from the front of the house, leading Simon.

His black beard looked thicker, and the cap perched on the back of his head had gold embroidery along the seams. She was surprised how pleased she was that he was dressing better. Simon looked like a well-to-do young scholar, just as Rabbi Nicodemus' assistant was expected to look.

"Sarai." Simon's handsome face lit up as he smiled at her.

Her heart sank with that odd guilt she always felt toward him. She liked him, despite how he disagreed with her father's teaching. She liked how his smile made her feel she was the only person he saw at that moment. Yet she knew better than to give even a tiny piece of her heart to a man who would not be her husband.

"Good morning, Simon. My father is about to resume lessons, but I believe he will take the time to speak with you." She gestured at the five boys entering the courtyard, their arms full of scrolls and slates.

"I came to see you, Sarai." Simon glanced at Caleb, who offered a sad smile. Simon had been well-liked by all her family's servants.

"You know that is not proper. You are no longer a student or a member of our household." She took a step backwards. "Please, do not make me order you to leave and not come back."

"You could never be cruel." He bowed again, a soft smile making his face so handsome it sent a pang through her chest. When he stood straight again, he held out a box of olive wood, carved in the shape of a rose. "I promised you a box for your treasures, do you remember?"

The momentary tightness in her throat was so strong, she couldn't breathe, let alone speak. Sarai blinked away a ridiculous urge for tears and took a step backward. Another pang hit her heart when the light left Simon's eyes.

"It is not proper for you to give me gifts." She stopped his protest with a raised hand. "My father permitted it when I was just a little girl. It is indecent, now that I am a woman." If only she could say she was betrothed to Jude. Surely that would stop him. When would Jude keep his promise? "My father will never give me to you. Be a man. Show the wisdom that made him so proud of you."

She turned sharply and hurried into the house. Behind her, she heard her father's weary voice speak Simon's name.

~~~~~

Thoughts of Simon and Jude swirled through Sarai's head. Why was the acceptable man so slow in keeping his promises, and the man her father refused so persistent? She was tired, but couldn't sleep, her head humming with irritation and worry.

The best way to quiet her mind was to work with her hands. Old Dinah smiled when Sarai entered the kitchen and joined her on the long bench where she spent her days. The frail old woman understood her even better than Miriam did, and said nothing about Simon's visit. That was kind of her. Sarai suspected some household servants, who had been with them long enough to be considered family, thought Simon a better choice for husband than Jude. Enoch had even told her Jude's father was too much in fear of High Priest Annas to permit the marriage.

She worked hard in the kitchen, scalding and then plucking the ducks for the evening meal, then kneading bread. Anticipating her father's pleasure with her industriousness restored her morning calm. Sarai had just picked up a pomegranate to cut open the rind when Enoch came to the kitchen to fetch her.

"Jude ben Boaz is here," he whispered, as he led her down the hall to the courtyard.

Sarai muffled a squeak of mortification. She had flour streaks on her dress. Her hair had come out of its braids and clung to the sides of her face in damp tendrils.

Some consolation, though. Enoch had said nothing about Jude's father, Boaz, being here. There would be no talk of a betrothal on this visit. At least Jude had come to see her. At last.

"Ah, my daughter, busy in the kitchen?" Eliakim nodded, his face bright with approval when Sarai stepped into the courtyard. He held out a hand to beckon her to sit with him.

She tugged her veil into place and stole a glance at Jude as she hurried to join her father. He was still as slim and carelessly elegant as ever, with his sandy hair and his fine clothes. His honey-colored eyes were bright as he smiled and bowed to Sarai. No flicker of distaste marred his expression and she laughed at her relief.

"I am leaving on another trip, Sarai, and your father permits me to give you a gift, to apologize for not visiting sooner."

She murmured her thanks and hoped she kept her disappointment from her expression. Her friend Ruth, the cloth merchant's daughter, would tell her to be grateful Jude knew he needed to apologize. Then she gasped with delight as he opened a shallow wooden box to reveal pins for her hair, shaped like birds, made of silver and brilliantly colored glass. Her pleasure in the gift faded as she listened to the men discuss Jude's upcoming return to Britannia, to trade for tin. She was glad for him, because it showed his father trusted him with delicate tasks, but the long trip meant Jude would be gone for months. Again.

Sarai knew better than to show disappointment. She thanked Jude for his gift and took some encouragement from the warmth of her father's words of farewell.

"He will be good to you, my dear," Rabbi Eliakim said, after he walked Jude to the household gates and returned to the courtyard.

"Yes, Father." Sarai took the red bird out of her hair and put it back in the box.

"I long for the day he finalizes our agreement." He laughed, a weary sound, when Sarai inhaled sharply. "Yes, we have spoken of the day he will make you his wife. Nothing definite, but a good foundation. Are you pleased with this?"

"Yes, Father." She pressed her hands against her warming

cheeks. "You know I am."

He sank down on the bench next to her and patted her knee. "I wish Jude had already asked for you. Many cruel things could happen between now and that happy day when I see you stand under the marriage canopy with your husband. I need to be sure someone will take care of you, should anything happen to me."

"But Father, Joseph --"

"Your brother loves you, yes, but his associates …" He sighed. "I will not speak of such things even in the safety of our house. Rome punishes a man's entire family for his crimes, or simply choosing the wrong friends. I admire Malachi ben Joachim, who can protect his family even as he stands on his principles."

Malachi, Norah's father, ran a prosperous inn on the edge of Jerusalem, on Spindle Street. Norah was famous for her cookery, which had helped build the fame of Malachi's inn. Recently, some of the Sanhedrin had been speaking against him. He refused to ban Gentiles from his inn. They now insinuated that Norah's popularity came not from her cooking skills, but because she and the inn's serving girls were playing the harlot. Malachi faced down some of them in the outer courts of the Temple and demanded justice. Either they bring proof of their words, slandering his daughter, or they pay a penalty. Of course, the young Pharisees couldn't bring any proof. When people mocked them, they played the injured party, pretending to be aghast that their word alone wasn't enough to condemn the young women to be stoned. In response, Malachi amused and scandalized Jerusalem by setting up Norah in her own household and business, to create feasts for weddings and births and other celebrations.

Abner and other suspected Zealots were known to meet at the inn on Spindle Street. Several Roman officers friendly to Malachi had warned him to send them away. They didn't want him to be penalized, if those young men were caught acting against Rome.

"Joseph … has promised he will be careful." Sarai understood too clearly her father's reluctance to even speak about her brother's activities. "Besides, nothing will happen to you." She took hold of his hand and pressed it to her cheek. "You will live to have your grandsons as your students and watch them stand under the same marriage canopy where I stood."

"You make me believe life will always be kind to us," her father murmured. He turned his hand in her grasp, to cup her cheek. "Troubled times are upon us, my child, and I am an old man whose health is not as strong as it once was. The cruel truth is that I do not trust your brother to guard you as you deserve."

"Father --"

"Joseph makes promises, but his anger overcomes his common sense. He thinks he keeps his actions and friends secret from me. However, ignorance is no protection against Rome's wrath."

~~~~~

Caiaphas came to the house that evening. Sarai was in her room, reading her new scroll. She heard the semi-familiar male voice, raised in anger, rolling through the house, and she shuddered. There were few men arrogant enough to raise their voices to Rabbi Eliakim ben Levi in his own house.

She crept out of her room to look down into the courtyard and verify her suspicious. Yes, it was Caiaphas. She agreed with Ruth. Caiaphas had taken on more of the authority he would wear when he was confirmed as High Priest, after his father-in-law, Annas. If he chose to expel Rabbi Eliakim from the synagogue in Bethany, or even prohibit him from entering the Temple in Jerusalem, would anyone stand against him? Would anyone speak up for her father? Annas had reprimanded Rabbi Eliakim several times over the years, accusing him of entertaining heresy. Surely her father hadn't written or taught anything in months that would bring Caiaphas to their house to rebuke him. What had brought Caiaphas to Bethany at this time of the evening, to speak with such anger?

Sarai heard Caiaphas speak her name and nearly cried out. She gripped the railing and strained to hear through the thudding of her heart. Fury accompanied her fear when she heard Lydia's name and she understood. Lydia's uncle was a tax collector. That besmirched the entire family. Caiaphas didn't condemn Huldah, Sarai noticed, for attending the birth this morning. Yet it was unseemly for Sarai to act as midwife for Lydia.

"Some have asked how you can condone your daughter acting as a midwife. A virgin should know nothing of such things." Caiaphas tipped his head back, his sneer even more pronounced and clear in the torchlight and shadows streaking the courtyard. "Perhaps you permit her this because she is no longer a virgin?"

Sarai pressed both hands over her mouth to stifle her gasp. Yes, she had heard the muttering, the criticism. Not for an unmarried girl to work as a healer, but for the daughter of a wealthy rabbi to "soil her hands with the unwashed and lowly," in the words of several women Sarai tried to avoid. Huldah had been criticized several times, in front of Sarai, for taking her as a student. She always quoted the words of many rabbis, about wasting the gifts given by Adonai. Which was the greater sin? To let talents that would benefit others sit idle? To let mere men determine the best time to use those talents? To let an intelligent young woman see the suffering and pain of the world, and the results of the joining of man and woman, which was blessed by Adonai?

"Father?" Joseph's shout cut through Sarai's spinning thoughts.

She raced down the stairs and into the courtyard, shoving aside servants who got in her way. The scene seemed all the more unreal in the flickering light of the lanterns and the long, wavering spill of shadows. Sarai found her father, sprawled in a trembling heap on the paving stones. With a cry, she went to her knees next to him. Joseph knelt on Rabbi Eliakim's other side, grasping his shoulders, trying to hold him flat. Their father's face was gray, his mouth twisted with pain. His left arm and leg stuck out stiffly, trembling, while his right side lay limp and pale.

"What did you do to him?" She stared up at Caiaphas.

His lip curled up on one side. "I would not soil my hands." He turned with a swirl of his robes and faced their staring, muttering servants. "Take heed. This is the punishment reserved for those who blaspheme against --"

With a roaring cry, Joseph leaped to his feet and lunged at Caiaphas. Two manservants caught him, stopping him before he could lay hands on the priest. Spitting and cursing, Joseph struggled to get free. Caiaphas sneered at him and stalked out of the courtyard.

Chapter Two

For the next three days, the only time Sarai left her father's side was to consult her small library of scrolls. Surely somewhere in all that collected knowledge, there was a treatment for the paralysis, the gray skin? She thought she would gladly trade all her education, all her scrolls, for one simple recipe that would return her father's control over his body.

She sang psalms to him, and when her throat hurt from dryness, she played the small flute of olive wood Simon had carved for her years ago. Rabbi Eliakim managed to smile for her, but nothing more.

When she wasn't searching or brewing new potions, she didn't leave his side. Not to wash or sleep or eat. She refused to leave when the physician came to examine him and when priests came to anoint Rabbi Eliakim with oil and say prayers over him for healing. She thought of her lovely new hair pins and vowed to give all her jewelry to the Temple, if Yahweh would heal her father.

On the fourth day, Rabbi Eliakim managed to raise his right hand to touch hers, when she spooned broth into his mouth. Sarai was so startled, she dropped the bowl on herself. A crooked smile twitched the right side of her father's mouth, but the left side stayed twisted, as if the flesh had frozen that way. Sarai wept and laughed as she called Miriam to get more broth.

When her father finished eating, he made a rasping, gargled sound that might have been her name, closed his eyes and went to sleep. Sarai spread blankets on the floor next to his bed and allowed herself to sleep. Surely the healing had begun.

Three hours later, the utter stillness of the house woke her. She washed her face in the stale water sitting in the basin and went to see what had changed.

Her father's students were gone. Men sent by the Sanhedrin took the boys back to their parents and posted a notice on the gates. Rabbi Eliakim ben Levi had been forbidden to take students. He was henceforth banned from the Temple for speaking heresy and perverting the Scriptures.

Sarai searched for her brother to learn what they should do about the judgment. Joseph had left the household and none of the servants knew where he had gone. They could guess, though.

He had snarled under his breath about the Sanhedrin playing Rome's games, saying they would sell their own parents to the slave galleys if it would keep the peace with Rome. "No peace while there's a single Roman in Judea," he had growled, before taking his cloak and marching away.

~~~~~

For two months, Sarai rarely saw her brother. Their father's care demanded all her time and energy. Joseph tended to the household's business, looking after the fields and orchards and vineyard. Nothing mattered but preserving the household just as it was, against the day their father could rise from his sickbed and return to his daily routine.

Rabbi Eliakim did not rise from his bed. As the moon waxed and waned, he gradually lost the daily struggle to feed himself and to speak. He spent more time asleep, tormented by pain or unhappy dreams that made him whimper like a child. At the new moon, his spirit quietly slipped away in the night.

There were few mourners beyond his children and servants to follow the body to the tomb cut into the hillside outside of Bethany. Sarai didn't care about the absence of her father's last students or their parents. They were already proven cowards. She tried not to care about the absence of her father's grown students. So many of them lived far from Jerusalem and Bethany and couldn't come back in time for the burial. She cared deeply about the absence of the scribes and scholars who had spent many hours at her father's table, discussing matters of prophecy and law. Despite their long friendship with Rabbi Eliakim ben Levi, they didn't send even a word of sorrow or sympathy to his children. None of them but Rabbi Nicodemus. He alone had visited Eliakim in his decline, and now brought jars of myrrh and aloes for the burial spices, in a final gesture of love and respect.

However, Simon's presence, standing between Enoch and Caleb, surprised her. She was sure Simon cared more about the approval of High Priest Annas than the loyalty he owed to the rabbi who had made him an educated man. His gaze met hers once, he bowed, then walked away. Something shriveled inside her. Despite the Sanhedrin, he *had* come to honor her father. She was grateful. Yet he would not speak words of comfort and mourning to her. What was wrong with her to want some sweetness from him?

Jude did not appear. Not at the tomb, and not once during the days of mourning when guests were permitted to come to the house to eat and sit in silence with the bereaved. Joseph's Zealot friends came openly, and Norah, but not Ruth. No one said if Jude had returned from his long journey. Sarai refused to ask after him.

Word came that Annas and Caiaphas said Yahweh had struck Rabbi Eliakim for his heresy. Joseph laughed once, when a Zealot friend brought the news. He said that explained much about the absence of so many people who once claimed to revere their father. Everyone cared more about their position in the Sanhedrin than they did about a man who had fed and taught and comforted them in times of pain and loss.

Joseph went out at all hours of the day and night. He brought his Zealot friends home with him, to grumble and plot and draw maps of Roman fortresses and discuss troop movements. Sarai retired to her rooms when those quietly angry men came into the house. She worked on her mother's loom or tried to play her flute, because she had lost all love for her studies. She shuddered when she heard several men ask Joseph, "Your pretty sister, she's not married or betrothed, is she?" Or other questions in similar lines.

Still, Jude did not come.

~~~~~

The days drifted by in a fog, and Sarai couldn't shake off the malady in her spirit. Then, nearly a full month after her father died, Simon came. She heard him arguing with Joseph at the gates of the house. Later, she could almost laugh at herself, how her heart skipped a few beats and the gray feeling left her spirit at the sound of Simon's voice. Something warmed inside her at the thought that Simon respected his former teacher enough to defy the edict against his household. She crept down the stairs to hide in the shadows and listen. Simon announced he wished to take her as his wife.

"My father refused you, for many reasons you know," Joseph said. A gate hinge creaked, and Sarai imagined him stepping back, already pushing the panel closed.

"I offer her honorable marriage, and a safe future," Simon said, a tinge of anger in his voice. "You put her at risk of being sold as a slave, if the Romans discover what you and your friends have been doing. Or worse. Pretty girls have been given to an entire barracks to share, to punish their fathers or brothers or husbands."

"Aaron will take good care of my sister."

Sarai thought through Joseph's Zealot friends. At least Aaron didn't frighten her or make her feel filthy and weak when he looked at her. She had even spoken to him a few times about healing salves and powders. He seemed to value her training as a healer. Was that why Joseph had agreed to give her to him? But why hadn't her brother at least warned her what he intended to do?

"How, when one mistake will have all of you crucified, or at best slaving on a rower's bench? You wouldn't risk your sister's life, her honor, if you didn't need his father's skill as a blacksmith, for weapons. Or his brother's caravans to smuggle people and weapons and stolen supplies." Simon's beautiful voice cracked in fury. "Mark my words, Joseph, you'll destroy yourself if you continue with Barabbas. You'll destroy Sarai. Don't you have any love for her?"

"My sister is none of your concern. Sometimes even family comes second to scouring the Roman filth from Israel."

Sarai backed away, trembling, while the men continued to argue, and ended up in the kitchen. She was proud that she didn't burst into useless tears, but she shuddered and looked so pale that Dinah cried out in alarm. Quickly, the words poured out, sharing what she had heard, what she guessed, in the men's argument.

"I overheard enough, but I didn't want to believe it was true," Dinah said, her voice lowered and as grave as her expression. "Aaron wants to send you to one of the Zealot fortresses to tend the men injured in raids."

Sarai shuddered, and wished she could feel flattered. Some friends of her father had disagreed with his decision to educate her. Several insisted that pursuing the healing knowledge of Gentiles would endanger her. Perhaps they were right? Would Aaron want her as his wife if she wasn't useful to the Zealot cause?

"You need to go to Jude ben Boaz, and if you have to, shame him into honoring his agreement with your father," Dinah said, with a sharp, decisive nod for punctuation.

Sarai choked on something thick rising up in her throat, laughter and tears and panic combined. "I can't simply confront --"

"No, but you haven't seen your friends in Jerusalem since before your father fell ill. You and Miriam and Caleb should go into Jerusalem, tomorrow morning. Visit your friends. Stop at Ruth's shop to get cloth for new clothes for the household." The old woman had a glint of mischief in her eyes. "That might be all you need to do. Let her do the fighting for you."

Sarai's mouth hurt, but she smiled. Ruth was an incurable gossip. With her cloth shop in the middle of the marketplace, she saw and spoke to almost everyone, eventually.

"Then," Dinah continued, "visit Norah, and ask her advice. Maybe her father will speak to his friends among the merchants. I'm sure by the end of the day, Jude will be here with ten donkeys full of gifts, to persuade your brother."

~~~~~

The next morning, Sarai woke to the sound of hammering on the gates of the house. A voice demanded that they open in the name of Caesar. She scrambled out of bed and hurried to dress. Soldiers filled the house by the time she put on her sandals and came down the stairs.

"Where is Eliakim ben Levi?" a soldier holding a scroll demanded. The servants gathered before him, shoved and dragged into the courtyard by soldiers.

"My father is dead." Sarai raised her voice to be heard above the sobs and whispers. Caleb had bruises on his face and his tunic was torn. Enoch knelt, head bowed. Blood dripped from his nose, onto the tiles. Miriam and Dinah huddled together, sobbing softly.

"Then who is in charge of this household?"

"When my brother returns --"

"Joseph ben Eliakim will not return to this house." He shoved the scroll into his belt. "He and other Zealots were captured last night. Everything within these walls is now forfeit to Rome."

Dinah cried out, staggering to her feet. She lunged at the soldier, hands bent into claws. Another soldier put himself between the old woman and his commander. A sword swung, stabbing upward. Dinah fell. Miriam and another woman screamed.

The world seemed to stop, all sound and movement vanishing, as Sarai stared at Dinah's blood, puddling on the brightly colored tiles. She couldn't think, couldn't hear, couldn't move, and didn't resist when a soldier caught hold of her wrist and led her away.

Sarai saw the blood, the woman's slack, lifeless face and nothing else, all the long walk to the Roman garrison. She was barely aware enough to obey, to sit or stand or walk when ordered. The ability to think, to feel, didn't return until late that night.

She sat in a stone cell lined with straw, in the company of six other women of varying ages. A low, ragged wail escaped her throat. Her cellmates ignored her until the guard outside demanded silence. Someone slapped her hard enough her head rapped against the rough stone wall. Sarai fell silent.

~~~~~

Dawn was a thin trickle of light through a narrow gap, high in the stone wall. The prison cell sat below street level. Sarai watched feet striding past, sometimes kicking debris down into the gap, to fall into the cell. The uneven rhythm of traffic, the shuffle and scrape of soles on the stone pavement of the garrison, the thick air inside the cell served to numb her, mind and senses. She didn't think to move when a man brought a bucket of water and several loaves of bread into the cell and dropped them into the filthy straw covering the floor. The other women dove onto the bread and water, and Sarai couldn't make herself care. One tossed her a scrap, little more than two mouthfuls. She couldn't make herself eat.

She was still holding the crust of dried bread when the door opened again, clanking and scraping where it dragged on the uneven pavement. The other women looked up, terror warping their faces, then hunched down. Several covered their heads with their sleeves or the ragged remnants of veils. The first shiver of feeling darted through Sarai. Fear put a metallic taste in her mouth.

"This is the fourth cell," a familiar voice drawled. "Surely you're not so disorganized that you can't -- ah, there she is. At last."

Long, ebony legs and the hem of a tunic embroidered with pomegranates moved into her field of vision. A massive, cream-colored palm moved in front of her eyes. She flinched back, expecting to be slapped again, and looked up.

Ebed's upper lip curled and he tipped his head to one side, looking her over with a sneer of dissatisfaction she had seen him use on a jar of ginger that had gone bad in transport.

"Is that the one?" a man asked in a bored voice, from beyond the cell.

"I almost hope not. Don't you know how to take care of

valuable merchandise?" Ebed held out his hand. Sarai stared at it. He growled and bent, grabbed her elbow, and yanked her to her feet. "I can't be sure of anything in the shadows here."

Sarai gasped, feet dragging as the merchant half-carried her out of the cell, down a short hallway, and out into bright daylight. He shoved her away from him. She struggled to stand up, despite the aches that kept her bent in half. He walked around her. That sneer grew sharper and he shook his head, looking her over head to foot.

"It's her, but ... Here, give me that."

He stepped away. Sarai turned to follow him, suddenly terrified that the only familiar face was abandoning her. A hard slap of water hit her in the face and chest. She staggered back, gasping, and distantly heard men laughing.

"Stand up straight." Ebed caught hold of her shoulders and pulled her upright, his face less than a handspan from hers. "Forgive me, little one," he whispered. "I had to claim your father owed me money and I wanted you in exchange. These barbarians want to keep the good favor of my shop."

"Ebed --" She choked on a trickle of dirty water.

"Trust me. For the sake of your father ..." His expression wrinkled in sorrow, then shifted back to his sneer. He kept one hand on her shoulder and turned to face the man who had followed them from the cell. "It's hard to believe, looking at her, but this bit of feathers can read. More than that, she has studied the healing arts from a dozen countries. I know, because I found the scrolls to provide that education. Since her father never paid me, I think I'm entitled to get back what I've lost by making use of what's been stored in her pretty little head." He nodded and winked at the big man in the robes of a clerk. "She can calculate and cypher, and I intend to use her to trick anyone who tries to get the better of me in trade. While all they see is a pretty face, she'll be studying their books right under their noses and ensuring I don't get cheated. If she knows what's good for her." He chucked her under her chin, hard enough to make her lose her balance. When she staggered, he caught hold of her again. "If she hasn't been damaged by whatever fools harvested her."

"You'd get more profit selling her to a brothel," the man said. "I know plenty of men who would pay for a taste of that pale skin."

He snorted. "Once she was cleaned up, of course."

"Hmm, maybe. Stand up straight, girl!" Ebed yanked hard on her arm, so she staggered out farther away from the doorway, across the courtyard. "Forgive me, little one," he whispered. He walked her out into the sunlight, and then back to the doorway. "Your brother is to be crucified. Your friend Norah's sweetheart is dead. Her father stands on the knife's edge between crucifixion or losing his inn, because Zealots met in his upper room. Some are dead, some managed to escape. The rest, I know not their fate. I am trying to win your freedom, but ..." He turned, shielding her from view of the doorway, and pressed a smooth rod into her hand. "From your sweetheart, who is tearing himself to pieces, trying to find a way to help you."

When her hands didn't seem to want to work, he guided her in hiding the rod inside her clothes, tucked inside her belt.

"Thank you," she whispered, and squeezed his hand before he handed her over, with a shove, into the grasp of the jailer.

Sarai followed the man back to her cell. She tried to rake the tangles from her damp hair, and paid more attention to her companions as she settled in to wait. How long would it take for Ebed to talk the officials into giving her to him?

Thank You, Adonai, for friends who come to us in our hour of despair.

Finally, when the other women slept or were distracted with conversations, Sarai took the rod out of hiding. She nearly cried out when she recognized her little wooden flute. Huldah had believed strongly in music and prayers to aid in the healing arts and had insisted Sarai learn to play some instrument to support sung prayers. Jude had called her the sweetest sparrow and promised her a much grander flute someday, made of silver and decorated with gemstones. That was another promise he had never fulfilled.

And yet ... Ebed had said her *sweetheart* had sent the flute. Who else but Jude would even remember she had played often at sunrise and sunset, when she made her prayers? It had to be a signal to her, a promise that he would come soon and rescue her. Perhaps even now, he stood before the Procurator, securing her freedom.

Sarai didn't dare play the flute. Someone would try to take it from her. There had been enough arguments and slapping and scratching over other women getting more than their fair share of water or bread. Sarai contented herself with holding the flute tight, hidden in both hands.

She knew better than to tie herself into knots, waiting for Jude to appear, but there was little else to do but hope. The day dragged on limping feet, punctuated by the whimpers and whispers of the women in the dark cell. Sarai tried to mark the hours by the angle of light and then shadow in the tiny gap in the wall. Dinner came before dark, more bread and warm water, but Ebed never returned. Jude never came. She tried not to weep, as hope trickled away with the daylight. Guilt and sorrow crept up on her with the shadows and nightfall.

How could she be so selfish, whining over the delay in gaining her freedom? Her brother was condemned to die the brutal death of crucifixion. What was wrong with her that when Ebed told her the news, she hadn't felt anything? She hadn't cared about Abner, or Malachi, or Norah. Joseph's Zealot friends were either dead or condemned to death, if they weren't hiding right now, in terror for their lives.

"Joseph," she whispered, so softly she barely felt the breath in her mouth. "Forgive me, brother. Forgive me, Adonai. I am selfish, and a coward."

She dreamed of Dinah's death multiple times that night. Each time, she woke up with a wail in her throat, but never released a single sound.

~~~~~

Sarai went before Procurator Decianius the next morning, to face formal judgment. All the household goods had been seized by Rome, the servants sold, the fields given to Roman officers. Sarai was to be sent to the Decapolis. Nothing was said about Ebed's claim on her. The jailer who led her back to her cell sneered about "that swaggering priest" who knew so much about the Rose of Sharon, owner of the largest brothel in the Decapolis. As a favor to him, Sarai would join her stable.

That night, she didn't cry. She trembled in fury and nausea that threatened to turn her inside out. Who else could "that swaggering priest" be, but Caiaphas? How could he claim he served Adonai, when he acted with such hatred? It wasn't enough that her father was dead, abandoned by all who had revered him. Caiaphas had to continue punishing him by shaming her with the life of a harlot.

Yet more chilling, so it dried up her tears, was the realization that if Jude had tried to rescue her, the jailer would have mocked her about that, too. His silence meant Jude hadn't thought her worth the cost or effort.

In the morning, when Sarai woke from her fitful sleep and before she opened her eyes, she prayed it was nothing but a nightmare that would soon be over.

She prayed the same prayer every night when she lay down, and every bitter morning when she woke, on the long trip by cart from Jerusalem to the Decapolis. With other girls condemned by their fathers' and brothers' and husbands' crimes to be sold as slaves.

Chapter Three

"Up."

A nudge with a booted foot started Sarai's day, in the gloomy gray before dawn. Morning was almost a relief. She had known no sleep. The air hadn't cooled with the fall of darkness, but stayed stifling and dusty from the previous day. She rolled over, too tired to moan as the stiff aches filling her body came alive. The blanket between her and the packed dirt of the inn courtyard had offered little beyond a sense of modesty and shelter. The cartload of women hadn't slept inside the inn where they stopped last night, but in the courtyard. From the sounds that filtered through the darkness from inside the building, Sarai was grateful. No woman was safe within those walls. Norah had told her, with scorn and dismay, about the brothels thinly disguised as inns throughout the land. Because of them, men constantly walked into her father's respectable inn and expected to have their pick of the serving girls. Sarai wondered if Malachi had suffered the same fate as Joseph. She prayed to Adonai that the separation between Malachi's inn and Norah's business had protected her friend.

Agabus stood over her now, a tall, skeletal man with scars crisscrossing his dark-tanned, leathery skin; his gray hair wrapped in a turban; a leather patch covering his left eye. He had stood over the girls every night and every morning since they had been given into his care to deliver to the slave market.

Sarai couldn't decide if he was trying to frighten them to ensure they didn't try to run away, or reassure them no one would hurt them. After all, he wouldn't get paid if the merchandise was stolen or damaged. Sarai didn't care. Nothing mattered anymore.

To his credit, Agabus treated his cargo slightly better than the donkeys that pulled the cart. Instead of using a rod, he guided the girls with short, clipped words. A sharp slap rewarded anyone who didn't respond the first time he spoke. The two soldiers who rode escort ignored the girls altogether, never speaking to anyone but each other, only responding to Agabus with gestures.

Sarai struggled to her knees, then to her feet, and stumbled with the others to the well in the inn's courtyard. The water in the shallow jar she pulled up with shaking hands was cloudy, but she still saw enough of herself to note that she looked even worse than yesterday. No one would recognize her as the treasured daughter of a rich rabbi. Her dark hair hung lank, dull with dust and sweat. Her delicate, pale skin was burned and peeling, despite the thin veil that hid her face and her shame. Her lips were swollen and cracked with thirst, and her gray eyes reddened with dust.

Dust, not tears.

No more tears for Sarai. She had given up weeping when she knelt in front of the Procurator and heard him pass sentence. Tears had only earned scorn during the long days in the prison cell, and now slaps from Agabus. He scowled enough to fill Sarai with fear when she had done nothing wrong. She knew she should be grateful he hadn't hit her, but gratitude had also been confiscated by the Romans.

Agabus called them to the cart before the four girls had time to draw up more than two jars of water from the deep, echoing well. They each took a drink and splashed water on their faces, ran their fingers through their hair, and hurried to climb into the cart. The threat of his rod was enough to make them scurry to avoid rousing his anger.

Two small, dry loaves of bread, tossed into the cart, served as breakfast. The nameless little hunchbacked man who drove the cart shared bread and cheese with Agabus. The soldiers brought food from the inn and ate in the saddle. They seemed to enjoy having the girls watch them eat, so Sarai refused to look at them. Before the amber curve of the sun peered over the horizon, their traveling party had left the inn and the tottering stone-and-clay walls of the little village far behind them.

Sarai huddled in on herself, ignoring her companions and ignored by them. Two girls were the daughters of merchants who had committed crimes against Roman laws or officials. The third was the daughter of a Roman official who had run afoul of his superiors. They had teased Sarai for her delicacy and her involuntary reaction to their crude language. When the heat battered them all to silence, Sarai had been glad.

Yet, the silence was in its own way a far worse torture than the taunting. She had only her thoughts for company, and memories of a life that seemed like a fable now. Once she had worn the finest clothes. Servants tended to her father's household, so she didn't need to concern herself. She had indulged in her studies, so learning ordinary housekeeping skills had been a diversion, to earn approval and help her beloved Dinah and Miriam.

She had been her father's treasure, destined to marry a rich man who would pamper her. Sarai had known it and was careful never to encourage any of her suitors. Except Jude. Had she been cruel to the other young men? Arrogant? Unfeeling?

Surely El Shaddai punished her only for her own crimes, rather than for the sins of her brother and father. Rabbi Eliakim had taught her that Yahweh was merciful as well as just. He wasn't like the Romans, whose idea of justice punished the entire family when a man committed a crime.

Please, Adonai, show Your great mercy to me now, and let me die before I am branded and sold as a slave. Even if I have harbored an impure heart, surely my suffering has purified me now, and You will allow me to journey to Abraham's Bosom before my family is shamed yet again?

"Play." Agabus looked back over his shoulder at Sarai. A flicker of a smile touched his mouth, and he nodded to her.

She didn't dare hesitate, but her mouth was dry as she took her flute out and scrambled to think of a song. At the start of the journey, she had thought to make friends with the other girls in their cart and alleviate the boredom of the journey. Agabus had asked her, gruffly and briefly, where she got the flute. She had feared punishment, but he had shrugged and let her keep it when she lied and said she had brought it into the prison. There had been no trouble until her simple tune, imitating a flock of birds dancing through the sky, had attracted the attention of a band of merchants. They had bought three of the original ten girls in the cart, and their leader had wanted Sarai, specifically because of her music. The escort soldiers had to intervene and show the merchant the orders with the seal of the Procurator, before he desisted. Agabus had told her to put the flute away and not cause trouble again.

His temper had mellowed a little after he sold three more girls at another stop, likely at a greater profit than the Procurator had expected. Sarai supposed he didn't fear trouble now that their destination was half a day's journey ahead of them. She played, but couldn't find it in herself to remember any joyful tunes.

~~~~~

The cart reached the outskirts of the city just before noon. The girls whispered in growing anxiety as they passed under arches and between high walls. Agabus stopped the cart in a small courtyard with a fountain and gestured for them to get out. Then he walked away, leaving them in the care of the hunchbacked driver and the two soldiers. The four girls slid out of the cart and hurried to scoop up water to wash and drink. Sarai drank her fill, ignoring the dust from her dirty face that tainted the water. Nothing had tasted so good, no water had ever felt so cool.

When the other three girls perched on the edge of the fountain, she chose to sit in the shadowy shelter of a wall. No one was in any mood to chatter. The other girls looked around in fearful anticipation she understood.

Nearby was the slave market, if they weren't already inside it. Sarai hesitated to take a deep breath, afraid she would smell the fear and pain and shame of those who were sold like cattle, to be abused and even killed at the whim of their owners.

Still, there was some relief in being here, in the Decapolis. In a matter of days, their fates would be settled, once and for all.

Please, Adonai, God of mercy and justice. Please, end my life in some dignity. I am weak and fearful, and I will shame my father's memory. Please, end my life, for I cannot endure any of this.

The Angel of the Lord didn't appear, though Sarai covered her head with her hands and prayed until Agabus returned. When he grunted his command, she got to her feet and followed the others, all silent. The soldiers did not come with them.

They walked down two streets, turned right, then another street, coming to a shadowy, quiet place; a half-roofed room of raw stone walls mortared with clay, and a floor of packed dirt. Agabus grunted an order for them to sit. He was done with them. Then he turned and walked away. Sarai suspected she would never see the taciturn, scarred man again. She trembled deep inside. Agabus was the last tie to her former life. Now, there was no going back.

Sarai heard men speaking somewhere beyond the walls enclosing them. There was laughter mixed with argument. The sound reminded her of her father's students as they argued long into the night over obscure passages from the Law and Prophets.

The handsome, young faces of her father's students flicked

through her mind. Benjamin, Joachim, Simon, Michael, Eleazar, and Jude. Rich and poor, equal recipients of her father's discipline. Equal competitors for her smiles.

Sarai cringed, remembering her father had been criticized for indulging her, educating her with the boys. Yet he had never permitted flirting. When she grew old enough to wear a veil, he had sent her to the roof. She could still listen and learn, but no longer sit in the courtyard with his students.

Not soon enough, though. Sarai knew now she had been cruel to Joachim and Simon when they showered her with pretty words and promises of future riches. She hadn't laughed when the other students taunted the two young men for their poverty, but neither had she done what was right and scolded them until they stopped. She was only a frail woman who thought with her heart instead of her head. No wonder Jude had abandoned her. All his promises and gifts of sweets and flowers and expensive skeins of thread were nothing but worthless trash.

Four women entered the roofless room. They wore indecently short dresses, with a slave brand on their exposed left arms, and no veils. Each stood before one of the four girls.

"Come," the woman standing before Sarai said.

"Where are we going?" Sarai's knees wobbled as she struggled to her feet again.

"You are to be washed and prepared for your buyer." She spoke with almost no feeling in her voice or expression.

Sarai wondered what had been done to this woman that she didn't care. She followed her through a maze of corridors, some of them roofless, others dark and echoing. She shuddered, loathing a new image of herself. Why had the thought of slavery meant nothing to her until she was a slave herself? Her father's slaves had been treated decently enough, but for the first time she wondered if anything could make up for the pain of being property. Why had she never considered the feelings of her slaves before? Where were her family's slaves now? Had they been sold to a kind master? Had the men been sold to farmers and merchants, or had they been sent to the mines or the galleys?

Blessed, most holy El Shaddai, forgive me my sins of cruelty and lack of mercy and pity. If I must suffer to pay for what I have done and not done, in Your mercy give me the strength to endure.

~~~~~

Rose-scented oil floated on the surface of the basin of warm water. Fresh bread, cheese, and grapes waited for Sarai after she finished washing. Mara, the woman in charge of her, put scented oil in her clean hair and brushed it until every tangle and frayed end vanished into silken, glossy smoothness.

Mara did not answer any of Sarai's questions, but told her what she needed to know. She explained the rules, which were simple: silence and instant obedience. Then she explained the beauty treatments she and the other three girls would undergo in preparation for the slave market.

"Some might say the treatments are wasted on you, since you're not to be a harlot."

"I'm not?" Sarai's voice broke, as if she had eaten sand.

"You're a healer, aren't you? Those are rare enough, even the Rose of Sharon wouldn't be so mad as to make you provide bed service. No, you'll spend your life tending the injuries the other girls get from the brutes, drugging the ones who try to suicide, and easing the sick ones out of their misery at the end." She shrugged and bent her head over Sarai's left arm, which she painted with henna designs.

"Healer ... to harlots." She shuddered, earning a half-hearted slap from Mara, for moving her arm.

"It's a better life than most will get. Especially the pretty ones. Some will argue to get use of you, so if you're wise, you'll stay away from the customers altogether, and hide your face when you can't." She paused as she dipped the pointed tip of the brush in the henna pot. "You may think I'm taunting you, but I'm warning you. The Rose of Sharon has demons. She'll coddle you as her own child one day, and toss you to an entire shipload of galley slaves the next, and laugh with the demons looking out through her eyes."

"Why ... all this?" Sarai gestured with her free hand at the supplies for the beauty treatments. She held as still as she could, when her legs ached to flee. Even if it meant running into Agabus and his rod, she needed to run. But she didn't.

"The Rose of Sharon has the best girls." Mara shrugged and gestured for Sarai to turn so she could paint her other arm. "Romans make her rich. Even if you don't provide bed services, you need to look good to support her image."

"Yes, but wouldn't a bath and clean clothes and a veil be enough?" She could finally put it into words, if only for herself. The beauty treatments seemed to make a lie of the assurance she would not be forced to be a harlot.

"If she doesn't take you, the auction master will offer you to other brothels, or he might send you directly to the auction block."

"Which is better?" Sarai could almost laugh at how calm her voice sounded, when she trembled inside so much she thought her bowels might empty.

"Whatever gods you pray to, ask them to send you to the market. It's far easier to have only one master, no matter how cruel. At least then, you know what to expect. Harlots have new masters every night." Mara tipped her head to one side and studied Sarai with her empty eyes.

~~~~~

Sarai paused in playing her flute and praying. Voices in the next room broke through the mournful notes.

A girl sobbed. A man laughed.

Another man snapped out, "Strip and be quick about it," punctuated with a curse and the sound of a slap.

Sarai remembered the things Mara had so casually told her an hour ago. All her muscles stiffened so she couldn't have fled if she wanted.

The brothel owners had come to inspect the girls and make their bids.

Flesh smacked against flesh again. The girl yelped. Her sobs stopped. Wood scraped across the tiled floor. It sounded like furniture being moved. All the rooms in this part of the preparation house were exactly alike: a pallet bed placed against the wall, a bench against the opposite wall, and a table in the middle of the room. Sarai clutched the edge of her pallet bed and shuddered.

"Please." The girl's voice cracked. "Don't."

"Hands off," a man said.

Sarai had heard his voice earlier, talking to the other women preparing the girls. Mara had said he was the eunuch Phoebus, her master. His voice was icy calm, stealing the breath from Sarai's body.

"You can't use her until you've paid for her."

"Adonai, save me," Sarai whispered. She bowed her head and

raised her hands to cover her ears.

Was the buyer going to rape her right there?

"Break her in," was the term Mara had used. She had said after three or four times, a girl learned how to help the man using her, so it didn't hurt. A smart girl, she said, learned to pretend she enjoyed whatever the man did to her, so he would be pleased and perhaps give her an extra coin or a trinket, beyond what he paid her owner. She would never save enough to buy her freedom, but she could make her life a little more pleasant.

"You call on Adonai? So, you're a Jew?" a low, rich, laughing female voice asked.

Sarai raised her head. A tall, red-haired woman leaned against the doorframe. Her scarlet, gold-trimmed skirt was slit so one leg showed from the knee down. She wore jeweled bangles on her ankle and trinkets tied around her leg below her knee. Henna designs covered her bared flesh. Her curly, thick hair hung loose, twined with fine silver chains. Only harlots wore their hair loose in public, even among the Greeks and Romans.

Kohl outlined her enormous gray eyes. Her sleeves were slit, revealing henna-painted arms hung with numerous bracelets and bands of gold and silver. Her dress clung to her body, revealing a voluptuous shape that made Sarai feel like an adolescent boy by comparison.

"Yes," Sarai said, when the woman just waited, with a patience no one had displayed toward her in what felt like months.

"Why are you here?"

A scream shattered the air in the next room before Sarai could answer. Low, wracking sobs followed. One man laughed, and another made grunting noises like a stubborn bull.

"Those fools have no idea how to handle a woman." The stranger shook her head and sauntered into the room.

Before the door curtain fell back into place, Sarai saw a Nubian standing out in the hall. He wore little more than an Egyptian-style kilt, stark white against his blue-black skin, and bronze bands on his wrists and ankles.

"He's mine," the woman said, as she settled onto the bench. "A woman in my -- *our* profession, needs a bodyguard, or idiots like those three next door will try to control us." She shook her head. "They're taking turns with that poor girl, using brute force instead of coaxing her. She won't be good for anything for at least a week, and that's bad for business.

"Now, for you, I'd make sure a kind man had you your first time. One who sees himself as a seducer of virgins and prides himself on his skill. If you have fun, the customer has fun. And you're willing and eager -- and undamaged -- for the next man." She smiled and raised her hands, palms up, as if inviting Sarai to agree with her logic. "However, Decianius says you're a skilled healer, and he's sent you to me because he owes me many favors. I won't ask you to service anyone." She chuckled. "But you might enjoy it. You could become rich, if you're clever. How does that sound?"

This was the Rose of Sharon? The demon-possessed mistress of harlots?

Yet she was beautiful, richly dressed, coherent. Maybe people just said she was demon-possessed to be cruel? Sarai dared hope for the first time since Ebed's attempt at rescue failed.

"I don't want --"

"Why are you here? Decianius didn't even tell me your name, only that your brother incurred Rome's wrath, so your entire family paid the price."

"Joseph, my brother was a Zealot. With Barabbas. They were trying to steal a Roman supply wagon, on the road to Jerusalem."

"Sweet child -- not Joseph ben Eliakim, of Bethany?"

"You heard of him?" Sarai swallowed down a sob in the face of this unexpected sympathy.

"Heard of him? I knew him. He carried messages to me from Barabbas."

"He did?"

"Do you believe in what your brother did? What he lived and died for?"

"I hate the Romans, if that's what you mean."

"Partly." She chuckled and held out a hand, gesturing for Sarai to join her on the bench. "Joseph told me about you, Sarai, how clever you are. A woman who can read and write and calculate -- as well as a healer."

"He was proud of me?" Warmth filling her chest threatened to turn into tears. Sarai blinked to fight them back. She feared if she allowed the tears to fall, she would never stop.

She had harbored angry feelings against her brother, before and after he had been caught by the Romans. He had taunted Simon for his dreams of rising to leadership in the Sanhedrin. He had despised Jude for his wealth, and called him a weakling who would always defer to his father for the sake of his inheritance. He had said one too many times that Jude would never marry her because his father feared Annas' judgment against Rabbi Eliakim. And yes, she was angry because his actions had brought her to this place, speaking with a demon-possessed harlot. Yet at least she was alive -- Joseph was dead.

Joseph, forgive me. Adonai, please forgive my unforgiving heart.

"This is your chance to take vengeance for your brother. Join me in aiding the Zealots," the Rose of Sharon said.

"But --" Sarai shook her head. Words tangled in her mouth. Too many questions and doubts.

"But how can I help the Zealots, since I'm only a woman? Little dove, the common soldiers in the Roman army can't bring their wives with them, if they're allowed to marry at all. The officers have their wives, of course, and several mistresses. But Roman soldiers need women as much as they need food and weapons. They need women -- I provide women.

"Romans think most women are mindless husks, existing to give them pleasure and sons and to decorate their homes. Men say many things they shouldn't, in a woman's arms. I tell Barabbas many useful things, and I get rich off Roman gold."

In the next room, the girl had stopped crying. Sarai thought of letting a man touch her, as only a husband should touch his wife, to obtain information to help push the Romans out of Judea. It would be revenge for what they had done to Joseph and to her.

Her father, however, had condemned the Zealots. "If the Lord does not build the house," he would quote to Joseph and his restless friends, time and again, "the builders work in vain. You must wait for the Messiah. When Messiah comes, with the power of Yahweh, Rome will flee Israel and crumple into the dust."

"I -- can't." Sarai bowed her head as her face burned. She suspected she would be so terrified or repulsed by the touch of a stranger, she would never remember anything he said.

"Think of all the admirers you'll gather, starving for a smile, a sweet word, an hour of your time," the woman whispered. Her lips curved in a mischievous, lush smile. "You could have prefects and centurions, procurators and governors. Imagine all the things they'd tell you, boasting to impress you with their power."

"I'm a healer," Sarai blurted. "Not --"

"Not a whore?" The Rose of Sharon shrugged and tipped her head back with a laugh that went from smooth and rich to harsh and crackling. "There's no escaping. Choose the path that will make you rich quickly. You'll never have to go where a man tells you or wear what he decrees or stay home and silent. You won't have to birth baby after baby until you're worn out or dead in childbirth."

As if a mask fell away, fire flickered in her eyes and her face twisted in a grotesque parody of her former sweetness and beauty. Her graceful hands stiffened into talons, digging into the bench's sides. Two long nails snapped. Her head jerked back and forth a dozen times in as many heartbeats.

Gibberish spilled from her lips and foam speckled them. Sarai let out a tiny shriek and stumbled backwards until she pressed her back against the opposite wall. The Nubian darted into the room and caught the woman as she slid off the bench. She thrashed, twisting to get free, but he held tightly to her and stretched her out on the floor, holding her flat.

"Don't hope for the Messiah, stupid little girl," the woman snarled. Her voice grated, low and deep, as if a man tried to speak through her.

How had the Rose known she had been remembering her father's words? Sarai pressed both hands to her mouth to keep from shrieking. The action pressed her flute into her cheekbone.

Huldah had said she played sweetly enough to drive out demons, as David's playing on the harp had banished the evil spirits tormenting King Saul. Did she dare try?

"Join us. Fight the invaders. Get revenge for your brother. He's calling from the grave for you to avenge him. You're wasting your time, hoping for Jude to come save you. Silly child, silly dreamer. You adored him. Stupid child. Jude doesn't want you. He wants his gold more than he wants you. If he loved you, he'd be here, buying your freedom."

Fury and sorrow fought in Sarai's chest. She took a deep breath and brought the flute to her lips. A psalm of lament, calling down Yahweh's justice, ran through her mind as she played the first note.

Cackling laughter tore through the woman's body, twisting her and raising her from the floor in convulsions. Sarai played louder, praying with all her might for Adonai's protection.

The Rose of Sharon let out one shriek, then went still, collapsing like a rag doll. Staring at her, the Nubian fumbled to gather up his mistress in his muscular arms. Sarai lowered the flute to her lap as the big man hurried from the room.

Sarai sank down to her pallet and wrapped her arms tightly around herself. She closed her eyes and rocked slowly, shivering. How had this woman known about Jude? Had Joseph told her? Yet how had she known Sarai had been thinking of the Messiah and her father's words only moments ago?

Surely, demons had been speaking through her.

If Sarai joined her, using her body and beauty to spy on the Romans, to help the Zealots, would demons reside in her, as well?

"El Shaddai, please, protect me." Sarai's voice cracked on a sob she refused to release. "Let me die before I come to such a path. Please, haven't I paid enough of a price for my sins? Blessed Redeemer of Israel, protect me."

Chapter Four

Sarai closed her eyes against tears and bowed her head, resting her face on her bent knees. She released a shuddering breath and tried to push her thoughts in other directions. When she was only a small child, just after her mother died, her father had taught her psalms to recite when she needed comfort. Try as she might, the only one that came to her mind began with the plaint, "My God, my God, why have You forsaken me?"

Another shuddering breath. She listened to the silence beyond her thudding heart. Only later, when the evening shadows closed in and Mara brought her bread and goat's milk for the evening meal, did she realize a miracle had occurred.

The buyers for the brothels hadn't come into her room. If the Rose of Sharon did not come claim her, she would go to the auction block. She told herself to praise God for that miracle, that reprieve. Even if she was sold as a concubine, a field worker, the most menial of slaves, surely that was better than to be sold into harlotry.

~~~~~

The next day, a man with the face of Simon ben Micah walked among the men trickling into the slave market. Sarai stared from behind the shelter of her pale blue veil and prayed she was wrong. That man couldn't be Simon, only someone who looked like him.

A man with the same wide shoulders and square jaw? Who stood a head taller than nearly everyone gathering around the raised wooden platform in the center of the slave market? Wearing his faded, purple-striped coat, with sleeves that didn't quite reach his wrists?

A sob filled her throat. Sarai fought to swallow it before it erupted.

Simon was here. A man who couldn't even buy a donkey when he left her father's house. He couldn't have come to buy a slave. Had he come to see her humiliated? Would he watch her be sold, and remind her that if she and her father had not been so proud, she might be safe, his wife, at this very moment?

An ache throbbed through her heart. Had he taken the long

journey from Jerusalem to the Decapolis, just to watch her final degradation? She had thought so much better of him, when he was her father's student. No, she refused to believe he would make such effort just to see her humiliation. Perhaps he was in the Decapolis on business for Rabbi Nicodemus.

Simon had been the most apt of her father's pupils. He could argue the finest points of teaching without growing angry or resorting to cruel remarks to humiliate his opponents, like other students sometimes did. He wouldn't be so cruel to be here merely out of curiosity. Or had working with the Sanhedrin changed him so much already?

Sarai flinched and her hand crept up to the flute tucked inside her belt, hidden by her outer robe. Jude had flattered her when she played the flute, but Simon had *made* the flute for her. How could she have forgotten?

He didn't look any different from the last time she saw him. He was still handsome, with glossy, curly black hair and large eyes. He had wide shoulders and long-fingered hands that handled the scrolls with reverence. His skill with pen and ink had earned her father's praise. He was kind to the servants and had a voice worthy to serve in the Temple, reading the holy words to the gathered worshipers.

His only flaw was his lack of family and wealth -- and yes, agreeing with Caiaphas, when he criticized her father. She wouldn't be surprised if Simon was here at the behest of Caiaphas, to ensure she was humiliated and thus finalize the punishment for Rabbi Eliakim ben Levi.

Did any of that truly matter? Sarai waited to be sold in the slave market and Simon stood among the buyers. The boy who had smiled at her now was a grim-faced man who watched the slaves step up onto the auction block, one after another.

Simon never moved, never spoke a word, as the male slaves, destined for the galleys, the fields, the Roman mines, were brought to the auction block one after another. Sarai barely heard as the auctioneer listed each man's skills, his age, his crimes, and then began the bidding.

She prayed her veil hid her features, and Simon would go away before the men were all sold. Then it would be the turn of the women destined to be concubines, household slaves, and harlots.

Sarai prayed. The Pharisees taught that Holy God didn't listen to women's prayers, but El Shaddai was merciful, wasn't He? Surely He would hear and notice her fear and pain, despite her status as a woman. She watched Simon as her group stepped up to the end of the platform. She held her breath, waiting for the Angel of God to appear and intervene. Whether El Shaddai snatched her away to another place or struck her dead in that moment, she didn't care, as long as she didn't have to stand on the auction block.

She didn't die, when Phoebus grabbed her by the elbow and guided her up onto the knee-high block of wood. Her tears deserted her, when the eunuch yanked the shielding veil from her head and nudged her chin with his fist, so she had to raise her head and look at the grinning, murmuring mass of men. Sarai refused to look at Simon. She prayed he had grown bored by now and walked away.

The scribe read aloud the sentence that brought her to the slave market, then her list of skills. Men on one side of the market called out crude remarks, some in languages she didn't understand. She could guess what they meant. Several men stepped closer, arguing with Phoebus for not putting her with the girls destined for the brothels. They didn't want to pay the higher price demanded for a skilled healer, a woman who could read and write and handle household accounts.

Some grew angry enough, Sarai thought they would rush the platform, maybe attack Phoebus or even her, and drag her away. Then movement from the corners of the market square stilled the argument. Sarai turned her head enough to see the tall, scarred men with swords, who stared directly at the loudest arguers.

Phoebus gestured to the scribe, who read her sentence and skills again. The men who wanted her to be a harlot moved back into the crowd, and the bidding began.

"Ten shekels," a cracked voice called from Sarai's right.

"Eleven shekels," another man said, only a heartbeat later.

She ignored the slowly mounting bids. Sarai had never asked how much her father had paid for the slaves who did all the work in their house and vineyard and fields. She didn't want to know.

A flicker of movement caught her attention. Despite her resolve to see and hear and feel nothing, Sarai looked. Simon stood only five paces away, directly in front of her. When their gazes met, he nodded to her.

Sarai's vision blurred, but she refused to blink and let the tears trickle down her cheeks.

"Twenty-two shekels," a deep, male voiced called. Sarai turned to look at the man, just to escape Simon's gaze.

Her stomach knotted. Silence filled the market. No one else called out a bid to top the twenty-two. She could barely think a prayer of denial as she stared at the man.

Bare-chested, he gleamed, filthy with grease in the matted hair on his chest and arms. His beard was a tangled mass, streaked with gray among the dirty brown. Tattoos decorated his cheeks above his beard. He wore a scimitar slung from the belt of bronze disks hung low around his hips. His belly protruded over his belt. He licked his lips as he looked Sarai up and down.

When the auctioneer asked for more bids and no one responded, the swordsman chuckled and rubbed his hands together in anticipation. He stepped closer to the platform and held out one hand, visibly claiming her before the bidding had ended.

"Half a talent of silver."

Sarai froze. Hope told her that was Simon's clear, musical voice. The threadbare rags of her pride prayed it wasn't him.

"I agree the girl is beautiful, young master." The auctioneer laughed. Behind him, Phoebus snickered. "But no woman is worth so much money. Not even if she were Caesar's daughter."

Laughter rippled through the market. Sarai's face burned. She clenched her fists inside her sleeves. Why hadn't El Shaddai rescued her? Why hadn't the Angel of God struck her dead, in mercy?

"She's a virgin," Phoebus said. "A cringing Jewish virgin. You'll get no pleasure of her for weeks. If ever."

"Half a talent of silver," Simon repeated. "And if you have lied and she isn't a virgin, if I find one unwarranted bruise on her, I want all my money back. And I keep the woman."

"Concubine," Sarai whispered, so softly she barely even heard herself.

Of course. That was the only answer. She almost smiled at the cool sense of relief that washed over her at the thought. Simon would make her his concubine.

He had a bright future among the Pharisees, in the Sanhedrin. He would be influential, and eventually rich. Important men would offer him their daughters as his wife. Simon could never make Sarai his wife because of her father's conflict with Annas.

She had bruised Simon's heart and damaged his pride in her mistaken attempts to be kind and discourage him. Her brother had mocked him. Now, Simon would be avenged on their family, by making Sarai a lowly concubine.

Sarai knew Simon wouldn't be cruel. She would be safe. He would never love her, but that didn't matter. She had thought Jude loved her, but he hadn't rescued her, had he?

Silence rang through the slave market for a few heartbeats more. Sarai cringed when Phoebus crossed the platform in front of her. He and the auctioneer conferred for a few seconds. She couldn't hear them through the buzzing hum that filled her head and made her knees turn to whey. Whispers and mutters trickled into the waiting silence.

"Does anyone bid more?" the auctioneer asked.

Sarai could breathe again when the men crowded around the platform took a step or two away, and most shook their heads. The swordsman scowled. He didn't step away.

"Sold! To the rich young man. A nobleman perhaps?" the auctioneer mocked.

Simon wore that faded coat, after all. He had no slaves following him, no fat purse of money hanging from his belt. It was wrong of them to mock him.

What had it cost him, to gather half a talent of silver to buy her? Where had he got the money?

"A scholar," Simon said.

"A rich one, to pay so much for one slave."

"I sold everything I owned to buy her." He stepped up to the block and held out his hand to Sarai.

"She'll have to serve you fifty years, to get your money's worth out of her." Phoebus handed over a roll of parchment, listing the particulars of her sentence and slavery.

"I'm a scholar, not a fool," Simon said. "She's not mine until you sign it and stamp it with Caesar's crest. Otherwise, you could arrest me tonight and claim I stole her."

"Ah, a truly wise man." Phoebus nodded and gestured across the market square, to the gate, where another scribe waited at a long, low table.

Simon's touch was gentle as he grasped Sarai's elbow and guided her down from the block. He didn't release her as they stepped off the platform and walked across the dusty, crowded square of disgruntled men. Sarai kept her head bowed, refusing to look at anyone, half-afraid Phoebus would send guards after them to stop Simon and drag her back to the block. Or one of those men who wanted her sold to be a harlot would snatch her away. Maybe several. They would rape her before Simon could rescue her, and then she would have no choice but make her living as a harlot, ruined for the rest of her life.

Or the Rose of Sharon would appear, negate the sale, and take back her gift from Jerusalem's procurator.

Yet Simon led her to the table and the scribe, and nothing went wrong. Would they leave the market in peace? He switched his hold on her to his left hand, so he could sign the parchment and hand over the small bag with half a talent of silver.

He had sold everything, to buy her? Sarai couldn't wrap her mind around the thought. Why would Simon do such a thing?

What about his service to Rabbi Nicodemus? How could he have obtained permission to leave his studies, his duties, and travel all this way to find her and buy her? Had he jeopardized his future, to do this?

"Cover yourself, Sarai. You do not walk in shame any longer." Simon snatched her discarded veil from the table, where Phoebus had dropped it, and handed it to her. When her hands didn't want to work, he draped it over her head.

Then he took the parchment of her condemnation and the bill of sale, resumed his grip on her arm, nodded to Phoebus and the scribe, and walked away. He never spoke to her or looked at her. Sarai stumbled along beside him as best she could.

"You -- scholar! Hold a moment." The swordsman caught up with them half a street away from the slave market.

The wind blew from behind him. Sarai gagged at the filthy, salty, sour stench that hit her in the face. She thought a prayer of thanks that she hadn't been sold to him.

"You sold everything to have her?" the man continued, when Simon stopped and turned to him. "You need money? Let me have her for one night. Two shekels. It's more than even the Rose of Sharon charges, and she's skilled." He grinned, revealing blackened teeth. He reached for Sarai's veil. Simon slapped his hand away.

"If you try to touch her again, you'll regret it." Simon's voice cut through the warm, dusty air like lightning dipped in ice.

"All right, you can have her first. Is that your problem? I don't care if she's virgin or not, I just want one night to feast on her." The swordsman's grin widened, but he did step away.

"The Scriptures condemn a man who makes his daughter a prostitute. How much worse condemnation for a man who sends his wife into harlotry?" Simon spoke in cool tones, but Sarai heard the power of his rhetoric and years of training in the Law, waiting to be unleashed on this filthy Gentile.

"Wife?" The man spluttered and staggered back another step. "Ares save me -- a fool, hidden in the robes of a scholar!" He looked Sarai up and down one more time, then turned away, roaring laughter.

Sarai barely noticed when Simon tugged on her arm and resumed walking.

Wife? Surely, Simon hadn't meant it. She was his property. No one would expect him to make her his wife, when she had been so thoroughly disgraced.

No, he had only said that to send the man away before he tried something.

"Come, Sarai." Simon gently led her around a corner.

He didn't look at her, didn't speak to her, as they walked down more streets, through fountain squares, past houses that slowly grew larger and more ornate.

Soon, the doors didn't open onto the street, but had narrow courtyards and gates between them and the foot traffic. Through the gaps in the walls and gates, Sarai glimpsed fountains, flowers and trees, paving tiles and benches.

Gradually, the large, fancy houses grew smaller again, less luxurious. Sarai hardly dared to study her new surroundings but concentrated on Simon. She had to anticipate his next move, his first order.

"Master?" she said, when they paused to wait for a cart blocking an intersection to move out of the way.

"Sarai." Simon sighed, but smiled when he turned to her. "Didn't you hear me, when I sent that filthy idiot away? You are my wife. Or you soon will be."

41

"Forgive me?" She went to her knees and pressed her veiled forehead to the toes of his sandals. "I was a fool. I knew you were the best of my father's students, but I only saw your lack of family and wealth. I did not treasure you. This is my punishment."

"No. Sarai, don't ever kneel to me. You are my wife. " His toes twitched under the weight of her forehead. " Yes, I bought you. I paid to free you, because you are the greatest treasure in my heart." He bent to grasp her arms and lift her to her feet. "Not my slave."

"Your concubine. That is the best that I deserve." She blinked and hot wet trickled down her cheeks. Her veil stuck to the trails of her tears. "I will gladly serve you all the days of my life. You will never regret freeing me. I will tend your house and you will be proud of me. You will hold your head high in the city gates."

"Love me, and I will always hold my head high," he whispered. His somber look brightened to a grin. He glanced to the side and nodded. "We can go on now."

The way had cleared. Sarai flinched when he took hold of her hand this time, but she rather liked the dry strength in his grip. He had no calluses from hard, physical work. That meant he had spent all his time in scholarly studies since leaving her father's household. The other students had teased him because he performed manual labor to pay for his education. Simon had chopped wood and helped with the harvest and plowing. Sarai wondered how anyone could be such a fool to mock a man who worked for what he valued.

El Shaddai, the One who sees me, purify me through what I have endured. Make me worthy of this man. Make me a joy to him and not a torment.

Simon's hands could soon become hard and rough and calloused again, if he had to work to support them. He had left his duties with Rabbi Nicodemus to come find and redeem her. Common sense said he had lost his position, just for shaming his master. No one would take him on as an assistant and scribe. Simon would have to start all over, working his way up through the ranks. It wasn't right. It wasn't fair. Why should he have to suffer because of her? What had he risked or lost, to come find and buy her?

The house where Simon finally stopped had faded stains of blood on the lintels, and tiny boxes nailed to them. Sarai marveled at the sight of them in the midst of the Decapolis. The decorated boxes held slips of papyrus with the scriptures written on them.

Even without the neatly painted words of blessing over the door, she would have recognized the markings of a priest's household.

She finally believed Simon's words. He would make her his wife. Why would he take her to a priest, except to marry her?

"Welcome." The woman who opened the door to Simon's knock was dressed all in black, with a gray veil covering her head. She stood with hunched shoulders and was thin as a stick, but her hands were warm and steady as she reached for Sarai's hands. "Come inside, child. Praise to the Lord Most High that you have been found. A thousand blessings on you, Simon ben Micah, for the great and good thing you have done."

As Sarai stepped over the threshold, her flute slid out of her belt and clattered onto the tiles of the entryway. She hurried to pick it up and lost her breath in a moment of understanding.

"You gave this to Ebed," she whispered, as Simon drew her back upright. "He told me ... my sweetheart was trying to free me." She blinked back tears, silently scolding herself for her foolishness in thinking Jude had made even that much effort for her sake.

"Adonai will recompense you both for the trials you have endured," the old woman said. "Come in, come in, we have much to do if we are to have a wedding feast today!"

~~~~~

The old woman was Haddaseh. Widowed nearly twenty years now, with no children to look after her, she was housekeeper for her brother, Hananiah, a retired priest. He had served in the Temple, helping with the sacrifices. When the stiffness in his joints grew too painful to allow him to continue, he had come to live near his daughter's family in the Decapolis.

"It is the will of the Living God that brings us so far from our home, into this land of evil ways and strange tongues." Haddaseh shook her head and clucked her tongue, but her eyes sparkled, belying her words. Her voice was soft and sweet, making it easy to listen to the bits of gossip that meant nothing to Sarai. "Time and again, we have been able to help many Jews in their time of need. Who would help them if we were not here?" She finished pouring warm water into a basin set up on a table in the small, clean upstairs room where she had led Sarai. "There. A bride should have a bath with scented oil and rose petals, on her wedding day, but --"

"But this is a taste of Paradise and more than I thought I would have today," Sarai hurried to say. She rested her hand on the old woman's, where she gripped the handle of the water jug. "Thank you. I can't express how much I appreciate all you have done for me."

She gestured around the clean, white-painted room, and her gesture took in the entire household, the sympathy, the wash water, the welcome. Sarai knew what could have awaited her this night. She had seen it in the swordsman's face, heard it in the sobs from the girl in the next room, saw it in the demons looking at her through the eyes of the Rose of Sharon.

Blessed El Shaddai, I thank You with all my heart and soul and strength. My life is Yours, in thanksgiving.

"We are more than glad to help. It's like a young girl's most wishful dream. A tale of heroes and adventure. The handsome young scholar who gives up everything he has to travel the world and find the innocent maiden, stolen by cruel enemies." Haddaseh clasped her hands together against her bosom, closed her eyes, and sighed. Then her eyes popped open and a mischievous smile tweaked her lips.

Sarai laughed with her hostess. Strange, how foreign laughter sounded and felt in her mouth. She had thought she would never laugh again.

As she washed and put on the finely woven, pale blue dress and sheer veil Haddaseh had provided, her hostess told her something of Simon's side of the tale.

Simon knew the old priest and his sister, because Sarai's father had sent him to the Decapolis on errands several times. Even after he learned she was to be sold to the Rose of Sharon, he had dared to hope, and asked Hananiah and Hadasseh for help. They had been delighted to do so.

"We offered to loan him money, but he had already sold everything," the old woman said with a sigh and a shake of her head. "Young men are so impetuous. He sold all his fine clothes, his scrolls. Now, how can he work among the Sanhedrin? Bad enough they will mock him for abandoning his duties for the sake of a woman." She clucked her tongue three times. "But he will compound the mockery, dressed in clothes that should have been tossed to the beggars months ago. We would have gladly helped him, given him all the money as a gift, for your father's sake alone."

"You knew my father?" Saraih choked on the honey cake she had been nibbling. The old woman's words shocked her out of the whirlpool of guilt she felt over Simon's sacrifices.

"Ah, yes. Before you were born, my brother chose to remove himself from that pit of foolish vipers ruling the Sanhedrin. He shared your father's belief that the Messiah will suffer first, before He drives our enemies from Israel. My brother keeps his beliefs to himself, and waits until wiser minds and hearts come to power in the Temple and the Sanhedrin."

"If you had known about Joseph --"

"We would have come to help you immediately. As it is, all has worked out well. I can host a wedding feast as if for my own daughter." She patted Sarai's head and then hurried out of the room, muttering about keeping the ducks from burning on the spit.

"All has worked out well." Sarai hiccupped once, caught in emotions she couldn't understand. Then she bent forward, rested her forehead on her clasped hands and laughed.

She had no idea how she should feel at this moment. Her life had been spared, changed, transported to a haven of peace. Gratitude and joy, she knew, were appropriate feelings now. There was no reason for anything but gladness today. Tonight was her bridal feast. Hananiah would lead her to stand under the marriage canopy and put her hand into Simon's. He would speak words of blessing on them and read to them from the Law. The four of them would feast together and laugh and perhaps sing.

After such a great miracle, Sarai knew she would have nothing to fear when Simon led her to their bedchamber. He had proven the truth of the sweet words he had spoken in more innocent times. He had sacrificed greatly to save her and win her. Tonight, instead of tears and terror and pain, she would gladly yield herself to her husband's desire.

She would not think of Jude. She would put away her silly, childish dreams of Jude's hand holding hers, his whispered words of adoration. After all, Jude had abandoned her to the Romans.

Simon had saved her. Simon had proven the love he had promised her in more innocent, foolish days.

Chapter Five

Their first morning of marriage started sweetly. Simon smiled at her when she woke up and rolled over to look for him. He had held her all night, and Sarai discovered that she missed the warmth and shelter of his arms, even when he still lay beside her. His face showed honest regret when he climbed out of their bed.

"Must you leave?" she asked, before she could even consider the words.

Sarai blushed. Her face grew even hotter when Simon smiled, as if her thoughts were written on a scroll. Then, he leaned down over their bed and kissed her, and Sarai decided she didn't care how wanton her thoughts might have been. Was it not right, a gift from El Shaddai, for a woman to take delight in her husband?

"I would gladly stay all day alone with you, my wife." Simon's eyes sparkled, and his voice put an extra caress on those last two words. "However, I must look for some kind of work. Hananiah is a great and good man, but it would be wrong to impose on his hospitality for more than a few days."

"Simon? How much have I ..." She swallowed hard, refusing to burst into tears. She was a wife now. She had to be strong for her husband. "How much have I destroyed your future?"

"You are my future, sweet Sarai. Adonai led me to find you and gave me the means to save you and make you my wife. So I know our God will provide me with a livelihood to shelter and protect you. My treasure." He caressed her hair, then turned away to dress. In moments, he was gone.

Sarai hurried to wash and dress. While Simon looked for work, she should do all she could to repay their hosts. She was glad she had learned household skills, though there had never been any need. Until now. She would need them in the days and years to come. There would be no servants in Simon's household.

Hadasseh only protested once, when Sarai came to help her with the baking and the mending. Then she accepted the new bride's help. They chattered happily, as if they had known each other for years. The sound of their voices brought Hananiah to join them in the kitchen.

After less than a day, Sarai wished she and Simon could stay with Hananiah and Hadasseh. This was, she decided, the proper kind of riches for a household. No slaves or servants, but filled with laughter and honest caring that made up for the lack of fine clothes and expensive food. It didn't matter that most of their neighbors only called on Hadasseh or Hananiah when they needed them for something, and the High Priest would never come to ask his opinion on matters of interpretation or history.

Hananiah and Hadasseh were nearly twins. Sarai would have taken them for siblings even if she had never been introduced to them. Thin and gray-haired, they had the same sparkling eyes and equally sparkling wits. The old priest settled into the corner of Hadasseh's kitchen and joined their talk as the two women mended and cooked and baked. He told them the latest market news, the official proclamations from the Roman overlords, the neighborhood gossip.

He teased them, throwing one riddle after another at them. Sarai was delighted to find a priest so comfortable in the presence of a woman not of his household. Pharisees had always studiously ignored her when they visited her father's household, as if they thought a woman's presence would contaminate them and make them unworthy of serving Adonai.

Hananiah was not like that. He was like her father, believing that a woman had just as much wit as a man. He certainly tested Sarai's, with his riddles and puzzles. He laughed just like Hadasseh, a warm, buzzing sound that made Sarai feel safe.

He rocked back and forth on his stool, seriously threatening the stability its legs as their discussion grew more intense. He laughed at Sarai the first time she called warning to him and teased her just as he did his sister. Hananiah hooted in delight when Sarai answered his questions and then challenged him in turn.

Talk eventually turned to prophecies of trouble for Israel. Sarai nearly dropped the loaf of bread dough she held on a long-handled board, when Hadasseh mentioned a specific passage in a specific scroll she had read.

"What's wrong, child?" the old priest asked.

He reached for a pile of dates Hadasseh had just finished splitting and pitting, to put up on the roof for drying. His sister slapped his hand without even looking at him. He winked at Sarai and settled back against the wall, balanced on two stool legs.

"Hadasseh, you can read, too?" Sarai took a deep breath to steady herself and slid the loaf into the beehive-shaped oven that sat just outside the kitchen door.

"Hananiah taught me." Hadasseh nodded, settled down at the table and reached for a bowl of almonds to crack.

"Did you think your father was the only man brave enough to teach a woman to read?" Hananiah said with a chuckle. "Of course I've been teaching my sister to read and understand the Scriptures. What else are two old folks to do? We can either study and improve our minds, or get into trouble gossiping and complaining."

Hananiah snickered when his sister let out a muffled snort at his words. "Idleness leads to illness and a sour spirit. Training and honing the mind is just as important as keeping the body useful and strong and healthy." He leaned closer to Sarai and lowered his voice to a rasping whisper, which was loud enough to be heard in the next room. "Don't tell her, but she's the best pupil I ever had."

The three laughed together and Sarai settled down at the table to take up another task. She had never fully realized how much work there was to providing for even a small household. All the many steps to preparing a meal and looking ahead to the next few meals. Or mending, or preparing to wash clothes, or the endless cleaning required of a proper Jewish household. She supposed with all her father's servants, the chores hadn't seemed endless. Sarai told herself to be grateful there would only be herself and Simon to care for.

Until, of course, she gave him children. Every man needed several strong sons, to support him in his old age. Sarai wanted to give Simon sons to be proud of, but would children be a blessing, or only add to the burden on his life?

She set those thoughts aside, refusing to let them darken her pleasant day. She had to learn to trust El Shaddai for everything. Hadn't He already proven merciful and generous and faithful? She would put the future in the hands of the Almighty God.

The kitchen talk turned to Sarai's father and the many years Hananiah had known Rabbi Eliakim. The old priest confirmed what Hadasseh had told her the day before. They would have gladly helped her, simply because her father was an old friend.

Never mind that Rome's cruel justice outraged them.

"But don't let such treatment justify any foolish actions against Romans in the future," Hananiah warned. He let the stool drop back down onto the front leg with a thud. "You might think, why not help the Zealots, to take revenge on the Romans? Many would agree with such thinking. Yet look at the harm their raids have done. Would the Romans have sent you to be a slave, if Joseph had not been caught among them?"

Strike against the Romans? Unbidden, memories spilled into Sarai's mind. She thought of the Rose of Sharon, the woman's pride in tricking the Romans and making a profit off them while they spilled their secrets to seemingly harmless, mindless women.

Sarai remembered how she had seriously considered the woman's words. For a moment, the offer made sense. Was it a noble cause? Did the defense of Israel truly justify a sinful action?

"Child?" Hadasseh touched Sarai's chin, making her lift her head so the old woman could look her in the eye. "Something troubles you. Have you already done something to strike back?"

"I?" A startled bubble of laughter escaped her. Sarai blushed. "No, I wouldn't have had the courage, even if I had the opportunity. And ... I think I did have the opportunity. But Adonai intervened. I believe our God truly did save me." She shivered and turned to pick up a dish she had just washed, to dry it. Hadasseh intervened, taking it from her hand.

"Tell us. I think the memory of it troubles your spirit. It will wear a sore spot if you do not let it go."

Sarai glanced at Hananiah. The elderly priest nodded. His gentle smile promised forgiveness, no matter how foolishly she had acted. The tenderness in his eyes and the laughter they had shared assured Sarai that he would never consider her tarnished by simply being in the same room as the harlot.

Her father, though he loved her dearly, would have been more mightily upset with Sarai than with the Rose of Sharon. That realization surprised her and cast a shadow of sadness over her memories. Her father, for all his wisdom, would have been disappointed, perhaps even angry with her that she had listened, had been tempted for a few heartbeats.

She loved these two elderly folk, who had opened their hearts and home to her and to Simon. Sarai found the courage to tell them exactly what had happened. She told them about the Rose of Sharon's visit, the discovery that the harlot knew her brother, and how the woman encouraged her to welcome a life of harlotry to spy on the Romans. Neither brother nor sister showed any signs of being shocked. Sarai wondered if such easiness in spirit came with age, and she envied them.

"Yes, perhaps she does think she is doing some good for Israel." Hananiah nodded. "There are even some among the priests who would approve of the end results of her actions, even as they condemned her for harlotry, and offering other women to the Romans."

"Patriotism does not wipe away or justify physical and spiritual uncleanness," Hadasseh said, and clucked her tongue. She turned back to drying the dishes.

"Which is the worse impurity?" Sarai almost laughed as she realized the words came from her mouth. "To be a harlot with Jewish men, or to go to the Romans?"

Both elderly folk stared at her a moment. Then, to her surprise, Hananiah laughed.

"You should have gone to study law. You would have made your father immeasurably proud, little Sarai." He chuckled a few more times, nodding. Then his expression turned somber.

"I agree with your father, that the Zealots only cause more trouble for Israel. Yet I think Laila, the Rose of Sharon does some good with her spying. She helps keep foolish young men alive with the information she steals. Still, what good does it do her? Her evil ways have opened her soul to demons. What good are riches and good deeds and protecting your country, if your body and soul are unclean on the Day of Judgment?"

"Even if she took the very best care of you, child," Hadasseh said, "it would still be a life of misery. Even if every man who enjoyed your body was kind and gentle, it would torment your soul. The demons who control her would make her hurt you. Child?" She put down the last dish and wrapped her arms around Sarai, who shivered. "What is it? Oh, don't let my pessimistic words frighten you. You're safe. Simon is a good man."

"Not that." Sarai forced her lips into a smile, to reassure both her concerned hosts. "When she was speaking to me, the demons struck her. She talked strangely. She fell to the ground and shook all over. How can she be happy in that life, filled with demons?"

"We are foolish, weak, sinful creatures. Imperfect, formed of clay, easily shattered." Hananiah got up from his stool and crossed over to stand before Sarai. He rested his hands on her shoulders. "Laila chooses to believe she is happy, because to admit the poverty and illness of her soul would be to destroy herself utterly. Allow her to cling to her illusion of doing good, because there is no hope for her. No one with the power to cast out demons would have compassion on a harlot, so there is no one to help her."

There should be, Sarai decided, deep in her soul. If El Shaddai had heard her prayers and allowed Simon to rescue her, surely the merciful Creator would send someone to lift Laila from her greater misery and torment.

~~~~~

Simon returned just before sunset, dusty and weary from traveling through the city, asking for work. Sarai's heart clenched at the sight of him. For her, he was reduced to such a humble position. He should still be in Jerusalem, assisting Rabbi Nicodemus. His days of coming home dusty and sunburned and sweaty should have ended years ago.

Sarai insisted on warming water and helping Simon wash and change his clothes. She washed his dusty feet and rubbed them, as she had rubbed her father's feet during his last illness. When she rose from her knees, she found Simon staring at her as if he had never seen her before.

"My husband, have I done something to offend you?" she half-whispered.

"Offend? Not at all." His smile grew wider. He caught up both her hands in his and tugged her closer. "You surprise me. I have always seen you as a lovely, delicate flower, to be protected from a harsh world. Instead, you ..." He shook his head.

"I am not a useless decoration?" Sarai tried to smile, though she suspected she might cry. Did Simon truly think her so helpless, so useless? He seemed pleased, but how could she know? She had ample proof that she had badly misjudged him many times before. "Forgive me."

"Forgive you for being a delight to me?" Simon slipped his arms around her and stood, drawing her snug against his chest.

She sighed and closed her eyes and gladly rested her head

against his shoulder. There were many good parts to marriage, she had discovered already. This quiet sense of rest and completion was one of them.

"I only want to make you happy. To be a good wife, to meet your needs and ease your burdens."

"What would make me happy, my treasure, is to give you the life you knew in your father's household, with servants so you never have to do anything." Simon pressed a kiss against her forehead. "Nothing but be beautiful and love me, of course."

Sarai pressed her face closer into the pleasantly musky warmth of his robe and squeezed her eyes tighter against treacherous tears that burned to escape. Simon would never have riches, because of her. Whatever work he found, she vowed she would labor twice as hard, to keep him happy. She would take in sewing and do extra baking, whatever she could find to do, to earn money to help him. She vowed to delight him in every way possible, to make up for that loss. She would love him all the days of her life.

~~~~~

That night, Sarai went up to the flat roof of the house, intending to sit with Simon and Hananiah in the cool dusk before retiring to bed. She paused on the stairs, hearing the seriousness in the men's voices, and hesitated to join them.

"It isn't the end of life," Hananiah said.

"No, but it does threaten my chances here," Simon countered.

His tired voice held an edge that made Sarai flinch and clutch at the wall where the roof met the stairs.

"He laughed at me, when I told him of my training. He said I was a fool to leave my secure position to rescue the daughter of a fool. I wished I had a sword, to cut out his filthy tongue. He laughed at my anger when he mocked Rabbi Eliakim. Then he laughed and said Sarai deserved to be a slave, because of her father. Why should she be punished for his sins?"

"Did he indeed sin?" the old priest asked.

The serenity of his voice restored the cool tranquility of the evening shadows. Sarai sat down on the top step to listen.

"I don't care. What does the Messiah have to do with me? Whether He comes as a suffering servant and shepherd, or He comes as the victorious warrior to destroy our enemies, the Messiah is not coming for many years, yet."

"How can you be sure of that?"

"How can anyone be sure?" Simon sighed, the sound turning into a groan. "What matters is that I wanted to hurt him, for what he said about my beloved teacher and my wife. He said everyone in the Decapolis knows about Rabbi Eliakim and the High Priest's decree. If I say he was my teacher, I will be sent away. If I say that I once worked for Rabbi Nicodemus and willingly left him, everyone will laugh at me. No one will hire me."

Sarai closed her eyes tight against tears. She had done this to Simon. What could she ever do to repay him for all he had lost?

"Yes, it will be hard for you both, but persevere. You have done well in the eyes of Adonai, and that is all that matters. You will be blessed for your righteous deeds, if you keep your heart pure and act with patience and trust."

"What sort of blessing is it for Sarai, after all she has gone through, to make her live in the streets?"

"Is she living in the streets now?" The old priest sighed, and Sarai heard laughter in the sound.

"No, but we cannot live on your hospitality forever. I must provide for my wife. If I cannot find work as a scribe in the Decapolis, then I must journey until I find work and a good home for us. I must rise to a position of respect, and prove to everyone in Jerusalem and Bethany that I was no fool."

"Ah. Then your pride is your reason. Pity."

"What do you mean?"

Sarai hurried down the stairs. The thudding of her heart in her ears muffled the men's voices. She took deep, trembling breaths to fight her tears and blinked quickly when her vision blurred.

She stumbled into Hadasseh, returning from tending her herb garden in the inner courtyard. Sarai said nothing, but her hostess seemed to understand. She led the younger woman to the kitchen and gave her a honey cake. They sat on a bench quietly for a few moments.

"Men think they are so much stronger if they don't tell us the troubles of the world," the older woman observed.

Sarai hiccupped in surprise.

"You blame yourself for your husband's troubles, don't you?" Hadasseh just gave her a serene look when Sarai could only goggle at her. "Sound carries very well at night, and I heard everything they said, up on the roof. Did you force Simon to give up his studies and his secure position, and come looking for you? Did you threaten to shame him before all Israel if he didn't redeem you?"

"No," Sarai whispered.

"No, you did not. He is your husband. He is a man. You, so very young, cannot force him to do anything he does not truly want to do. He chooses, and he must face the consequences of his choices. You cannot be punished for what he has chosen to do, though the Romans certainly punish everyone around him for a man's stupidity."

Those wry words startled a tiny gasp, almost like laughter, from Sarai. The older woman nodded. A smile tugged at the corner of her mouth.

"Yes, you are the reason he did such things, but they were of his choosing. Do not shame him and do not add to his burden by wailing and blaming yourself. Your duty as his wife now is to give him all your loyalty and love, to give him joy and strength among his burdens. Remember this moment, when the days are long and hard, and quell your complaints.

"Turn your back on all that you knew before Simon redeemed you and made you his wife. Devote your life and heart solely to him. This will please Adonai, and our God will bless you, and by blessing you, your husband will be blessed as well. That, my child, is how you may repay your husband for the sacrifices made for your sake."

"I swear it. Simon is the center of my life." Sarai's voice trembled, but the threat of tears had left her eyes. "I was a foolish child. I gave to the poor, but I did not truly pity them. I looked at my father's slaves and did not pity them for their destroyed lives. Now, I have been sold as a slave, and perhaps I will become a beggar. That is the will of our God. I am glad to serve my husband with my hands and prove to him my love and loyalty." Her voice caught, nearly breaking. "I'm only sorry that I cost him so much."

"You did not cost him anything he was unwilling to pay." Hadasseh pressed her hands on either side of Sarai's face and tipped her head down, to kiss her forehead. "I think even now, so discouraged, he will gladly say he has the better part of the bargain."

Please, El Shaddai, give me the strength and wisdom to ensure Simon always believes so.

~~~~~

Sarai accompanied Hadasseh to the marketplace the next day. She met several women who lived on the same street. They were kind and welcoming and didn't press when Hadasseh didn't offer many details about why Simon and Sarai were staying with her and Hananiah. It was uncomfortable enough the women knew she was a new bride. They gave her knowing smiles, and several whispered advice for dealing with a new husband.

However, two days later, when Sarai went out alone to spare Hadasseh, who had a headache, the women she encountered seemed to know everything. Women she hadn't met yet knew who she was. They commended Sarai for capturing the heart of a man who would risk so much for her sake. They expressed their sympathy over the loss of her father and brother. She reflected that it would be nice if their menfolk held the same opinion about Simon's actions. Every morning, her husband went out to seek work, and every evening he came back to the house, more discouraged. She ached for him when he confessed to Hananiah that he considered returning to laboring in the fields. Several men had commented on his strong physique and recommended he develop a reputation that depended on his strength and not his skill with a pen. As if a scribe did nothing but write.

An older woman, Elisheva, walked home from the market with Sarai. Her silence was more comforting than the words spoken by the other women. They were two streets away from Hadasseh's home when Elisheva's breathing grew labored. She smiled and tried to assure Sarai that this was nothing to worry about. She often had this tightness in her chest and thickness in her throat. All she needed to do was sit down, and it would pass. Fortunately, they were only a few steps away from her door.

"A few steps" turned out to be another ten minutes, creeping down the street. Sarai insisted on supporting the older woman. She carried her basket, half-full of fruit and vegetables and bread still warm from the baker's oven. All the while, Sarai's mind raced, trying to remember what she had read about breathing problems. Yet she had read advice and cures and speculations about the causes of illnesses of the lungs in *so many* scrolls. Sadly, she didn't have her scrolls any longer, to consult them. She helped Elisheva into her house and had the elderly woman sit. Then she went to the covered pitcher sitting in a shadowed niche, where it would stay cool, to get her a cup of water.

Elisheva's house was small, but set at the perfect angle to allow sunlight to fill her courtyard most of the day. Three looms were set up in the courtyard, which was twice the size of the house. Each had projects in some stage of completion. The air was fragrant with many pots of plants, all herbs used for seasoning and for healing. They sat on stands and shelves everywhere in the sunlight. The shelves partially hid large copper cauldrons set over fire pits. The cauldrons were dusty with disuse and no aroma hung in the air to indicate their former use.

"Forgive me if I seem rude, but what do you use to help your breathing?" she asked, after handing Elisheva the cup. Sarai tried to prepare words to offer some of the remedies she knew, but how to do it without implying that whatever the elderly woman was doing now was useless?

"What can I use?" Elisheva shrugged and made a little upward gesture with the cup, in thanks, and raised it to her pale lips with shaking hands, to sip. "I rest. I sit still far too much. I pray."

"Many of your herbs can be used to ease the tightness in your lungs."

"They can?" She frowned and looked out the open doorway into the courtyard, as if she saw the rows and shelves of pots of green growing things for the first time. "I know that sometimes the smell makes me feel better. I always feel stronger when my weaving students are here, but ..." Another shrug. "I let my niece grow her cooking spices here, because she has such poor light in her home. I know about plants to make dye, not for cooking."

That explained the copper cauldrons. The dust coating them indicated how long Elisheva's breathing problems had interfered with that occupation.

"Would she mind if I used a few leaves to create a potion to help you?"

"Even if she did, and she's not the selfish kind, thank Yahweh, well we wouldn't tell her, that's all." A bit of color returned to Elisheva's pale, thin cheeks, and a sparkle of humor in her eyes.

When Sarai left an hour later, Elisheva's color was better and she no longer wheezed. The elderly woman assured her that her nephew and his sons could all read. They would help her follow the instructions Sarai had written, for preparing the leaves, roots, and seeds, to create several potions. She had chosen an herbal brew that Elisheva could drink, as well as inhaling the steam. Then she wrote down several more to try. She had to laugh that the woman was more impressed that Sarai could read and write, than she was over her knowledge of herbals and healing potions. The instructions had to be scratched into the plaster coating the wall next to the door into the courtyard. There was no parchment or ink in the house. Elisheva promised that her nephew or his sons would transfer the instructions and the recipes onto papyrus, to make sure they weren't lost.

Sarai explained to Hadasseh what she had done and why she was late returning from the market. The elder woman shook her head and smiled and declared that Adonai had repaid her for the help given to Sarai and Simon. Elisheva was one of her dearest friends, and she worried for her constantly because of her breathing problems. Fortunately, the elderly woman had many relatives and students who looked in on her. That was little comfort when her lungs were heavy and she couldn't catch her breath. She was highly regarded in the community because of her skill creating dyes in highly prized colors. She hadn't been able to do the work herself, for several years now because of her breathing problems, but she still took in students for weaving, and oversaw several nieces who had taken up the dye work. Even if she couldn't earn a living, her family were good people who loved and looked after her.

Chapter Six

That evening, Benjamin, Elisheva's nephew, came to call on Sarai and thank her for her help. He brought a heavy skein of thread dyed deep blue with purple overtones. Now Sarai understood why Elisheva was so highly regarded, if she knew the secret to creating such vibrant color.

Simon came into the courtyard while she and Hadasseh were talking with Benjamin. Their visitor seemed startled to see him. Simon merely nodded greeting, when Hadasseh introduced them to each other. He rested a hand on Sarai's shoulder and stood behind the bench where she sat. The gesture felt somehow protective, with some emotion she couldn't define.

"May I ask -- where did you gain such healing knowledge?" Benjamin said, after a few seconds of silence that threatened to become uncomfortable.

Sarai had the oddest feeling he almost didn't want to ask.

"My father was a wealthy rabbi with many friends who prized knowledge above all else," she said carefully. Simon's complaints and self-recrimination, which she had overheard, seemed to echo in her head. "He indulged my curiosity by seeking out scrolls with healing knowledge from all over the world. I believe I made my father very proud with my skill, which I shared with all in our village, as is only right before Adonai."

"Yes," he murmured, and his gaze flicked away from meeting Simon's over her head. "As is only right. I had heard of your father, but ... didn't make the connection until now." He cleared his throat, thanked her again, and stumbled through a few pleasantries before making his departure.

"That man can be a pompous fool sometimes," Hadasseh said, coming back into the courtyard after seeing Benjamin out. "But I know he has a good heart. Something happened between you two. I can tell. Benjamin isn't good with words, despite his beautiful delivery when he reads scripture in the synagogue. He had a speech prepared, and seeing you, Simon, knocked it entirely out of his head." She chuckled. "He is hopeless when it comes to speaking or thinking on his feet."

"What happened?" Sarai asked.

"Interesting," Simon said after a moment.

He squeezed Sarai's shoulder and finally stepped around from behind her. His expression was thoughtful and touched with pain. It reminded her of the days when the other students tried to "put him in his place, the dirt-grubber," according to Michael, after Simon had earned high praise from Rabbi Eliakim.

"He didn't have any problem with knowing what to say, when I approached him about work as a scribe several days ago." He managed a thin smile, nodded to both women, and left the courtyard.

"Oh, dear." Hadasseh watched him go. "What do you wager that Benjamin came to ask you to consider staying here, as a healer? We have very few in this part of the city, and none are Jewish, or care about obeying the laws of purity. We need someone with your skills. Benjamin couldn't in all conscience suggest such a thing if he had an unpleasant meeting with Simon, could he?" She sighed. "Adonai warns us against pride, doesn't He?"

Sarai went in search of Simon, though she wasn't sure what to say. She found him on the roof, leaning against the wall, staring south across the city, to the dark horizon. She imagined he was looking toward Jerusalem, seeing the life he should have been living right that moment. Secure in the approval of the leaders of the Sanhedrin, with a bright future ahead of him.

He flinched when she pressed herself against his back and wrapped her arms around his waist. For a long moment he held perfectly still, not even breathing. Then, carefully, he turned around in her embrace and enfolded her in his arms. They stood together in silence.

~~~~

Word spread about how Sarai had given Elisheva relief and put color back into the elderly woman's cheeks. Several women came to ask her advice and were astonished when she offered to write out instructions for them. They admitted their husbands couldn't read, or their fathers, but thought they knew someone who could do the job. Then they suggested she consider staying and establishing herself as a healer. Sarai thanked them and responded as only a dutiful wife could: she did not know her husband's intentions, but he was awaiting word on several opportunities and inquiries he had made.

Hadasseh chuckled over the gossip she overheard in the marketplace, and the whispers in the women's gallery in the synagogue. Every woman Sarai helped added their voices to the insistence that she be persuaded to stay as their healer. Then they added their voices to the exasperation being heaped against the foolish men who had turned down Simon when he sought honorable work. Only a highly intelligent and scholarly man could be married to a woman gifted with such valuable healing skills.

The laughter stopped when Hananiah had a visit from several men who asked him to intervene with Simon. Hadasseh threw up her hands in exasperation when none of the men apologized for the unkind things they had said to Simon, or the criticism they had heaped on Rabbi Eliakim.

"Such fools, it would never occur to them to think how they would feel, if other men told them to their faces, 'Oh, yes, we think you are an idiot, but your wife is so talented, we will allow you to stay among us.' Adonai save us from proud men!"

Sarai smiled and thanked the women who came to her for advice and to make potions for them. They brought necessary bits and pieces to express their gratitude. New sandals, lengths of cloth, needle and thread, sweets. She always gave the same answer when they pressed her to settle among them: She waited on her husband's decision. After a while, the gifts grew inconvenient. How could she and Simon carry so many things when they left, on foot? They didn't have the money for a donkey, much less a wagon for it to pull.

After their second Sabbath in Hananiah's home, Simon announced they would journey toward Jerusalem, and seek Yahweh's will for their lives along the way. Sarai was not surprised. She ached for his troubles and the burden he carried. She scolded herself silently, for feeling exasperation and longing to stay right where they were. Yes, she was happy, and knew many women who could become her friends. They had to leave for Simon's sense of pride, just as irritating as the pride of the men who refused to apologize while trying to persuade him to stay so Sarai could become their healer. She confessed her own pride to Adonai, and vowed to prove herself a worthy, virtuous, and obedient wife to

Simon, and give him no cause to regret the choices and sacrifices he had made.

Hananiah and Hadasseh discretely sold the small pile of household items Sarai and Simon could not carry with them. They provided a purse to hold the resulting coins, and a list of friends in towns and villages along the way to Jerusalem, who would help the young couple for their sake. Elisheva's niece insisted on giving them a bag containing many healing herbs and roots and seeds, carefully dried or powdered, and flasks of vinegar and oil, wrapped in cloth, to use in creating healing potions. She apologized, laughing a little, at the heaviness of the bag, but insisted the contents would come in handy along the way.

The morning Sarai and Simon parted from their hosts, in the chill before dawn, all four held back tears. Hananiah prayed Adonai's blessing on them. Hadasseh made them promise to send word when they had found a place to settle, and to remember brother and sister in their prayers.

Sarai did remember them in her prayers, as they headed south and west, toward the Jordan River crossing. She prayed for Simon, that he would find work worthy of him. Sarai prayed she would be a blessing and not a burden to her husband.

They developed a pattern when they approached a village or town. If a friend of Hananiah and Hadasseh lived there, they went to that house first and gave greetings from the elderly priest and his sister. Then they followed the advice of their hosts.

If there was no one there to call on, they walked through the market to learn the size and prosperity of the town. Sarai talked to mothers with young children, while Simon listened at the gates where the elders talked and passed judgments. He inquired where the richest men lived, people who might require the services of a scribe or even a private tutor for their sons. Sarai sought out a virtuous older woman who would let her stay in her courtyard in safety while Simon looked for employment.

Plenty of farmers and carpenters looked at his wide shoulders and large, capable hands, and offered him work. As the long, dusty days wore on, Sarai feared Simon would accept, simply out of desperation. He saw no shame in working with his hands and back, but he had worked too hard for his education to let those years of work go to waste.

Several times, she offered her help and healing knowledge, and the contents of the bag of herbals, to people traveling the road with them, or in a village marketplace. Usually that earned some praise, an offer of hospitality, even a coin or fresh bread in gratitude.

Once, someone suggested she stay and establish herself as a healer, because their village had none. That village's synagogue leader told Simon he was being punished by Adonai for choosing a heretic as his teacher. Sarai didn't know if Simon had admitted what he had done to rescue her. She didn't ask. After hearing their host for that night criticize the religious leaders in the village, it didn't matter. Neither she nor Simon would have stayed if all the village elders begged them. The division in the village would engulf them and force them to take sides.

Simon's face grew grim and hard as their journey continued and his search yielded no results. A cold trembling settled in Sarai at times, yet she forced herself to smile for him and chattered about the beauty of the sky, the warmth of the weather, the sweet perfume of the fields and trees around them. Anything, no matter how silly she sounded to herself, to convince her husband that she had no worries or complaints.

If it weren't for Simon's determination to find work that would set them up in a fine home, and the dwindling number of coins in the purse on his belt, Sarai thought she could be happy in this life. When he wasn't worried about food or shelter or the men who looked too long at her, as if trying to see through her veil, Simon was a pleasant companion. He answered all her questions and told her stories he had heard about the places they passed. She loved to listen to his strong, clear, rich voice.

Though she prayed against it, constant disappointment turned their steps more surely toward Jerusalem with each day that passed. As they climbed up the Jordan River valley, the landscape grew increasingly hilly. By mid-afternoon, her legs protested the uphill climb. There seemed to be far more uphill slopes than downhill. When she saw a particularly inviting, cool green meadow by the side of the road, she couldn't resist asking to stop and rest. Just for a little while.

"I'm sorry." Simon held her hand and guided her in stepping over the narrow ditch that separated the road from the meadow. It wasn't a Roman-built road by any means, but it was decent enough.

"Sorry for what?" Sarai sighed as she sank down into the cool grass and slid her sandals off her feet.

"You should have a cart to ride in, or at least a donkey. You should have grapes to eat, not bread and water." He made a disgusted face as he untied the mouth of their water skin. He offered her the first drink, as he always did.

Sarai laughed after taking a sip. The water was still cool. The bread last night's host gave them that morning was still soft, and she sighed after taking a tiny bite. She laughed again when Simon frowned at her, visibly confused.

"Simon, I was almost slave and now I am free," she said, trying to explain what still wasn't clear in her heart. "I will never complain about small things. Besides, the bread is fresh and the water is cool, and there are many who don't have this much. I will always remember how it was to have no hope, to be a slave on the auction block, and I will be happy no matter what." She took his hand and pressed his knuckles to her cheek. The gesture always pleased him, and his troubled look faded. "You are my dear husband and you treat me far better than I deserve. How can I be anything but happy? I am with you."

"You deserve far better. We both do. Things should be far different. Your father should not have died. If he had not been ridiculed and ostracized, he might still be alive. Some have said your brother deserved to die, following the Zealots. You were innocent, Sarai. You didn't deserve to be enslaved for their crimes."

"The innocent suffer for sins they did not commit, and the guilty live in luxury and ease. My father taught me, on the Judgment Day, atonement will be made. To have the approval of El Shaddai, who would not choose to suffer a little while in this life?"

"That sounds like something Jude would have said." Simon snorted. He yanked on the thong as he rewrapped it around the mouth of their water skin. "A fine one he was, to talk like that. With his father's wealth, he will never know a moment of unjust suffering. When I think what he said on the day --"

He leaped to his feet, instantly alert. Sarai turned, looking for what had alarmed him. A knot of men came over a small hill, heading down the road toward the village she and Simon had just passed through. She glanced up at Simon. He watched the oncoming men.

Sarai wrapped her veil more securely around herself, to hide everything but her eyes. She hunched her shoulders, trying to make herself appear smaller, harder to notice. Simon glanced down at her. Some of the alert hardness in his face relaxed.

"Master, will you explain the story about the weeds and wheat?" a man said, as the group drew closer to where Simon and Sarai sat.

"The harvest is the end of the age," the man in the center of the group said.

He gestured at the long stretch of grass on the other side of the road. He and the men, nearly a dozen, stepped over the ditch and sat down. They arranged themselves so their leader sat higher up the slope and they all turned to face him.

Sarai trembled inside at the sound of His voice. He was not a handsome man; pleasant looking, yes, with big, dark eyes that seemed to see everything and to caress the world as He studied it. His clothes in the dull, earthen tones of rough-spun cloth, indicated He came of ordinary stock. His voice, however, flowed out smooth and sweet, like rich honey.

"And the harvesters are angels," the man continued.

Sarai strained her ears to hear, hungry for such teacher-student discussions again. Her eyes threatened to tear up, as memories of her father with his students interfered with listening.

"As the weeds are pulled up and burned in the fire, so it will be at the end of the age. The Son of Man will send His angels, and they will weed out of His kingdom all who do evil. They will throw them into the fiery furnace, where there will be weeping and gnashing of teeth. He who has ears, let him hear."

The men muttered among themselves while their teacher waited, smiling, for their questions.

"Interesting," Simon murmured. "Sarai --"

"I will be all right. Don't worry for me." She bit back the urge to ask him to take her with him. It wouldn't be seemly.

Her father had received criticism for letting her sit with his students even as a little girl. She refused to shame her husband for one moment, even if it was before strangers.

"Are you sure?" The concern that dug furrows in his forehead vanished in eagerness. Simon caught up her hand and kissed her fingertips, then hurried to cross the road to join the men on the other side.

"Who is your teacher?" Simon asked a man who sat at the edge of the group, closest to the road. He frowned at the others and didn't join in the discussion.

"That is the Nazarene." The big, tanned man laughed when Simon frowned in confusion.

He had a booming laugh and voice, like the fishermen Sarai had seen when she was very young, traveling with her father to the shore of the Sea of Galilee. What kind of a man was this rabbi, to draw a fisherman away from a quite lucrative livelihood? Sarai hoped Simon asked good questions and the men spoke loudly enough she could hear the answers.

The teacher stood and gestured for them to get up and continue on their way. Still, no one had asked Him any questions. Sarai thought that was rather odd.

"I'm not sure if I've heard of Him," Simon said.

"He's the son of a simple carpenter, but we, His disciples, believe He has been sent by God, and God speaks through Him."

Sarai felt as if ice had fastened her immovably to the ground. Little enough she knew of the world, but she knew that men who claimed they heard Yahweh's voice and spoke His words invariably died, killed by the very people they had come to teach.

"But how do you know?" Simon asked. "How can anyone know such a thing?"

She barely heard his voice through the rapid thudding of her heart.

"As Jesus just said." The big fisherman gestured at his rabbi as He and the other men stepped onto the road again. "He who has ears, let him hear."

Jesus stopped after He stepped over the ditch and looked directly at Simon. For just a moment, his gaze shifted from Simon to Sarai, sitting in the grass. He smiled, and she felt as if a warm arm had wrapped around her. She looked into Jesus' big, dark eyes and something hard and tight and sore inside her softened and healed.

"The Kingdom of Heaven," Jesus said, turning back to Simon, "is like a merchant looking for fine pearls. When he found one of great value, he went away, sold everything he had and bought it."

Jesus waited, a hand stretched out as if inviting Simon to say something, ask a question. Simon stayed silent. Sarai couldn't see his face, but she could easily imagine his stunned expression. What kind of teacher was this, who used stories to teach men who were not His disciples?

"He knew what was of greater value," Jesus said, as He turned to leave. His voice rang with warmth and joy. "And he sacrificed everything else he possessed to obtain it." Nodding farewell, He continued down the road. His disciples followed silently.

Simon stared after them, long after they disappeared behind another gentle rise in the landscape. Sarai waited. When she had looked into Jesus' eyes, she wasn't sure what she sensed, but she liked it, despite the sensation that He knew all her hopes and dreams and lies and petty cruelties.

That was what she felt: accepted, known, *loved*, despite all her flaws and failures.

Yet how could that be? Jesus was only another rabbi, another teacher wandering the land, gathering disciples and sharing the bits of truth He had learned, the insights He had gained through hours of prayer and fasting and study, and waiting on El Shaddai.

"Did you hear that?" Simon's voice cracked. He held out a hand to Sarai and she hurried to join him. His hand felt hot and shook slightly when he grasped hers. "I know I've heard of this Jesus. I know I've heard the name spoken in the Sanhedrin, but ... I could almost believe He came from Yahweh. It was as if He knew about us, what I sacrificed to free you." His face glowed, making him so handsome and full of life, Sarai shivered. "I think we should find out more about this Nazarene."

"Where is He going, do you think?" she asked.

"Where else? Every prophet eventually goes to Jerusalem. I think this is a sign from Adonai. We are meant to be in Jerusalem. No more stopping in every small town for a day or two, and humbling ourselves to beg for work." His smile gentled and he raised his other hand to tug back her veil. "Sweet Sarai, can you be strong a little longer, until we are in Jerusalem?"

"You are my husband. Where you go, I will go. Your God is my God. Where you live, I will live, and where you die, there is where I will be buried."

"My treasure," he whispered. "My pearl of great price." He bent his head and brushed his lips ever so gently against hers.

Sarai closed her eyes and returned his kiss. She knew she had not quoted from the Scriptures properly, but she believed El Shaddai would forgive her. This was her husband. Did she not owe him everything?

~~~~~

Simon asked about Jesus at the next village. Sarai listened, fascinated by tales of the sick He had healed when He stopped there several days before, and the lessons He had taught about serving Yahweh and having faith. However, she noticed that Simon did not appear happy to have so much information. She couldn't be sure, but she thought the eagerness with which some people talked about Jesus bothered him. Especially the people who were healed.

"*Claimed* to be healed," Simon said, when she asked him in a quiet moment.

In mid-afternoon, the village well was momentarily deserted and made a good place to rest and speak privately. A shelter had been built over it, with a few benches, making it a gathering spot for the village women when they came to draw water in the morning and evening.

"They *claim* He healed them, or they at least *believe* they had some illness He remedied. I'm sure if I talk to wiser folk, those who know the people of this village and can see through the excitement, they'll tell me they are the kind who constantly imagine all sorts of illnesses. Like Old Thomas, the vinedresser who used to work for your father. You remember him, don't you? One moment he's full of aches and pains, sure that he's going to collapse and asking to see his burial shroud before he closes his eyes. The next moment, he hears about a festival in the next village and he's ready to drop his pruning knife and go running off to join in the singing and dancing."

Simon snorted and shook his head. His gaze darkened and focused on something in the distance. "I am afraid that I have heard more about this Jesus from Nazareth than was discussed in the Sanhedrin, and very little of it is good."

"But the people here --" Sarai began.

"We have only talked to the common people, not the leaders of this village. Certainly not the synagogue rulers. Besides, you were tired and hot, and we were just sitting down to rest when this Jesus came by. So was I. I'm not really sure what we heard."

"You said I was your pearl of great price, like Jesus talked about in His story. You were sure His words were a sign from Yahweh that we were to return to Jerusalem," Sarai half-whispered.

"Hmm ... well, as Michael used to say, if Adonai was willing to speak through Balaam's donkey, He will speak through anything and everything." Simon's grave expression brightened. He might have laughed in another moment. Instead, weariness settled over his features again. "This is a quiet, sheltered spot," he said, looking around the roughly paved area surrounding the well. "Stay here, and I will seek out those who know the truth of the situation. I have a duty to investigate these troubling stories. I'm sure the Sanhedrin will be grateful to know what this Jesus is doing and saying, away where they can't keep watch. Away from their influence."

"And what if you ask your questions and find out that these people weren't mistaken? What if everyone acknowledges they were truly ill, and now Jesus has given them health? What if it's true that He gave sight to a man who was blind for twenty years?"

"As I said, Yahweh works through many vessels and instruments, even dumb animals. I am sure our God is wise enough and strong enough to even work through ..." He sighed and rubbed his temples.

"You know what my father taught. Giving sight to the blind is a sign of --"

"No!" The sharpness of his tone seemed to surprise him as much as it did her. For a few long seconds, Simon stared at her.

She stared at him. She felt as if the darkness of the Roman prison cell once again closed around her, while her mind and body were numb with shock and grief.

Simon took a deep breath.

"No, my sweet Sarai. There is no possibility this Jesus, this untaught carpenter from Nazareth, of all places -- no possibility He could be the Messiah." He raised a hand, stopping her when she opened her mouth to protest, to offer more of her father's teachings.

Sarai caught her breath, more startled by the sudden thought that Simon could grow angry enough to strike her, than by the actual fear of being struck.

"You loved your father, and it is only right that you hold to his teachings, that you stay loyal to all he taught you. But think, Sarai.

69

Wouldn't the High Priest, who stands closest to Adonai, know better than anyone the true signs of the Messiah's coming? If Annas says Jesus is not the Messiah, a prophet, or instrument of God, then we must show humility and wisdom and accept his judgment."

Simon kissed her and left without giving her a chance to think of a response. Sarai said a silent prayer that he would learn the truth, and be satisfied, when he found the synagogue leaders.

She made use of the privacy and the shade, and the clay jar in a netting of rope, to draw up some water. First she drank, then she washed her face and hands and braided her hair. The shadows hadn't moved much across the pavement by then, and she calculated she had another two hours before the first of the women came to draw the evening water. She hadn't played her flute since that nightmarish encounter with the Rose of Sharon in the slave market, and right now she needed the comfort of music. A psalm had frightened the demons, and perhaps had influenced the brothel owner to abandon her. More worship songs would surely do her good and soothe her spirit.

Chapter Seven

Recalling the notes and trying to lose herself in memories of happier times, singing the psalm with her mother, helped to distract Sarai for a short time. Too soon, though, she thought about Simon's words and his tone of voice and expression. She scolded herself not to be disappointed. She knew Simon disagreed with her father's teachings about the Messiah first coming as the Suffering Servant.

I just didn't think he was so ... angry in his disagreement.

In the years since Simon had ended his studies with her father, just how much had his attitude and loyalties changed? Perhaps he had changed far more than she had guessed, from the determined, studious, intelligent boy she remembered.

You're a fool, Sarai beth Eliakim. You hear a man speak only once, you look into His eyes, you imagine that He knows your soul, He seems to speak with God's wisdom and insight beyond all mortal hearts ... how can you so easily believe He could be the Messiah? Simon is right. There are more details of the story than we heard, and the blind man who was healed perhaps wasn't truly ...

Sarai sighed and put down her flute. What was she thinking? Surely if a man was blind, he would know it? Surely the people who knew him, lived with him for years, would know if he was blind rather than pretending, malingering, playing a game? Life was not kind to the blind, not even if they came from a wealthy family and had servants to guide them and attend to their every need. Chances were stronger that a man who had been blind for twenty years was a beggar, and his family had been reduced to threadbare circumstances if he was the provider. Why would someone *pretend* to be blind?

So if Jesus had truly healed a blind man ...

She shivered, hearing her father's voice in her mind, echoes from many overheard discussions with his scholarly friends. Despite their many disagreements, they all had to agree: restoring sight to the blind was a sure, undeniable sign the Messiah had come among them.

So how could Simon refuse to believe? Surely, after he talked to the leaders in this village, he would have proof and he would be convinced?

Sarai raised her flute back to her lips and chose a new song, a happier one. She would be smiling and rested and ready to make Simon smile when he returned for her.

"Hello."

The voice was soft, weary. The woman who stepped up to the bench a third of the way around the well pavement looked even more weary than her voice. She appeared a few years older than Sarai, dressed in clothes that looked new, the colors still bright, no frayed edges or faded spots. She carried a child cradled in a sling of cloth. It was knotted on her left shoulder and hung across her chest, with the child curled up against her right side. Her right arm braced the child, and her left hand held a large basket, the contents covered with a cloth. She had likely come from the marketplace, two streets away from this quiet spot. A village this large would have several wells. The market had likely formed around the largest one.

"Elohim's blessings on you," Sarai said.

"Are you new-come to our village?" The woman put down the basket, then bent and set the child down on the bench. "I don't know your face, and we have certainly grown enough in the last few years that I wouldn't know everyone."

"We are travelers, my husband and I." She guessed what the mother was about to do, when she lifted the sling off over her head. Sarai hurried to pick up the jar that sat on the well lip and lowered it on its rope. "Let me."

"Thank you." She settled down next to the child and drew back the enfolding cloth. "I am Adah. This is Elias."

She slid her arm under the little boy and raised him up. Sarai held out the jar. She couldn't see anything for the boy to drink from other than the jar.

"Wait a moment, this should make it easier." She put down the jar on the bench and hurried to dig through the bag that she had put down on the pavement under the bench.

In a moment she had a small wooden cup Simon had carved for her one night when they had taken shelter with a woodworker and his apprentices. Sarai nearly fumbled the cup, stunned with the strength of her wish that Simon had accepted the carpenter's invitation to stay and join in his thriving business. All based on the beauty of the cup, and a box shaped like an apple he had made that same night. The skill of Simon's hands had earned great admiration from the woodworker.

Her hand didn't shake as she dipped up water in the cup and held it out to Adah to let her son drink.

"You are very kind. Usually I am prepared, but I took longer at the market than I planned, and he is so thirsty … the fever is worse today. I thought after so long, it would have run its course and …" A strangled sob, badly muffled, choked off Adah's voice.

"How long has he been ill?" Sarai stepped closer. She studied the little boy's pale face, the sweat beading his forehead, the parched lips, the sharpness of his cheekbones and collar bone. His limbs would also show signs of emaciation from fever and likely from being unable to eat.

"It feels like years. Perhaps ten days. How can a child be so full of life one day, and the next shivering and unable to keep down any food?"

"But he can still drink," Sarai said. "That is always a good sign." She offered the boy a smile. Elias tried to smile around the lip of the cup. His frail hand pressed against his mother's as she held it to his mouth.

"Is it?" Adah looked up at her. "How can you be sure?"

"I … have had some training in healing. Do you know how he fell ill? I mean, did he injure himself? Were there sick people around him? Did he touch a dead body? Some filth, out in the fields or forest?"

Adah flinched when Sarai said "injure." She pulled back the blanket to show a discolored, crusted bandage wrapped around the boy's calf. Sarai flinched even before the stench of the liquid oozing through the bandage reached her nose. The words of numerous texts, from different countries and teachers, spilled through her mind. Common sense said the wound had gone bad and poisoned the boy's blood. If she cleansed the wound, that would give the boy a chance to heal.

"I will try to help him, if you will trust me," she said, and reached for the bag again. She thanked Elisheva's grateful family and the gift of all the healing herbs.

As Huldah had taught her, Sarai hummed a psalm as she lay out the ingredients she would need. That caught Elias' attention and he smiled a little as his mother stretched him out on the bench. Sarai asked Adah to fetch more water, because washing was the largest part of the healing process. She tried not to complain, even just in her head, about the thoughtless person who had bungled the initial treatment of the injury, and let it go bad. Likely Adah didn't know any better, but surely someone in the village should know the laws of cleanliness spelled out in scripture? That should have prevented half the problem right away. Huldah had spoken for some length on the simple solution of cleansing a wound thoroughly, pouring on wine to purify and oil to seal and moisten and soothe the torn flesh.

Sarai stopped humming and recited one psalm after another, choosing the ones that always helped when tending wounds as foul-smelling and messy as this otherwise simple gash. She chose psalms with a catchy rhythm and big words that always seemed to entertain the children. Elias whispered the words with her. The recitation seemed to distract him from the painful process of cleansing the wound.

"Ah, there, you see?" Sarai held out two fingers for Adah to see pieces of grit and what looked like a soggy, thick splinter of wood that measured from the tip of her finger to the first joint. "The wound was dirty, and held onto the sickness. That is why all the ugly weeping of the flesh. But you are very brave. That must have hurt terribly, but you are brave and strong, aren't you?" She patted Elias' shoulder. The boy nodded, and his smile grew a little wider.

"The big, arrogant fool," Adah whispered, with tears in her eyes. "Jehu, his father -- he let his grandmother tend Elias, instead of taking him to the midwife when he first hurt his leg. She insisted on covering the wound with clay and wrapping a cloth soaked in wine around it and told us not to remove it." She shuddered, clearly furious, and wiped tears away with the heels of both hands. "She shrieked at me when I tried to wash the wound first. She's just a crazy old woman who believes she should have gone to serve in the Temple. She says angels speak with her, and she's constantly throwing curses at anyone who disagrees with her. Jehu is terrified of her. He wouldn't listen to me." A sob escaped her. "He wouldn't even let me take our son to Jesus, when He was here."

"Do you think Jesus would have healed him?" Sarai asked, as she sprinkled powdered herbs into the cleansed wound. According to the texts she had read, they would fight the sickness in the flesh and dry the wound, so it would begin to heal and close.

"It doesn't matter. Jehu is just as much afraid of the synagogue leaders, even though they contradict everything his grandmother says. They have orders from the Sanhedrin, just come to our village five days ago. Have nothing to do with this new rabbi, Jesus of Nazareth. They won't say why. Jehu thinks the Sanhedrin isn't sure yet what to do with Him, so they just say stay away from Him." Adah smiled through her tears. "Ah, but you are a gift from Adonai. I prayed for so long. I was so afraid Elias would grow up lame, or … or worse."

"He is not healed yet," Sarai said, after wrapping some clean cloth around the wound. "If the grandmother finds out what I did for him, what will she do?"

"Oh, she will try to chase you from the village, calling down a thousand curses on you. Demand the angels make you barren. Threaten you with a dozen demons to eat your soul." Adah shook her head. "If I could, I would leave this village. At least until she joins her ancestors."

"Do you have any relatives in other villages you could go visit?" Sarai nearly laughed when Adah sat up straight, eyes widening, looking as stunned as if she had been hit in the face with a board. Clearly, the woman did have relatives elsewhere, and had never thought to take shelter among them.

Sarai was exhausted by the time Adah had gathered up Elias to go home. She gave the grateful mother several bundles of powdered herbs, wrapped in bits of cloth. Two were to sprinkle in the wound when she washed it with water and wine and sealed with oil, three times a day. The third, she was to mix with warmed wine to have Elias drink in the morning and before he went to bed, to strengthen his blood. The fourth was a powder of willow bark, to fight pain and fever. She gave Adah instructions to give the boy anything he wanted to eat, as much as he wanted. Huldah had always insisted that the body knew what would do it the most good. People needed to learn to listen to their bodies, just as much as they needed to learn to listen to the Spirit of Adonai.

When she was alone again, Sarai closed her eyes and played a

75

soft, slow tune to refresh her spirit, and she prayed. She had tried to forget that bitter future that had awaited her when she went to the Decapolis. At the time, the thought of spending her life as a healer for harlots didn't seem much better than being a harlot. Certainly even harlots deserved some mercy and help? Most didn't choose the life but were forced into it as slaves. Just as she might have been, if another man had bought her in the slave market.

She much preferred being a healer and midwife, but had considered letting her gifts go unused, to protect Simon. They hadn't discussed how Benjamin had insulted him and then nearly asked Sarai to stay as a healer for the small Jewish community in the Decapolis. How could she in all good conscience perform as a midwife and healer in a place where her husband was mocked? In a place where he was not respected for his talents?

She couldn't.

Yet she longed to use her gifts. What was wrong with using the skills and knowledge Adonai had given her to help others, as she had helped Adah and Elias just now? Wouldn't Adonai bless them and bring her and Simon to a new home where he would be respected as a man of learning, and she could be a healer?

Adah returned to the well shelter before Simon did. Her husband carried Elias, and she carried a basket of provisions for Sarai, in thanks. Fresh bread, raisin cakes, honey cakes, dried meat, and a skin of wine. Jehu was a big man, full of muscles, tanned dark by farm work. He handled his sick little son with a gentle tenderness that brought tears to Sarai's eyes when she thought about the family later. He had sheets of papyrus and a small cake of ink and a quill, to have Sarai write her instructions, and the recipe for more of the potion and powdered herbs. He couldn't read, himself, but he had a cousin who was a scribe in another village, a full day's journey away. This cousin could read the instructions and make sure the family followed them. Jehu agreed with Adah, they would go visit his cousin and stay there until Elias was well, and safe from his grandmother's interference.

Simon joined them just as Sarai finished writing out the instructions. He approached quietly and did not demand to know what was going on, as Sarai had seen other men do. He gravely nodded acknowledgement, when Jehu thanked him for the help Sarai had given Elias. Simon flushed a little when the big farmer said they were a gift from Adonai. Sarai went cold inside, when Jehu said they were a reward for obeying the synagogue leaders and not taking Elias to Jesus for healing.

When the family left, Simon gathered up his bag and Sarai's, and let her carry the basket of food. He merely said he had found a place for them to spend the night and led her away from the well. Just in time, because women were approaching with their water jars. The shadows of sunset were stretching across the sparse paving stones and packed dirt. He walked more swiftly than usual, his legs stretching out in longer steps than Sarai could match.

She waited until they had gone down two streets and made two turns and were on a third street before venturing to ask, "Are you displeased with me?"

"Displeased?" Simon went pale and he stopped so suddenly she nearly ran into him. "Sarai ..." He exhaled loudly and bowed his head. "No, my dearest, I am not displeased. I am ... I am not sure what I am thinking or feeling. I should be proud of how you offered help." He tried to smile.

Should be? Her mind seemed to snag on the odd wording. Did that mean Simon wasn't proud of her? What had she done wrong?

"You are kind and generous and pure of heart, and in any other situation ..." Simon sighed again and turned, gesturing for them to resume walking. "The sad truth is that your father was condemned for indulging your unusual education."

"Yes, I heard Caiaphas criticize my father. He said it was indecent, allowing me to serve as a midwife when I was still a virgin. He questioned whether I was no longer a virgin. I am sure that brought on the fit that eventually killed my father."

Her lips seemed to burn after releasing those words. Sarai had thought them often during the long months of her father's illness, but she had never dared to speak them aloud.

"I am sure he was not truly angry about that. No, what worried him were all those scrolls of Gentile teachings and beliefs." Simon's shoulders hunched briefly, and his mouth flattened. He gained speed again. "I will not order you to stop serving as a midwife. I will only ask you to refrain from using what you have learned from Gentiles, what you read in the scrolls. Use the knowledge Huldah imparted to you. I am proud of your healing skills, but only use the clean wisdom that comes from our own people. And do it quietly.

You do not want to attract the attention of the Sanhedrin while they still remember your father in anger."

He is afraid. He risked so much for me ... but maybe not all? Sarai immediately gave herself a mental slap for such thoughts. Who was she to grudge Simon some sadness and second thoughts over all he had sacrificed?

"I will be circumspect and avoid notice whenever possible. Will that please you, my husband?"

"Everything you do pleases me, Sarai." He turned and smiled at her. Then he tipped his head back and sighed loudly. "I am sorry." He slowed his pace so she could keep up with him.

Before she could sort out some of the thoughts swirling through her head, Simon told her where they were going. Their hosts for the night were Ananias and Naomi. He was a former leader of the synagogue. Blind now, he was a teacher for the boys who wanted to go on to advanced studies with rabbis in larger towns. Sarai braced herself for a warning not to talk about Jesus, or perhaps not even talk about Adah, Elias and Jehu. It didn't come, but she kept quiet during their stay, and waited for Simon to introduce any subjects that were safe for discussion.

They stayed two days with Ananias and Naomi, who were pleasant hosts, if reserved. Sarai longed to ask about the people in the village, their reaction to Jesus' visit, His teachings, and especially if the people He had healed had truly been sick. Simon did not bring up the subject, so she didn't dare. She heard little gossip about the villagers, and never left the house's luxurious courtyard with its two olive trees and a tiny fountain.

When she and Simon left the village, they rode with a merchant caravan that was making a wide circle to the west before turning toward Jerusalem. They would reach the city several days after they would have arrived if they had gone on foot. Ananias insisted they conserve their strength and ride. The caravan leader was his sister's oldest son, and he would feel much better about their safety if they stayed with his nephew. Sarai was not surprised to learn later that Ananias had entrusted Simon with a written report, compiled by all the synagogue leaders, of everything Jesus had said and done while He was in their village. She was a little disappointed, though, and suspected their benefactor cared more about the delivery of the report than he did about their continued welfare.

~~~~~

Sarai trembled, that hot afternoon as they entered Jerusalem. Riding with the merchant caravan gave her too much leisure to anticipate and worry. All the thoughts she had avoided on their journey besieged her now. How would people react when they saw and recognized her? People who knew how her father had been condemned by the Sanhedrin. Who knew of Joseph and the Zealots and the failed raid that had led to his crucifixion.

The dust and shadows cast by the tall buildings enclosed her, as if swallowing her alive. Then the thickening crowds of Jerusalem did swallow her. She startled every time she thought she heard a half-familiar voice. She told herself she only feared for Simon's dignity, and the mockery others would heap on him when they recognized him.

She vowed not to care about the shame, the gossip, the speculative looks that would surround her once someone recognized her. The fact that she had been rescued, that she had been sold for Joseph's crimes, wouldn't matter to some people. She would always be soiled, unworthy in their eyes. She remembered now what the jailer had told her, that a priest had asked that she be sent to the Rose of Sharon. If that was so, her enemy might have spread the news deliberately, to add to her shame. All of Jerusalem could already be convinced she was a harlot right that moment, enslaved to a demon-possessed woman. It wouldn't matter how many times Simon swore she was a virgin on their bridal night, she would always be considered unclean.

Sarai could only pray that if Caiaphas was the one who had condemned her because of her father's heresy, that he had told no one. How could he explain that he knew of the Rose of Sharon and her brothel, without smearing himself with a little of the filth he tried to use to cover Sarai?

She vowed she would accept all the humiliation that came her way, for her father's sake, but she would not let Simon be punished for his goodness to her. He had done a great and noble thing, and he deserved to be praised and rewarded. If the only way to protect Simon was to stay in their home, to never let anyone see her face, or have anyone know her name or her father's name, then so be it.

As they walked into the heart of Jerusalem, she wrapped her veil closer and bowed her head and struggled to keep up with

Simon's long-legged stride. She told herself she didn't care how people speculated on her treatment when the Romans confiscated everything after Joseph's arrest. Many people preferred vicious lies to the truth, because the lies were always more exciting.

Simon took her to the market in the lower quarter of the city. Sarai wondered if he were going to try to find a job as a stonemason or a stable worker or some other occupation he knew. Not to make a living for the rest of his life. No, only to fill the gap until he found someone kind and generous, to give him work that suited his talents. He had been a blessing from Adonai when he was her father's student, because he did so many tasks well. It was late in the day, too late to meet up with the men who came to the market to hire laborers by the day. Perhaps Simon was here simply to hear the news of what large building projects were in the making or who needed workers. He would return in the morning to find work.

She remembered that report he had promised to deliver to the Sanhedrin, and she shivered. What would result from that errand? Would Simon meet anyone who looked on him with kindness? Maybe someone who would give them shelter for a few days, until he could find work and a place for them to live? Or would all his service to the Sanhedrin be outweighed by her father's heresy?

While she was pondering the possibilities, they passed right through the fountain square where the hiring was done. Sarai pressed her parched lips together and ignored the dusty feeling in her mouth and throat. What was Simon doing? What did he intend? They were going the wrong way if he was going to the Sanhedrin. She had vowed silently, many times along the way, she would never question him. The need to ask him what he intended burned in her head, exacerbating the dusty, hot feeling that sapped her strength and bowed her shoulders.

He studied different people as he led her down the crowded, narrow pathways between the stalls, the carts piled with fruits and vegetables, the cages with ducks and chickens ready for butchering. They passed out of that portion of the marketplace. Now she saw stalls with sandals, veils, belts, other items of clothing. They kept walking.

"Can that be Sarai?"

A scratchy, high voice broke through her musing. Sarai cringed as she realized her veil had slipped back on her head, revealing her face. She glanced around, searching for the familiar voice, half-longing for that friend and half-fearing to see her.

Simon had led her to the quarter of the market where the cloth and jewelry merchants displayed their wares. Yes, that was Ruth in the stall her father had owned for nearly thirty years, only a few steps away and staring.

The slightly younger woman had come since childhood with her father to hand-deliver cloth to Rabbi Eliakim's household. Sarai had always looked forward to those deliveries, when she could take her friend aside and giggle and play and learn about the latest news in Jerusalem. Ruth had been delighted to be considered her friend and boasted of their friendship, and that she would attend Sarai when she married.

Ruth stood half-hidden in the shadows of her stall. One raised hand clutched a length of pale blue cloth, so fine it glistened in the afternoon light. Plump, red-cheeked, with tightly curled black hair and an incongruously pointed nose that twitched whenever something roused her interest. She had always been outspoken, quick to pass judgment on people.

"Yes." The woman standing in front of her stall had a narrow, sharp-boned face that glowed with a delighted smile. Norah. "It is her."

Market gossip said a man might shy away from marrying Norah because she wasn't pretty, all skin and bones, with dusty, limp hair, but he would be the luckiest man in Jerusalem because of her cooking and her calm, reasonable personality. Norah, however, had refused every suitor until Abner came to the inn on Spindle Street, and Malachi had never forced her. He was a hard, strong man when it came to his inn, but soft when it came to his daughter's happiness. No one had made Norah smile like Abner did.

Abner had died in the failed raid. Sarai cringed, half-expecting Norah's smile to shatter in another moment, reminded of his death. Abner had brought Joseph into the Zealots, but Norah might still be so hurt she would blame Joseph for her pain. Abner might have married her two years ago, if he hadn't become so devoted to traveling the length of Judea, spying for the Zealots.

"I want to believe it's her." Ruth's voice rose, sharpening until it made the hairs on Sarai's arms stand up. "But it can't be. Sarai was

81

taken as a slave more than a month ago."

"I'm positive that's Sarai." Norah took a step away from the stall and her smile widened when she saw Sarai looking at them. "That man with her is Simon."

"Simon's never coming back to Jerusalem," Ruth retorted with a sniff. She put down the cloth and straightened the folds. "He embarrassed Rabbi Nicodemus. If Simon has any intelligence left, he won't show his face in Jerusalem for the rest of his life."

Sarai looked around, and nearly laughed with relief when she saw Simon had moved so far ahead of her, he couldn't possibly have heard Ruth's words.

"Then I pray he has no sense," Norah said with a laugh. She stepped across the gap in the crowd and held out a hand. "Sarai? Is that really you?"

Before Sarai could answer, Norah laughed and flung her arms around her. Tears filled Sarai's eyes and she could scarcely take a breath for the trembling that washed through her body. Amazingly, she felt like laughing as she returned her friend's embrace.

"Praise be to Yahweh!" Ruth exclaimed. She scurried out of the stall and joined them, wrapping her plump arms around both women. "It is you! I told you so, Norah. This woman has no faith in our God's goodness."

Sarai choked on laughter. Ruth would never change, and she was heartily glad of it. Over Norah's shoulder, she saw Simon looking around, worry starting to touch his face. She raised a hand to get his attention.

"What happened? How are you here?" Norah demanded.

"Simon found and rescued and married me, and now we are to make our home in Jerusalem. He is my husband and I am proud to belong to him," she added, reacting to the lingering sting of Ruth's words. Sarai wiped the tears from her eyes and turned to Simon as he joined them in front of Ruth's stall.

Chapter Eight

Her heart seemed to stop short when she looked into his eyes and saw such joy in his face, he seemed to glow. An aching filled her chest. She wanted him to be forever happy, forever looking at her with that expression in his eyes.

"But where will you live?" Ruth demanded. "How will you make a living? Simon, you can't expect Rabbi Nicodemus to take you back, after you embarrassed him in front of the Sanhedrin."

"Our God helped me find Sarai." Simon took hold of her hand. The simple gesture drew happy tears to warm her eyes. "I believe He will provide for us. I have an errand to run. Will you watch over my Sarai until I return?"

"She's like a sister to us. Of course, we'll watch over her." Norah gestured for Sarai to step into the shelter of the cloth stall.

Simon put down their bags, retrieved the packet of papyrus sheets Ananias had entrusted to him, made his farewells, and hurried away.

Bolts of the most expensive, fragile fabrics waited in the shade, along with stools to sit on and Ruth's provisions for the day. Sarai laughed, wondering how she could have forgotten. Ruth couldn't tend to the stall without a basket of fruit, a pitcher of watered wine, and a platter of honey cakes to nibble on during the day.

For the first time in her life, she was heartily glad for her friend's habits. Without asking, Norah filled cups for them all and handed Sarai the honey cakes. Ruth didn't make a single murmur of protest, which was a sure sign of her interest in hearing all the details. Sarai sighed and tried not to gulp the entire contents of the cup. She watched Simon hurry away, through the marketplace, heading in the direction of the more expensive, aristocratic homes in Jerusalem. She shivered and said a silent prayer that when he turned in that report, he would only encounter friends. Not those who would punish him for rescuing her.

"Where is he going?" Ruth took the platter of honey cakes.

"I think …" Sarai sighed. Would she threaten his chances, bringing ill luck down on Simon if she spoke her thoughts? "He promised a rabbi in another village to deliver a report to the Sanhedrin. After that, I think he hopes to speak with Rabbi Nicodemus. He doesn't hope to become his apprentice again." She knew that was true. However, Nicodemus was known as a forgiving, generous man. "But Simon is a good scribe and will work hard. Rabbi Nicodemus has so much work, so many responsibilities, surely there will be something he can give Simon to do, to earn a living. God has already blessed us so much, who are we to doubt Him?"

"But what happened to you? We heard the Romans took you away to sell as a slave. Everyone was so sure you would be sold to a general or a centurion to be his mistress. You could have gone to Rome!" She shivered, but her eyes sparkled, so Sarai couldn't decide if Ruth was horrified or envious of such a fate.

"Be quiet and let her tell us," Norah said with a chuckle. She refilled Sarai's cup and settled on the last stool.

Sarai told them. About the hot, dry, bruising trip. How Agabus kept such tight, careful watch over them. Watching the other girls be sold off along the way. Arriving in the market in the Decapolis and being washed and prepared for the market. What Mara had told her. She even told them a little about Laila, the Rose of Sharon, her partnership with the Zealots, and what Hananiah and Hadasseh had told her. Sarai shivered a little and decided not to tell them her suspicions that Caiaphas was responsible for her being sent to serve Laila's brothel, or what happened when the demon spoke through her.

Her two friends sighed and smiled when she told them how Simon bought her in the slave market and took her to Hananiah to be married.

"You do lead an exciting life," Ruth said with another sigh. She had been so caught up in Sarai's story, she forgot the honey cake sitting in her hand.

"Yahweh protect me from that kind of excitement," Norah muttered. She turned her head so their plump friend couldn't see and rolled her eyes expressively.

Sarai choked, inhaling a crumb of honey cake when she tried not to laugh. In the silence while the three smiled at each other, the rising clamor of voices came clearly through the marketplace.

"Can you see what's going on?" Norah tried to peer around the side of the stall, but Ruth had a far better view.

She leaned over the shelf of the stall, sticking her head out into the sunshine. She rested her elbows carelessly on piles of fine cloth. An excited giggle escaped her, and her whole body wriggled like a happy puppy.

"It looks like that rabbi from Nazareth again," Ruth reported. "He's been traveling the countryside for so long. Do you know when He returned to Jerusalem?" she hurried on before either one could answer. "I hope He stops here. He says such interesting things!"

Yes, interesting things, just as my life was exciting. Sarai caught her breath, wondering how she could be so cynical. Yet, after what she had gone through, who would not be cynical or even bitter?

Then Ruth's words finally made sense in her mind. She gasped a little louder.

"Jesus from Nazareth? He's in Jerusalem?" She stood and tried to lean out of the stall to look. Her heart warmed as she remembered that single glance she and Jesus had shared, that day by the side of the road.

"Where else would the Messiah come, but to Jerusalem?" Norah said with a shrug.

"Talk like that could get you in trouble with the Sanhedrin." Ruth settled down on her stool and gestured out into the street. "And here they come now!"

Sarai froze as Caiaphas stalked down the street. The elegant, dark-haired man wore the same blue, white, and gold robes he had worn the day her father had his fit. The same scowl. The same blue tassels on the corners of his robe and his prayer shawl. His eyes blazed with the same fury he had unleashed on her father.

Would Caiaphas grow red-faced, nearly spitting as he spewed fury at Jesus? His elegant facade had slipped loose several times when he came to deliver Annas' condemnation, even as her father calmly quoted Scripture that supported his teachings.

Five handsomely dressed men followed in his wake. Sarai remembered her father's words one particularly unhappy night, when she crept through the darkness of the garden, shivering, to comfort him. He had sighed, laughed ruefully and embraced her.

"My precious child, I now have proof that those who wish to advance in power among men become foolish in the ways of the Almighty God.

They ignore what is clearly stated in Scriptures, to hold fast to teachings that permit them to walk in arrogance and self-righteousness. It is far easier to nod your head and agree with those in high positions, rather than to think for yourself and listen to the still, small voice of Adonai."

Sarai watched the five men following in Caiaphas' shadow and wondered if they dared to think for themselves. Had they chosen to affirm every word that came from Caiaphas' mouth? When had Caiaphas stopped thinking for himself and decided not to obey the still, small voice of truth that came from Adonai?

I have been out in the sun too long. I am only tired. Sarai shivered and settled down on her stool in the shade again.

Indeed, how could she think such thoughts? Her father had died in disgrace. Her brother had died for his rebellion. She had been humiliated and sold as a slave. If Adonai hadn't permitted it to punish her father through her, then perhaps He had allowed these things to happen to her to teach her to have more compassion. Who was she to judge anyone? How dared she, a mere woman, criticize and judge one of the religious leaders of Israel?

"I wonder what they're upset about now?" Ruth said with a giggle.

Norah hushed her. All three women held perfectly still, when the six men came to a stop nearly in front of the cloth stall. The three had a perfect view of their angry faces and no need to strain their ears to hear the conversation.

"What are we going to do, Caiaphas?" the tallest man said. "Nothing we've done yet has stopped this Jesus from teaching wherever He goes."

"The more He teaches," another said in a whining, scratchy voice, "the less people listen to us. Once we lose control of the people, Rome won't need us anymore." He stomped like a petulant child.

"If there's a revolt, Rome will blame us," the one standing at the far end of the line said, nodding. He was classically handsome, despite the streaks of silver in his prayer curls and the hair emerging from under his turban.

Sarai stared, shocked, when Ruth sighed and rested her elbows on the edge of the counter to stare at the speaker. A fatuous little smile brightened her face. The man was old enough to be her father and was undoubtedly married.

"We will deal with Jesus when the time is ripe." Caiaphas' voice rumbled soft and mellow, sounding eminently reasonable. Sarai shivered even more at the sound of it than when he had shouted at her father and his voice cracked with venom. "For now, we listen and gather evidence."

"There should be a great deal of evidence to gather," the tall man said as the commotion of laughing, calling voices grew louder. He pointed. Sarai looked between their shoulders and saw a knot of men come down the street.

Jesus led them. Sarai smiled just to see His kind face, the life and compassion in His eyes. A little barefoot boy darted out into the street from a merchant's shop. Jesus stopped to smile and speak a few words and rest His hand in blessing on the boy's head.

"Isn't that Simon?" Norah whispered. She pointed, further back in the crowd.

Sarai felt a tight, yet warm stirring in her chest. Indeed, Simon walked at the edge of the growing crowd. Jesus led the way, with His disciples in a cluster around Him. Then a handful of people followed, all talking to each other and pointing at Jesus, watching Him as if they expected Him to produce manna from thin air.

Three men seemed to stand out from the crowd. One was Simon. On his left walked Rabbi Nicodemus, his robes dark and dignified by their very simplicity, his neatly trimmed beard touched with more silver since the last time Sarai saw him.

Her heart jolted as she recognized the third man. Jude ben Boaz walked on Rabbi Nicodemus' left. Not nearly as tall as Simon, not nearly as broad-shouldered. He seemed barely out of childhood with his slim stature and swinging, easy stride.

No. It was wrong to let her mind dwell even for a few seconds on a man who was not her husband. Simon had risked all to save her. Jude could have saved her from the Romans and not felt a dent in his riches. Yet he was nowhere to be found when she truly needed him. She believed even more her brother's words, that Jude did not ask for her because his father feared Annas' condemnation. If Jude did not act against his father, and his father did not act without the approval of Annas, how could she have thought he would have saved her from the Romans?

Jesus settled down on the edge of the fountain in the middle of the market square. Someone in the crowd asked Him something.

Sarai couldn't hear the words, but others in the crowd called affirmation. Caiaphas and his sycophants scowled and muttered and moved away from the cloth stall.

Sarai leaned forward on the counter to see better. That one tiny story, overheard at the side of the road, had not been enough.

At a gesture from Jesus, the small crowd settled down on the cobblestones and the edge of the fountain. Children quieted. The disciples gathered around Jesus like a phalanx of guards. Sarai wondered if they feared for their rabbi's safety, or they simply wanted everyone to know they were His students.

"He's going to repeat it for us. My cousin was there on the hillside when he spoke," a woman called to another woman who stood only a few steps away from the cloth stall. She tugged a child onto her lap and leaned forward, visibly eager to hear whatever Jesus said.

"Blessed are those who hunger and thirst for righteousness, for they will be filled."

Jesus looked around the market square, as if He looked at each person individually. His gaze seemed to linger a few seconds on the three women in the stall. Sarai knew, with a certainty that warmed her, He saw her. Then His gaze slid on to touch Caiaphas and his followers.

"Blessed are the merciful," Jesus continued, "for they will be shown mercy. Blessed are those who are persecuted for righteousness, for theirs is the kingdom of heaven. Love your enemies, do good to those who hate you, pray for those who mistreat you. If you only do good to those who are good to you, how does that make you better than anyone else? Sinners do that. But love your enemies. Be merciful, just as your Father is merciful."

"What about justice and the Law?" the man with the whining voice called. "Moses gave us the Law."

"Ahaz only cares about the law when he can use it to bully others," Ruth muttered.

Norah hushed her and cast a worried glance at the six men. They were still close enough to hear the women speak, but Sarai thought they were so focused on Jesus, they wouldn't have heard.

"I have not come to abolish the Law or the Prophets, but to fulfill them." Jesus stood and turned to address the people sitting at His feet, looking at each face. "Unless your righteousness surpasses the religious leaders, you will not enter the Kingdom of Heaven."

"How can anyone do that?" the tall man among Caiaphas' followers called. His shoulders pulled back a little straighter and his scowl softened.

Sarai swallowed a giggle. Did he actually think Jesus was complimenting them? She knew instinctively He had not been speaking in approval.

"Who is he?" she whispered to Norah, nodding to the man.

"That's Rueben. He's Caiaphas' right hand," her friend whispered back.

"He says my father's cloth is the only cloth in the city fine enough for him," Ruth added. "Unfortunately, that's all he seems to notice when he comes to buy." She sighed and fluttered her eyelashes at the man.

Sarai muffled a giggle when Norah rolled her eyes again. Ruth focused too much on Reuben to notice their exchange.

"Be careful not to do your good deeds where people can see them." Jesus turned to look directly at the six men from the Sanhedrin. Or did He look into the cloth stall, speaking directly to the three women? "When you pray, go into your room and close the door. Then your Father, who sees what is done in secret, will reward you."

"How should we pray, then?" Rabbi Nicodemus said, stepping forward. He gave Jesus a little bow of respect. Warm relief flooded Sarai. She didn't know what she would have felt, if he condemned Jesus. It would have meant he had finally given in to Annas' teachings and agreed that the Messiah would only come in triumph. Never the Suffering Servant of her father's teachings.

"This is how you should pray." Jesus spread His arms, as if gathering everyone in the square close to Him. He bowed His head in humility and closed His eyes.

Sarai compared His actions and posture to that of the men of power she had seen all her life. Her own father had often prayed with his arms stretched to heaven, head tilted back and voice booming as he listed all the good deeds he had done since his last prayer. Did God need to be reminded, to reward people properly? Sarai had sometimes wondered, but had never dared to ask.

"Our Father in heaven," Jesus said, in the tones of one petitioning an official. "Holy and adored is Your name. May Your kingdom come among us. May Your will be done on Earth as it is done in Heaven. Give us today our daily bread. Forgive our offenses as we have forgiven those who offend us. And lead us not into testing and trials, but deliver us from Satan."

"Why should we forgive people who offend us?" a previously silent member of Caiaphas' group called out.

People muttered and cast wary, even angry glances. Sarai was shocked that even these men dared to interrupt the teaching of a rabbi. Did this show genuine interest in learning from Jesus, or just their lack of respect for Him?

"If you forgive men when they sin against you, your heavenly Father will also forgive you. But if you do not forgive men their sins, your Father will not forgive your sins," Jesus said, without hesitation or any sign that the question irritated Him.

"Who are you to speak for God?" The speaker's voice cracked and squeaked. Now Sarai remembered him. Menahem had wavered often between her father's teachings and following Annas. He had finally decided who was safer to support. "You are a false prophet. All you people, go home! Do not listen to this man!"

"What has He done?" a burly, sweat-stained man called from the crowd. "He's said nothing that isn't of God."

"He speaks against the Sanhedrin. His works are of the devil."

"Give us a sign to prove who you are!" Ahaz added.

"When evening comes," Jesus said after a moment, "you say, 'It will be fair weather tomorrow, for the sky is red.' You know how to interpret the sky, but you cannot interpret the signs of the times." He smiled gently as He spoke, and His tone was warm.

Caiaphas and his knot of followers muttered among themselves, as if Jesus had scolded them instead of responding with kindness. And a touch of humor.

Perhaps, Sarai thought, that angered them more. He didn't react in anger or fear but challenged their dignity by *refusing* to react in fear. That, she knew, was a greater sin in their sight than even murder or adultery.

Caiaphas and his followers stayed where they were, scowling and muttering among themselves, as more people in the crowd shouted questions. From the way they were phrased, Sarai guessed some of those questions were asking for explanation of things Jesus had taught at other times. When Simon came to retrieve her, would he be willing to talk and consider what Jesus taught? Or would he remain adamant that Jesus could not be from God, simply because Annas did not approve of Him?

"Master," a disciple asked, "if the way is so narrow and so few can find it, then who can be saved?"

"He's a good one to ask," Ruth said with a giggle. "That's Levi, the tax collector. People say he walked away from a houseful of treasures -- stolen from fellow Jews, of course -- to follow Jesus and be the scribe among His followers. If a tax collector can be allowed into Heaven, anyone can."

"With God all things are possible," Jesus said, in answer to His student's question.

"You're just upset because he didn't ask your father for you." Norah met Sarai's startled gaze and rolled her eyes, indicating she was teasing.

"Father wouldn't soil himself by selling cloth to a tax collector, much less let me marry one." Ruth sighed. "He is relatively handsome, but since he's no longer rich, why does it matter? Why does everyone condemn riches? Is it a sin to be rich? Isn't it a sign of Yahweh's blessing?"

Sarai thought of her father, and how little good his orchards and vineyards and fields had done for him. He had died abandoned by most of his peers, condemned by the High Priest for the things he taught directly from Scripture.

"Lord," a broad-shouldered, tanned disciple said, "we have given up everything to follow You."

"If anyone would come after Me," Jesus said, turning to address the entire crowd again, "he must deny himself and take up his cross and follow Me. For whoever wants to save his life will lose it, but whoever loses his life for Me and for the good news from Heaven will save it."

That sounded suspiciously like something the Zealots would say, to recruit foolish, hot-headed young men. Such words made the loss of life, the risk of imprisonment and torture and disgrace, sound honorable. Sarai clenched her fist, reducing the remains of her honey cake to crumbs. She didn't want to hear any more, if Jesus insisted on saying such things.

Only a few questions later, Jesus sent the crowd on their way. He and His disciples continued down the street, past the cloth stall.

The people who had been following Him scattered, some back to their shops, others back down the street, some to scoop up handfuls of water from the fountain and drink before wandering away. Caiaphas and his companions stalked away, headed a different direction from Jesus and His disciples.

Simon and Nicodemus talked, walking slowly through the dispersing crowd, headed toward the cloth stall. Jude hurried to catch up with them. A tight thread inside Sarai's chest relaxed when Simon smiled at him in welcome.

Had she expected her husband to be jealous of his former rival? Did she want him to be jealous? Perhaps she wanted a chance to scold Jude for abandoning her and turning all his pretty words into lies. Yet how could she say such things without hurting Simon?

Nicodemus said something Sarai didn't hear. It brought a rueful smile and a shrug from Jude, the same cheerful demeanor that had won her heart when she was just a child of ten. Then he turned and glanced at the women waiting in the shadows of the cloth stall. He smiled, nodding to each one in respectful greeting. His glance slid right over Sarai, who sat in the middle. Then he stood up straight and his mouth fell open.

"Sarai?" His voice squeaked and broke. "How are you here?"

"Sarai is my wife," Simon said.

"I was in Britannia, trading for tin. I didn't return to Jerusalem and hear about Joseph and the raid until after you'd been taken away," Jude hurried to say. "I swear to you, I would never have let them take you away."

"What could you have done?" Sarai heard her calm, quiet voice as if from far away. Strange, how she didn't tremble, didn't show any of the turmoil racing through her body.

Jude hadn't known about her family's tragedy until too late to do anything? He hadn't betrayed her?

Or so he said. She felt chilled for a moment, as that thought echoed in her head. She thought she had heard he had returned *before* her father's death, yet he never came to visit during the time of mourning, so how could she be sure?

"I could have bought your freedom."

"Simon found me and saved me." Sarai smiled at Simon and his answering smile of pride shattered a hard shell trying to squeeze her. "He risked his career, he sold everything he possessed, to buy my freedom. And then when he had every right to humiliate me by making me his concubine, he married me."

"Who would take him on now, after making a fool out of himself?" Ruth muttered. "You embarrassed your master, Simon. You'll be lucky to find work running errands for the scribes, forget about being one again. Certainly not in Jerusalem, where everyone knew what you did." She simpered and glanced at Rabbi Nicodemus, clearly asking him to confirm her judgment.

Sarai pushed down a surge of irritation. Simon ignored Ruth, but that did not help. How could Ruth speak so foolishly, and spoil this fine, bright feeling of unity with her rescuer, her husband? Why did she still consider Ruth a friend?

"He would be wasted as an errand runner." Rabbi Nicodemus rested a hand on Simon's shoulder and shook him a little, in affectionate reproof.

"But how is he to make a living?" Sarai said. "He is one of the finest students my father ever had. I heard him say so. To make him return to laboring in the fields or in carpentry would be cruel. He doesn't deserve such a punishment." She pressed her hands flat on the counter, to steady herself when her knees weakened.

Why did these warm, safe, joyous feelings never last very long?

"No need to worry, Sarai." Simon smiled wider and rested his hand on hers.

"I still need to train a successor for my place in the Sanhedrin." Rabbi Nicodemus nodded, his smile parting the dark and silver of his beard. "Despite marketplace gossip to the contrary --" His smile turned into a momentary, mocking glare directed at Ruth. "Those who know the truth of his sacrifice respect him."

"God has blessed us. I knew it was a sign, remember? I told you we would be blessed because of what I risked." Simon raised her hand to his lips and kissed the tips of her fingers, which wrung a gasp from Norah, a sigh from Ruth, a chuckle from Nicodemus, and a scowl from Jude. Sarai thought her face would burst into flames. "Soon, Sarai, you will have every comfort you deserve."

"And you, my friend, are a man who keeps his word." Jude shed his scowl so quickly, Sarai thought she had imagined it. He slapped Simon on the back and laughed. "Come, let's celebrate. Sarai's freedom and safety. Your marriage. Simon's restoration to the Sanhedrin. It is a time for rejoicing! Come, feast at my house."

He bowed to them and spread his arms wide in invitation.

Sarai looked to Simon, unsure what she wanted. Go to Jude's house to feast? Or find a quiet, dark room to sit and think? She should celebrate with her husband. Even if she hated the thought of anyone looking at her and knowing what she had endured, she would walk through the streets with Simon, so everyone would know his kindness and mercy.

Chapter Nine

"Child." Nicodemus rose from the padded bench in the hallway, when Sarai emerged from the guest quarters in Jude's grand house.

"Rabbi Nicodemus. I'm so glad to see you." Just in time, she stopped herself blurting how much she appreciated that he had come to her father's burial, risking censure from Annas and his followers. Sarai refused to ruin the joy of this day with sad memories.

"Are you? Truly?" He grasped her shoulders, his touch gentle, and studied her face. "I must beg your forgiveness. I did not hear what had happened to you, to Joseph and your household, until it was too late to do anything. The procurator was rather apologetic, when he understood I had some authority to stand in your father's stead. I should have been notified. I should have been allowed to redeem you."

"And risk being dragged downward by my father's enemies and detractors?" She tried to smile as she shook her head. "I know you would have moved the heavens and earth to save me, if you had known. That is enough for me."

Her smile grew a little easier as that wound was erased. She had tried not to toss Nicodemus into the same basket with all the other family friends who had abandoned her in her time of crisis.

"Hmm, it is not enough for me. I fear those enemies -- you know of whom I speak -- those enemies made sure I did not learn of your situation until it was too late to do anything."

He gestured to the doorway farther down the hall that opened into the courtyard. Sarai nodded and let him link their arms, to lead her out to join the others.

"One of my jailors said something that made me think ... Well, yes, my father's enemies continued to punish him through me."

"In what way?" Nicodemus paused them just a few steps shy of the sunshine and the talking, laughing people out in the courtyard.

"What are people saying about me, my fate? The punishment

95

for Joseph's crimes?"

"Only that you were sent to the Decapolis to be sold."

"No one wonders why I was sent so far?" She could almost laugh. Had Adonai answered prayers she hadn't even dared to make? Was it possible that no one knew she had been sent as a gift to the Rose of Sharon? Then again, wasn't slavery bad enough?

"Hmm, I just assumed it was to make rescue difficult, if anyone thought to try. Simon proved far more impetuous than I ever would have thought," he added with a smile. "I didn't hear where you went until a day or two after he vanished without, as I mistakenly believed, even leaving a message to explain himself."

"Mistakenly believed?"

"He did leave a note. I found it. I fear that your father's enemies need someone new to watch and criticize. My room in the halls of the Sanhedrin is regularly searched, likely for evidence that I teach heresy of one sort or another. Sometimes they hide their work, other times I think they make a mess deliberately, to warn me. A messy search took place about the time Simon ran off to rescue you. His message was buried with debris that I did not sort out and retrieve until just a few days ago."

He sighed, and it seemed as if a dozen years briefly settled on his shoulders and creased his features. Nicodemus summoned a smile and patted her hand, tucked in the crook of his arm.

"Believe me, my dear Sarai, if I had obtained the answers I needed in a timely fashion, I would have sent to the Decapolis to redeem you. I would have demanded the authority to retrieve you before you reached the slave market. We must both thank Adonai for Simon, who knows how to find answers everyone else is denied."

"Yes, we must." She smiled for him. "And I do believe you. I know you would do anything for my father's sake."

"And for you. Please, promise me, Sarai, you will look on me as your father, in his stead."

"Gladly."

Then they stepped out into the sunshine and joined the others for the celebration. Jude's servants were marvels of speed and efficiency. Just in the time Sarai had been washing up and changing into clean clothes, they had organized a feast.

Jude and Ruth insisted on knowing all the details of the rescue, how Simon had pried the information out of the soldiers and Roman officials involved in confiscating the family estate. Several times Jude muffled what were likely curses, every time Simon gave the name of someone who had helped him, but who, it turned out, had refused information to Jude. Sarai thought about Nicodemus' comment on Simon's ability to find answers no one could. Perhaps the information hadn't been withheld from Simon because no one thought he could do anything with it. Not like Jude and Rabbi Nicodemus, both wealthy men with resources and powerful connections. Perhaps other friends of her father had tried to rescue her also, and had been blocked and discouraged similarly?

Eventually, it was Sarai's turn to tell her side of the story. She flinched when Ruth insisted on calling it an adventure. Sarai tried to brush aside the questions. She had been able to talk freely with Hadasseh and Hananiah about meeting the Rose of Sharon. A possible life of healing harlots, and her narrow escape, couldn't be shared with the people who had grown up with her. She took comfort in knowing no one seemed to know that particular detail of her story. If she told Ruth, everyone in Jerusalem would know within a month that she had been sent as a gift to the Rose of Sharon. The truth wasn't nearly as exciting as the gossip and speculation that would result.

Norah didn't press for details, and she intervened when Ruth pressed for more information than what Sarai had already told them. Sarai was grateful when evening came and Ruth had to head home, grumbling about how her father would scold her for closing the cloth stall early. She wondered again why she considered Ruth a good friend, when she knew the other woman would likely blame her for her father's displeasure. Ruth had made her choice, hadn't she? No one forced her to come to Jude's house. Miss a party, no matter how small? Not Ruth.

The fewer visits Sarai made to the marketplace in days to come, and the fewer encounters with Ruth, the happier she would be.

Sarai wondered how soon she and Simon could find and settle into a home of their own. He certainly couldn't take her to live in his simple quarters in Rabbi Nicodemus' house. His status had changed considerably when he became a married man. She didn't care how simple their home would be. Sarai thought she would welcome all the work waiting for her, when they found a place to live. She wouldn't be able to run into the marketplace every day, as Ruth half-invited, half-ordered her to do. She was a wife now, and had many duties and chores resting on her shoulders. As soon as there was a household to tend.

Still, she would find time to visit Norah as often as she could. That would be a joy.

Adonai was good, bringing her home, safe in the care of Simon, who had proven his love and kept all his promises. Sarai vowed again she would make him happy.

~~~~~

Jude insisted that Simon and Sarai stay in his home until they found a place to live. Sarai wondered, but never spoke her thoughts aloud: Would he have brought them under his roof if his father were not in Egypt on business? Would he have been so generous to them if his mother were not with his father, unable to watch what he did and report when Boaz returned? Jude's mother had been one of the loudest voices criticizing Sarai for her education and serving as a healer. If Jude had married Sarai, likely his mother would have stopped her serving anyone but the family with her healing skills.

Another reason to consider Simon her rescuer.

Jude gave them fine clothes and furniture and called them wedding gifts. When Simon and Sarai both protested the abundance, Jude laughed at them.

"Consider them gifts from Adonai," he said, after friendly arguing with Simon. "I am simply obeying teaching I heard from Jesus a few days ago. To find Heaven, I must give away everything that weighs me down and keeps me from passing through the narrow gate.

"Simon, you have pleased our God. You sacrificed everything for the sake of another. Will you deprive me of the opportunity to act as Adonai's steward and replace some of what you have lost? What use are my riches, if I cannot give to my own friends when they have need?" He laughed, raising his hands to the dusky sky. "Right now, my duty is to provide for you."

Simon accepted the gifts Jude insisted on giving. Besides household goods and clothes fit to wear into the Temple, he found a woman to help Sarai with her household chores. Deborah's husband was to have been sold as a slave because of his debts. Jude had taken the elderly woman into his home to shelter her when her husband fled, so his creditors couldn't take her as a slave.

Sarai held her breath when Jude gave the quiet, tiny woman's story to her and Simon. She wanted Deborah in her house, simply because here was someone who understood the injustice and pain in the world. Sarai said nothing to influence Simon's decision, holding to the vow she had made in Hadasseh's kitchen.

"She will be a mother to Sarai," Simon said at last, "rather than consider her a servant."

"You, my friend, are a good man." Jude made a little bow of respect. "May Yahweh bless you for your mercy and protect you from arrogance and foolishness in the years to come."

Because of Jude, when they found a modest little home, Sarai and Simon had everything they needed. They lived in the section of Jerusalem between the homes of the scribes and teachers of the Law, and the marketplace. While the neighborhood of small, neat homes was safe and clean, it wasn't rich or fashionable. It suited Sarai perfectly. She and Deborah enjoyed their short walks to the market each day. They planted herbs on the flat roof of the little house. Deborah knew a man who had the skill to repair the screen around the roof, to give them privacy for hanging their washing, and sitting in the open air on hot days.

When Simon brought guests to their home, Sarai delighted in ensuring her husband had a comfortable, pleasant place he was proud to share with others. She only wished so many of her husband's friends were not Pharisees. They wouldn't sit in the same room with a woman. Some scowled at her when they spoke her father's name, as if judging her guilty of his alleged heresy. She learned to keep silent and to leave her husband's guests alone, and never spoke of her hurt feelings to Simon.

Sarai learned quickly that much had changed just in the short time since she was gone from Jerusalem and Bethany. Norah hadn't been visiting Ruth that day they met in the marketplace but had been delivering her daily order of honey cakes. Part of her living came from baking now. The income from her father's inn was gone. Malachi had not been imprisoned or crucified, but he did face censure and some punishment because the Zealots had met in his inn. He lost the inn on Spindle Street. The popularity of Norah's cooking and skills in arranging feasts protected her father. Many powerful people in Jerusalem, Jews and Gentiles, spoke up on his behalf, so he was not crucified with the Zealots, or sent to the galleys or mines. Norah was not punished with her father, and did not lose her home, which was separate from his before the failed raid. It became Malachi's refuge. Caiaphas and his followers in the Sanhedrin spoke against Malachi, however, and he refused to worship at the Temple or attend the small synagogue near Norah's home. The inn had been given to a tax collector to whom Procurator Decianius owed favors. Everyone who had worked for Malachi left because the new owner was a cheat and liar. In just two months' time, the inn's reputation had deteriorated. The new owner didn't want to make repairs or pay decent wages. Rumors were already circulating that he might abandon the inn. Malachi said nothing about taking it back.

Caiaphas was silent, but his followers spoke out against Norah, trying to discourage people from doing business with her. Malachi grumbled to his friends and those who were criticized for supporting him. He claimed the religious leaders were using Norah to punish him for not crumpling under their censure. If this affected her business, Norah wouldn't say. When the curious and the gossips and people who tried to stir up trouble asked her, she usually laughed and said she was too busy to know. She admitted to Sarai that the patronage from Romans and other Gentiles had increased, which in turn earned more scorn from the Sanhedrin.

Nowadays, Norah only put up with Ruth's preening and criticism because she was a good source of all the gossip in the marketplace. She confided in Sarai that her father was considering buying an inn in another city, to start over. Damascus sat on the major trade routes, far enough from Jerusalem that Annas and Caiaphas wouldn't have the influence to ruin their new lives. At least, Malachi and Norah hoped so. Time would tell. First, they needed to save up enough money, then find the right property, perhaps a house to convert to an inn.

Sarai encouraged Norah and endured Ruth's sharp tongue while trying not to give the cloth merchant any fodder for gossip to spread about her. She prayed that Adonai would bless them both. And perhaps provide a different plan, that wouldn't take Norah away. How could she endure without Norah? Few of Simon's friends had wives. Those who were married seemed reluctant to encourage friendship between their wives and Sarai. She had her speculations about why that was so, but never shared them with Simon. She didn't want to trouble him. He had too steep a climb to return to his former status and acceptance among the ranks of the Sanhedrin. She wouldn't let him risk all that again for her. Later, though, as she held back more thoughts and questions that might trouble Simon, she wondered if she kept silent because she feared he *wouldn't* be troubled on her behalf.

As the months passed by, Sarai made friends in the surrounding streets and gathering places. She offered her healing skills where she was able, and little by little, her reputation spread. She didn't ask for payment, to avoid censure from the unseen cloud of critics Simon seemed to fear. If she didn't expect payment, then the people who truly needed help and couldn't pay physicians would feel free to come to her. They weren't the sort to talk where the fault-finders could hear them. In this way, she reasoned she served Adonai and expressed her gratitude for the blessings in her life, yet without disobeying Simon. So, when someone gave her a loaf of bread, a skin of wine, a basket of apples or onions or radishes, or a length of cloth in gratitude for her help, she was touched and proud that she could contribute to the household.

The day she was called to help with a difficult birth, she knew she had made a place for herself in her new home and life. She sang over the newborn, and wept, and when she returned home, she brought out her flute to play songs of thanksgiving to El Shaddai.

Often, when she was out to buy herbs for healing, or to see if the potion or powder or poultice she had made for someone was helping, she overheard people talking about Jesus from Nazareth. When she could, she stopped to listen, but she always stayed at the edge of the crowd and never asked questions. If she never drew attention to herself, then Simon could not be endangered by what she did. Most often, the people she overheard discussed the miracles they claimed Jesus had performed. Healing. Casting out demons. Perhaps half as often, they discussed the religious leaders' reactions to Jesus' actions or the things He spoke about. Some laughed at the priests and other rabbis, who seemed mostly upset that Jesus was willing to teach anyone who came to Him, without charge. Annas limited his criticism of Jesus to pointing out that He had not studied in the best schools, with the best teachers. Sometimes Annas admitted he was waiting to see what came of

Jesus' teaching, and if He was fomenting trouble. Many men, he stated, started out doing and teaching good things, to honor Adonai. Then their popularity drove them mad, so they thought they had enough power to overthrow Rome. Usually they ended up dead, their followers scattered.

Many religious leaders disapproved of Jesus, but most of their criticism amounted to weak charges of blasphemy. Most people believed Caiaphas was purely jealous.

Sarai longed to hear the stories Jesus told, the lessons He taught, in the fields and the marketplace squares or sitting beside streams or rivers, or even one time sitting in a fisherman's boat, a few paces off the shore. She wanted to hear more stories. She wanted to learn from Him, to understand how He thought, the things He believed, and understand the silent message, the unspoken promise she had glimpsed when her eyes had met His.

Sometimes, she learned Jesus was teaching nearby, just a street or two away from where she had gone on errands. She tried to get close enough to listen, if only for a story or two. Or maybe three. Sarai disliked being out, away from home for too long. She worried about encountering people who knew who she was, knew what had happened to her, and still harbored hatred for her father and his teachings, even a year now after his death. Such people would be sure to gather around Jesus, to listen and collect evidence against Him. Just as men had come to listen to her father teach and build up evidence to accuse him of heresy. When Sarai thought she saw familiar faces in the crowds around Jesus, she slipped away, so they wouldn't see her. They were always there, and she wished she weren't so afraid, so she could stay longer and listen.

Over time, she wrote down bits and pieces of Jesus' teachings, from listening to Him and hearing what others repeated. Stories about seeds, about day laborers, farmers, lost coins, runaway sons, and even a curious story about a rich man and a beggar, and how their circumstances reversed after death. Someday, she hoped she would be free to sit and listen to Jesus for hours, to feed the hunger growing inside her. If she could ask Him all the questions she wanted, would she learn that He believed as her father taught, or would He disappoint her?

~~~~~

"Jedidiah is dead." Simon sank down onto the bench inside the kitchen and stared at the sheet of papyrus in his hand.

Just moments ago, the day had held the promise of laughter and peace, and perhaps good news in a few days. Sarai thought she might be with child, at long last. She and Deborah had been comparing signs and counting days. The best gift Sarai could give her husband was a son, but it was too soon to tell if she was pregnant. Deborah had counseled her to be careful with her food and sleep and chores for at least another two weeks, then they would know for certain.

Sarai had been delighted to see Simon come into the kitchen in the middle of the morning, until she saw his pale face.

"Who is Jedidiah?" Sarai asked after a few minutes of silence.

"My cousin."

Deborah gave her a questioning look. Sarai shook her head and pressed a finger to her lips to silence the elderly woman. She would have to explain later, when Simon had left.

Sarai didn't know his cousin's name, but she knew a little bit of the story. His father had a half-brother who had managed to obtain the entirety of their father's estate, even claiming what should have come to Micah. Some of that wealth should have by rights paid for Simon's education. How different would their lives be right now, if his father had received his inheritance? Would Eliakim have welcomed Simon as an acceptable suitor for Sarai? Would she have already been married to him before Joseph was captured and crucified?

A rough chuckle escaped Simon. Sarai glanced over at him and guessed he had seen the exchange between her and Deborah.

"You need to know, because our lives will be greatly changed from this day forward." Simon closed his eyes and tipped his head back, so it rested against the whitewashed wall. "My grandfather had two sons, born within days of each other. My father was the son of the first wife. My uncle was born to the widow of my grandfather's brother. A Levirate marriage. Grandfather certainly didn't want a second wife, but he did his duty to continue his brother's name.

"There was a chance my uncle was the son of the dead man, conceived just before he died. When Grandfather died, my uncle schemed to be named the firstborn of both men. He was born to perpetuate the name of the dead man, so he claimed that inheritance. Nobody argued with him. But he wanted the firstborn's share from my grandfather, as well. My father was firstborn. That didn't matter."

"But if he was the son of the dead man, he had no right to the firstborn's share. That should have gone to your father," Sarai said.

"Exactly. You cannot have it both ways. My uncle found several teachers of the Law, and even a few priests, who supported him. They twisted and interpreted the laws until everyone was dizzy. Even worse, they punished my father for protesting that he was firstborn and gave him even less than a second son would have received." Simon knuckled his eyes and sighed wearily. "I think that is why I was so determined to become a scribe and a teacher of the Law -- to make sure other innocent, good folk were never cheated out of what was rightfully theirs."

"And you will do that. Adonai knows your good heart and honors your wisdom and integrity. You will be a champion for the widows and orphans," Sarai whispered, and clasped his hand. Simon smiled at her. She felt lightheaded at this proof of her ability to ease his heart.

"Someday, I will. There is still much learning I must do. Who would come to me, still a very young man, to defend them before judges and against their enemies?" He sighed, but he didn't sound quite so burdened and bitter. "Be that as it may … Father was driven out of the family home. He had one son, me. My uncle had one son, Jedidiah.

"I believe they resented us, and perhaps feared my father would someday find a higher authority to re-examine the argument and give him justice against them. When I was growing up, Jedidiah and his father did things to make our way harder. They went to men who hired my father to work for them and paid them to cancel the contracts. When Father borrowed money, Uncle bought the loan, and then went to the same authorities who gave him the inheritance, to change the conditions and demand the money be repaid immediately. Father was beggared, paying usury that clearly went against the law. When Uncle died, Jedidiah continued his ways. They even tried to convince your father not to take me as a student."

"That doesn't matter." She squeezed his hand a little tighter. "Your cousin is dead. He cannot cause you any more troubles."

"Oh, yes he can, my dear wife. Jedidiah has a widow, Hannah, and she is childless. I am my cousin's closest living relative, and no matter how he tried to twist the laws, he could not change that, or cancel my rights. All his wealth, his fields and orchards and cattle, go to me. Along with his wife."

He turned to her. "Don't you see? I must marry Hannah. Her son will fight with our sons and steal their inheritance. And what if she is pregnant with Jedidiah's child?"

"Do not sleep with her for six months after you marry her. That will be proof enough." Sarai almost laughed at the astonished look he gave her. Sometimes men were very childlike in their grasp of how to handle problems. "How long were Hannah and Jedidiah married?"

"Three years."

"And in three years, she did not give him children? Perhaps she is barren."

Perhaps God had punished Jedidiah, and the lack of children was not Hannah's fault. Sarai knew better than to say that. It was always the woman's fault if she was childless, never the man's. Even if he had ten wives and none of them gave him sons, it was always the woman's fault.

"Oh, my wise, sweet wife." Simon's face regained that glow she loved to see. He caught up her hand and kissed her fingertips. "Adonai blessed me when He gave you to me. Yes, He has blessed me twenty times over for rescuing you. We will be rich! I have everything Jedidiah's father stole from my father, and our sons will inherit it all. My cousin's name will disappear from the earth. It is God's justice!" He laughed and leaped from the bench and swept her up in his arms.

Sarai tried not to squeal in alarm when her flying feet nearly hit the table and the tall amphora of olive oil in the corner. She smiled and said a silent prayer, begging Adonai that Hannah would not be a reflection of her scheming husband, and they would have peace in their household. She prayed that she was indeed pregnant. Her child would be the firstborn, and there would be no rival born until it was too late for Hannah's child to be a threat.

Only later, when Simon had run off to ask advice from Nicodemus, did Sarai have time to think through what had happened. It hurt a little to realize that Simon showed no concern for *her* feelings about another woman in the household. A rival wife. Someone else to tend to his needs and look after the household, to cook and clean and make his clothes. And walk beside him to the Temple on the Sabbath.

Had Simon forgotten that even if he never wanted to touch Hannah, he had a duty to her as her husband? The Law made it clear that a man had a duty to his wife, and could not deny her children, because the children of her womb would protect and support her in her old age. Didn't Holy God punish Judah's son Onan for denying his brother's widow a child? Just so, Simon would be punished if he refused Hannah her rights.

Sarai had learned much from her friends and listening to the old women in the marketplace. Men were rarely reasonable or consistent when it came to the hungers of their bodies. Someday when Simon wanted her in his bed and she was unavailable, he would turn to Hannah. Despite his resolve, Simon might father her child.

"Please, Blessed Adonai, let me be with child. Simon's firstborn. Let this battling in the family stop with this generation and let there be peace," she whispered.

Chapter Ten

Simon sent Sarai and Deborah to see to Hannah, inspect the property, give orders to the servants tending the fields and orchards, and bring her home with them. Sarai couldn't decide if he had simply been too busy to take care of such things, or he was afraid to see his new wife just yet. She tried to be glad Simon trusted her with such important duties for the household.

Hannah was small enough to be a child. Sarai pitied the white-blond, delicate woman who sat quietly in the darkened receiving room of the massive house and waited for others to dispose of her life. Perhaps it was best that women dealt with widowed Hannah, first. It couldn't be easy for her to be a widow, alone, with no children or relatives to look out for her welfare.

Standing on the verge of slavery and degradation had taught Sarai to look at the world differently. Perhaps more clearly. Pity eased the resentment and fears she had known since the news came. She wondered what sort of husband Jedidiah had been. Had he sheltered his wife, pampering her and surrounding her with servants, until she couldn't think for herself? Or had he criticized and hemmed her in with rules, so she didn't dare move without permission?

After Simon's words about his cousin, Sarai suspected Hannah wasn't so still and quiet because she mourned Jedidiah. Not the kind of mourning Rabbi Eliakim had shown for Sarai's mother. Their household had been under a dark cloud of sorrow and loss for what felt like months. Hannah was merely quiet. Waiting. Watchful. There was a heavy feeling in the air filling the house that Sarai suspected was fear. Did it overpower the sorrow of widowhood, or was there none of the expected grief?

"We will be sisters," Sarai said, when she and the pale, quiet woman had looked at each other for several long moments. She finally stepped into the room and held out a hand. Hannah gave her hand into Sarai's grasp and let her pull her to her feet. "Simon, our husband, is a good man. You have nothing to fear."

"My husband --" Hannah lowered her gaze. "Jedidiah said his

cousin would send me away and sell me as a harlot to take revenge on the dead."

"Did he know he was dying?" Sarai couldn't comprehend anyone being so cruel, especially to his wife who had endured everything at his side.

The steward for the household had come to report to Simon the day after he received news of his inheritance. He had answered many questions. Jedidiah had been ill for a long time. If he knew he was dying, had he planted seeds of fear in Hannah, to bring discord to their household? Or had he expected Simon to be just as cruel as he would have been if the situation were reversed? Perhaps his conscience had awakened in guilt as he lay dying, and he spoke from fear.

Otherwise, Jedidiah truly was as vicious and vengeful as Simon had said.

"He was sick more than two years." Hannah followed Sarai through the house. "The rabbis believe God punished Jedidiah for his father's sins."

"Adonai punishes us for our own sins. We have no right to punish others for the sins of their parents. Or their husbands." She waited until a hopeful glimmer of a smile lit Hannah's small, oval face. "Simon knows what it is to suffer injustice, to be falsely accused and deprived of what is rightfully his. He will not be cruel. He will not make you pay the penalty for another's crimes. He knows his duty and he knows what is right, and he will take care of you."

"Yes. His duty." She sighed again. "I will miss this house."

"It is pleasant." Sarai glanced around the main room as they passed through it. Open doors gave glimpses of tiled floors, painted or paneled walls, tables surrounded by dining couches in the Greek fashion. A luxurious house, filled with the best.

The best of everything hadn't kept life in Jedidiah's body. Sarai decided she and Simon had been far better off, with just enough to meet their needs and put aside a little against future troubles.

With Jedidiah's wealth, they might never need to worry about the future again, but Sarai wished to ignore that wealth. No house full of servants, no idle hours, no luxurious clothes to awaken envy. If she did not want to change in her heart and soul, she must not let her outward appearance or her habits change, either.

"Must Simon sell it to pay his debts?"

"Debts?" A startled burst of laughter escaped her. "Simon has no debts." She gestured through the doorway, to the inner courtyard, and led Hannah outside. They sat down on a bench where they could look at a pool lined with painted Roman tiles. "What did Jedidiah tell you about him?"

"He said he was a common laborer, a drunkard when he had the money, and gambled on Roman games." She closed her eyes and turned her face to the slanting rays of the sun that penetrated the sheltering, thick vines and leaves that clung to the walls of the courtyard. "He was wrong there as well, wasn't he?"

"Simon is a scholar, assistant to the esteemed Rabbi Nicodemus. He worked with his hands, yes, when he was a student, to provide for his own food and shelter. He does not indulge in wine or other strong drink. He does not gamble, and he will not even loan money to those who have lost theirs through gambling. And no, he will not sell this house. We will live in Jerusalem, because he assists Rabbi Nicodemus in the Sanhedrin. But Simon will not sell this house or the lands surrounding it. This is the land of his ancestors. It must go to his sons."

"His sons." Hannah opened her eyes. They were darkened with pain, but no tears. "Only *your* sons. Our husband will never give me children, so Jedidiah's name will vanish from the land."

"Simon will not be so cruel. You have a right to sons to look after you in your old age. He will be a husband to you for *your* sake, not for Jedidiah's." She took the other woman's hand and squeezed it. "I promise you, we will be friends. Simon will be good to you because he is a good man. The man who risked everything to rescue me from slavery will not punish you for evil you did not do."

~~~~~

The marriage feast, because Hannah was a recent widow, was necessarily quiet and small. Sarai and Deborah conspired to learn all Hannah's favorite foods and gifted her with a new dress for the occasion. By this time, they had learned much about the household from the servants before they were paid and dismissed. Neither woman was surprised to learn that Jedidiah had not permitted his wife to indulge in new clothes during his long illness.

The wedding ceremony and the feast took place in the courtyard of their new home. The small number of guests included

Nicodemus, Jude, the young scribes and rabbis who were Simon's friends, and their wives. Sarai felt only sympathy for Hannah, standing under the marriage canopy with Simon. How sad, to feel unwanted, to cringe in anticipation of unjust punishment.

She knew what that felt like. Sarai daily thanked God for Simon's steadfast love and his willingness to risk all for her. Even though she had been wrong, and she was not yet pregnant with Simon's firstborn, she vowed to make Hannah welcome, to treat her as a sister, to never let any rivalry poison their home.

Their new home. She smiled as she thought of it, and barely listened as the priest officiating over the marriage spoke words of admonition and blessing on Simon and Hannah.

Simon had determined which of Jedidiah's fields had been gained through unjust means, and he sold them at a third of their value back to the people who had originally owned them. He gained the friendship and gratitude of those people, and more important, the praise of Rabbi Nicodemus and other leading men in the Sanhedrin. With the money, he bought a new, larger house, closer to the wealthier section of Jerusalem.

The household now had a man, Saul, to do the heavier household work and run errands. They needed no other help, with Deborah to assist Sarai and Hannah with the daily cooking, cleaning, sewing and other chores. Simon had one wing of the house, with his bedroom, a room for his scrolls, where he could study in quiet, and another for meeting with his scholarly friends. Sarai and Hannah, Deborah and Saul occupied the other wing, large enough each of them could have their own room.

The kitchen was twice the size of the one in their previous home. There was a formal room for feasting, a receiving room to welcome and entertain guests, a larger inner courtyard, and a small garden on the flat roof. Sarai didn't feel rich, but she gloried in the comfort and luxuries she thought she would never see again.

Adonai, I thank You. Let me always be grateful and properly humble. Let me always be giving and never taking, Sarai prayed silently. She made herself pray that prayer every time she caught herself tallying up her new possessions. She never wanted to be complacent and thoughtless again.

A shout went up from the wedding guests. Sarai shook free of her thoughts and smiled as her husband lifted Hannah's veil to greet her as his wife with a kiss on both cheeks. Sarai's heart squeezed, for a brief moment, when Simon saw Hannah's small, pale face for the first time. He smiled, but Sarai saw nothing remotely like his joy the day he made her his wife.

Blessed Adonai, protect me from jealousy. Simon loves me. I am his first wife. I am the one he sacrificed for. I have nothing to fear from Hannah.

~~~~~

Hannah, though she was older than Sarai by two years, took the position of younger sister in the household. Deborah acted as a beloved aunt, rather than a servant. Sarai enjoyed the sheltered little world they created. They each had their strengths, their talents, and by unspoken agreement, they didn't discuss the family's bitter history. Hannah rarely mentioned her life with Jedidiah. Sarai only spoke twice of her father's shame and her brother's death, and her journey to be sold as a slave. They understood each other. Each of them had suffered and feared because of the actions and choices of others, but the past was gone, and they had many years to live together.

Sarai went to visit Norah only when she ran errands, and only stopped to visit Ruth when she couldn't avoid going down the street where the cloth stall sat. It wasn't good to let Ruth guess that someone she claimed as a friend preferred to avoid her and her tongue, which had grown so sharp. Reuben had taken a new wife. She was everything Ruth was not -- dainty and quiet, with a lovely singing voice. Ruth's temper was vile, and she produced waterfalls of tears if Norah and Sarai didn't express their sympathy every time they saw her. Sarai was grateful for the excuse of household chores for her absence. Ruth seemed to enjoy blaming Simon for Sarai's "neglect" of her friends.

Sarai gradually spent less time with Norah as she spent more time offering her healing skills to those in need. If anyone ever found out, they certainly couldn't accuse her of wasting time with idle gossip or shaming her husband. Simon's reputation was always uppermost in her mind. Still, sometimes she did indulge herself, and sent home Saul, his arms full of whatever she had purchased, so she could sit in Norah's kitchen for an hour.

One day while Sarai was visiting, Malachi came to bring Norah a cluster of figs she hadn't been able to buy earlier in the day in the marketplace. He also brought the newest gossip, streaking through Jerusalem faster than flames on oil. Procurator Decianius had fallen out of favor with Rome. The word among the perpetually squabbling government officials claimed his replacement was already on his way from Rome.

Sarai only half-listened, trying to focus on the figs as she helped Norah peel them. She didn't want to fall into the trap of feeling any nasty glee over the procurator's fate. His treatment of her more than a year ago had nothing personal about it. Not like Caiaphas' suspected involvement was personal. So when Malachi mentioned the Rose of Sharon, Sarai didn't know what he had been saying just before that. She fumbled the fig and nearly dropped it on the floor. She sat very still and hoped she didn't look pale. She felt cold.

Nothing would make her ask Malachi to repeat what he had said, because she would have to explain why she recognized the name.

On the walk home, she nearly missed two turns because she wasn't paying attention, her mind so caught up in trying to figure out what might have happened. If the procurator was Laila's patron, was he was being held responsible for something she had done? Under the influence of demon-possession? Had she finally been caught spying on the Romans and passing the information to Barabbas, and Decianius was suffering for his bad choices?

Sarai thought herself into a headache, then she nearly cried aloud her frustration. Why was she wasting time and energy fretting over this? Neither Decianius nor the Rose of Sharon could hurt her now.

Still … she wanted to know.

The next morning, Sarai woke with the answer, and nearly laughed at herself, and at the irony.

If she wanted to hear the freshest gossip in Jerusalem, she would go to Ruth, sit in the cloth stall, and let her talk until she was satisfied. Sarai didn't even need to ask any questions.

~~~~~

Ruth was snarling under her breath when Sarai arrived. Her face was pale. Her hands trembled as she arranged and rearranged the piles of cloth in the stall. Reuben's wife, whom Ruth still only referred to as "that thief," had been there just half an hour before.

While Ruth was delighted to have the special order for a massive quantity of cloth, it had taken all her energy to hold up the sparkling, sweet, servile manner she used for all her customers. She had devoured her entire day's provisions in the time between the woman's departure and Sarai's arrival.

Sarai considered offering to run to the baker's house or to Norah for some honey cakes, if having more to devour would calm Ruth. Then again, judging by the smears of crumbs and fruit juice stains on the front of the other woman's clothes, giving her more to eat might not be a good tactic. Tomorrow, when she had regained her balance, Ruth would need to blame someone for her disheveled appearance when customers came to the stall. That someone would be whoever provided her the food that stained her clothes, rather than her own messy habits. Sarai sometimes wished Ruth weren't quite so clever at dissembling and making every customer believe they were her favorite, and that seeing them was the delight of her day. The energy it took to hold up pretenses had to be draining. The more strained and irritated Ruth became from the effort, the nastier her comments and expressions when there were no customers.

Today's visit to the cloth stall might just be a waste of time. Ruth moved from one side to the other of the long display of cloth and swatches of dyed material, rearranging and neatening and refolding, constantly muttering. Sarai suspected her friend was delighted at the large profit she and her father looked forward to, and furious about the source, and finding more reasons why the special order was a bother and inconvenience. It had to be giving her a headache. Sadly, Sarai couldn't dredge up a bit of sympathy for Ruth. Not when she scrambled to find some way to start a conversation about the procurator. She didn't like gossip and had never truly learned how. Knowing she had been the subject of cruel gossip made it harder to do it to others.

A girl with auburn hair cropped short like a boy's came to the stall with a purse of coins and a wax slate. Ruth made no effort to put on her practiced smile and simpering mannerisms. That, and the copper bands on the girl's wrists told Sarai this was a slave, running an errand for her master or mistress. She said not a word, and Ruth said nothing to her before copying down the writing on the slate, then making a mark in the wax and giving it back to the girl.

"Poor thing," Ruth said, when the girl took the slate and left. "Sylva from the tanner's court says she's the daughter of some barbarian chieftain from far north, Gaul or Britannia. Doesn't speak a word of Roman or Greek. Her father and brothers did something that irritated the general who conquered their tribe. Slaughtered them and took her and her sisters as slaves."

Sarai could almost have laughed when Ruth didn't even give her a slightly apologetic look. She had long gotten over her feigned delicacy about Sarai's brush with slavery.

However, being able to gossip about the slave girl nudged Ruth out of her complaining. For the next half hour, she treated Sarai to all the gossip about the new government officials "slithering" into Jerusalem, in her words, to take advantage of the impending upheaval resulting from the change in authority. She said nothing about Decianius directly. Certainly nothing to indicate why the procurator was being replaced. For all Sarai knew, it had nothing to do with Decianius at all, except that the new procurator and governor and other officials all had better connections. Finally she gave up, made Ruth happy by implying Simon would be irritated if she spent too much time away from home, and left.

"Sarai." Jude slipped from the shadows of an overhang when Sarai turned onto the short street of potters. He touched her shoulder, his face bright with that half-bashful expression that no longer charmed her.

"I didn't know you were back in Jerusalem already," she said.

A moment later, she wondered if she shouldn't have said that. It really wasn't right, to pay attention to the comings and goings of a man who wasn't her husband. If Jude were just Simon's friend, a frequent guest in their home, that might not have mattered. However, that long ago understanding that she would someday be his wife now made everything slightly shady and sticky, somehow.

"To be truthful, I never left. One delay after another. Problems with the last caravan ..." He shrugged, then glanced over his shoulder. For all the world as if he thought someone might be watching or following them. "I thought you'd never escape Ruth's clutches."

"Escape?" She managed a chuckle, despite the shiver across her scalp. Had Jude been watching her, following her?

"I had to warn you. The Rose of Sharon is in Jerusalem. You

don't want to risk her seeing you."

"Why?" She caught her breath and looked around, afraid her single word had been too loud. "How do you know about her?"

Jude cringed, and he looked around too, very clearly afraid someone would overhear.

"Why would I be afraid of her seeing me?" Sarai pulled her shoulders straight and walked a little faster.

Too fast? Would she attract attention by walking faster, or slower? She nearly stumbled when understanding seemed to hit her at the juncture of her ribs.

"You know -- you knew I was sent to her. You know what happened. What should have happened to me."

There was something almost amusing in the realization that she had anticipated different feelings, when someone made the connection between her and the demon-possessed harlot. To be truthful, Sarai felt oddly empty, and somehow calm. Certainly not the shame she couldn't reason away. After all, it wasn't her fault her father's enemies had tried to destroy her, perhaps even hoping the demons would move Laila to harm or even kill her.

"I was there at the same time you were. I feel sick every time I think about it." Jude's voice lowered and took on a harsh note. He walked a step behind her, speaking over her shoulder, as they moved down the busy marketplace street. "I might even have passed you on my journey. I went to the Rose of Sharon to buy your freedom."

Sarai ached from the effort to keep looking ahead, when she wanted to turn and clutch at Jude's robe, look him in the eyes and determine if he told the truth. Perhaps even shake him until he told her the whole story.

No, she didn't want the story to spill out here, in the middle of the marketplace, where someone might hear. Even if they didn't understand what they heard, someone would gossip and warp the truth into something truly harmful and dangerous.

"She spent four days raving, the demons speaking through her. Sending her running around. Striking at everyone and everything or helpless on the ground. Laughing or trembling with fits." Jude caught hold of her sleeve, forcing Sarai to stop and look up at him. He was pale. "Sarai, the demons knew my name. They mocked me, called me weak and a fool, and taunted me that you were as good as dead, that I was too late."

"Yes," she managed to say, as she tugged her sleeve free and kept walking. If he stayed with her, she didn't look to see. "You just missed me."

She shuddered as the image filled her mind. Her prayers and the psalm she played on her flute had driven the demons into a fury. Laila had still been suffering under their control when Jude approached her.

Then another thought struck her. She turned to him. He walked beside her, head bowed, a flush in his cheeks, his gaze focused on the packed dirt of the street.

"You *knew*. You were there. So you *lied*, when you said you had men searching for me."

"Sarai! No!" Jude tried to smile. He moved to grasp her shoulders and she shifted sideways, out of arm's reach. "You can't believe anything demons tell you. I came back here and put men to work, finding out where I had been led astray. I had hope. You have to believe me."

She nodded, words to the contrary clogging on her tongue. When she came to the next street where she had to turn, she made a half-mumbled farewell, thanked him for the warning, and hurried away. Jude made no effort to follow her. She was grateful. If he said anything else, to try to fix things, to change his story, to convince her he hadn't given up hope … she wasn't sure what she would do or say.

Hannah and Deborah were busy in the kitchen when she returned home. They were laughing and chattering about the news of a wedding, and requests from the groom's doting mother and aunts for new recipes for the wedding feast. Sarai let them draw her into the discussion with some relief. For a few hours, she managed not to think of Laila and Jude and all the different reactions that clashed and intertwined until she could hardly feel anything.

When the house quieted in the afternoon, with Saul out running errands for Simon and both Hannah and Deborah napping, Sarai went to the roof to think. She brought her flute and played psalms and tried to remember old songs of petition and protection. Sometimes she went silent in her mind, in her soul, and let her fingers move randomly up and down the flute. Adonai understood what filled her soul with fear and anger and hurt and desperate surrender. She lay down in the shade to sleep, utterly worn out, and later couldn't remember what she dreamed. Yet she woke to a sense of peace filling her. Adonai had brought her through so much grief and loss and turmoil and danger already. How could she be ungrateful and wrap herself in fear again? She would trust and pray and take shelter in the shadow of El Shaddai.

~~~~~

Phoebe came to her two days later, asking for more of the salve Sarai had given her uncle. The sores had faded with regular application of the first pot of salve, but the old man hadn't obtained more when it ran out. The sores had returned. Now, Phoebe admitted their entire crowded household lived in fear what would happen if their neighbors knew his sores had returned.

Their family inheritance included a prosperous vineyard half a day's journey from Jerusalem. The tax collector, Nabel, wanted the vineyard. Phoebe's uncle was scrupulous about making sure his taxes were paid directly to the Roman official three steps higher than Nabel, so the man was unable to raise the taxes or accuse him of not paying. The only way he could force them to sell was through deceit and attacking indirectly.

Old Manasseh, a priest, had a reputation for being easily bought. He also had a reputation for falsely certifying people as unclean, so they had to pay fines to the Temple and exorbitant amounts for sacrifices and cleansing ceremonies. Manasseh had let them know, when the sores first started to plague Phoebe's uncle, that he feared leprosy was in the house. It would have to be torn down to its foundations, all the household possessions destroyed in fire. They would be forced to sell the vineyard to have money to survive. Or they could simply give Nabel the vineyard and Manasseh would forget his suspicion about leprosy altogether. Both men had been nasty to everyone in the family when the sores had faded the first time. Sarai could only speculate how they would have treated her, if they knew she had told Phoebe's uncle what salve to use.

Sarai sympathized with Phoebe, but not the girl's miserly uncle. He could have bought the salve from several healers in the marketplace. She had told him of five whom she trusted to make the salve properly, so it was effective. Now the stingy old man had been suffering the itching and bad odor of the sores for a week. It served him right. However, he had also endangered his family's livelihood and security because he wouldn't pay a half-copper for enough salve to last him a week.

Knowing the ridiculous old fool would just resist common sense harder, the more he was proven wrong, Sarai decided to appeal to his miserly nature. The thought of saving money would make him more willing to do as she instructed. Sarai proposed the plan in front of the whole household, to ensure no misunderstandings. Plus, she could depend on Phoebe's mother, aunt, and grandmother to put pressure on the old fool to comply.

She took Phoebe and two of her cousins to the marketplace and taught them what to buy to prepare their own salve. However, she hadn't anticipated catching the attention of several people who followed, listening as she pointed out the ingredients and told the three girls the steps to take. She didn't realize she had an audience until several laughed, after she instructed Phoebe to wash her uncle's sores in the morning and evening with strong, sour wine. The more the wine burned the open flesh, the better.

The number of people listening and commenting made Sarai worried that eventually Manasseh would hear some gossip. If he realized the sores had returned, he would follow through on his threats. All she could do was pray for the family's safety and encourage the girls to act as circumspectly as possible. And prayed further that the gossips would find something more interesting to catch their attention.

Sarai wondered if Adonai had heard her prayers, when several people from the marketplace asked her to teach them to make the salve for themselves. If that was the center of their thoughts, and not the predicament of Phoebe's uncle, then all was well. She agreed, but knew better than to invite those people to her home. She promised to meet them in that square in the marketplace the next afternoon

Chapter Eleven

When Sarai returned to the market square, instead of three women waiting to learn to make the salve, there were eight, and two men. Sarai nearly fled. Her first impulse was to lie, apologize, tell them she had to go home, and leave that place immediately. They gathered around her, asking questions, raising their voices to be heard over each other. Huldah's belief that she had a duty to Elohim to share her talent for healing fought with that need to flee. Her teacher's voice was louder in her head, and Sarai said a silent prayer for courage as she raised her hands to silence the clamor.

The ten quieted almost immediately, so she had to muffle a giggle of surprise. She walked over to sit on the edge of the fountain, and they followed her, settling down on the cobblestones.

She thought she caught a sneer, a glitter of something unpleasant in someone's eyes. Sarai fought down a shiver of apprehension. She would not be surprised if some of those sitting in front of her, wanting to learn, were actually there to cause trouble. Huldah had warned her she might encounter people who opposed healers. There were the ignorant ones who insisted that healing only came through fasting and prayer, therefore the salves and ointments, tisanes and cleansing rituals were witchcraft. Then there were the rivals who would attack her reputation as a healer so the ill would come to them for help. These people pretended to be healers for the sake of profit and not because Adonai had given them skill and understanding.

How could she decipher who was there to cause her trouble? They were all watching her. She had to speak or do something soon, or they would leave. Maybe she should encourage them all to leave, and give up on this?

"Aren't you worried to be learning from one so young?" she said, before the plan was entirely clear in her mind.

Several laughed, including both men. Several girls said they had heard she was quite skilled. Sarai asked where they had heard that, and they couldn't find an answer. That was suspicious.

"Why do you want to learn from me?"

"What's this?" Menahem, one of Caiaphas' followers, stomped up to the side of the fountain and glared down his bulbous nose at her. "Who do you think you are, sitting like a teacher? What arrogance gives you the right to teach men?"

Sarai choked on a need to laugh, because the scene did look like a rabbi sitting on a bench, with his students on the pavement before him. Several girls looked around, wide-eyed. If she gestured for them to move away, they would likely flee and never return.

"I did not invite any of them to come sit under me to learn," she said, standing. That took away his height advantage, and he couldn't claim that she didn't show him respect.

"Yes, you did," one of the men said. Sarai was sure now she had seen him sneer.

"I did not. I agreed to meet three women today, to share the recipe for a healing salve. The rest of you invited yourselves to come along. I've never seen most of you until today."

He opened his mouth and Sarai knew he was going to call her a liar. Two of the women confirmed her words as truth. Menahem's face darkened and his mouth worked as if he fought to find the right words.

Sarai had the awful suspicion he knew who she was, and he had sent those men to spy on her. Maybe even to tell lies. Whether he was trying to hurt Simon, or simply continuing the attacks on her father, did it matter? The end result would be the same.

"How amusing," a woman said, her voice a rich drawl, coming from behind Sarai. "An ugly old crow, cawing and making trouble. Why do you let him frighten you, children?"

A ripple of murmuring voices went around the marketplace square and then everything quieted. Sarai heard the bubbling and trickling of the water in the fountain. Menahem's mouth dropped open, his eyes widened, and his face darkened more as he looked over Sarai's shoulder.

She turned, and for a moment all she could see was scarlet and gold. Sarai blinked, and the blur of colors resolved into Laila, the Rose of Sharon, sauntering slowly across the market square. People moved back, some of them fleeing, others just shifting around the perimeter for a better view. The area around the fountain cleared, and most of Sarai's erstwhile students fled.

Laila tipped her head back and laughed. The sound turned

from smooth, rich ripples to harshness. When her gaze met Sarai's, something in her eyes glinted darkly.

"El Shaddai, the one who sees me, protect me," Sarai whispered.

"Little dove!" Laila wriggled as she took a few more steps and held out her arms. "How wonderful. I came to Jerusalem to take care of business, and what lovely news did I hear? You were here as well. So I came out looking for you today."

"Why?" Her voice cracked as she heard Menahem chuckle behind her.

This was even worse than she had first thought.

"Why?" The left side of Laila's face twisted into a momentary, ugly sneer. "Because you're my property, stupid child!"

"No, I am not!" Sarai looked around. There was not one familiar face among all these staring people. She caught a glimpse of Menahem's dark robes as he fled down the street. "I am the wife of Simon ben Micah, a respected member of the Sanhedrin, assistant to Rabbi Nicodemus. I am no slave!"

"You are my property," Laila snarled, "and I am here to claim you." She growled something in a foreign tongue, and from the shadows on the other side of the square stepped the Nubian. He bared his teeth in a white grin and glided around the side of the fountain to Sarai.

Laila laughed, the sound oily and yet sharp-edged. That was the demon speaking with her tongue, looking through her eyes. And Sarai didn't have her flute.

The Nubian grabbed hold of her wrist. Sarai screamed and the sound echoed off the stone of the fountain and the nearest stone wall. It sounded like a harp note, plucked hard and strong and penetrating.

A psalm spilled from her lips as the Nubian twisted her around, reaching for her other wrist. She fought him, dropping and letting her weight twist her to the side. She kept singing, though she was almost instantly out of breath.

He snarled something in his foreign tongue and drew back his free hand. He was going to slap her, hard enough to knock her unconscious. Sarai knew it. She kept singing and stared hard into his eyes.

Laila shrieked and there was fear in the madness twisting her voice. The Nubian snarled and flung Sarai away, so hard she hit the edge of the fountain and nearly went in head-first. She hit the edge hard with her ribs and couldn't breathe for several agonizing moments. When she looked up, more people had scattered, fleeing the square, and the Nubian knelt on the dusty pavement, holding down a writhing, screaming Laila.

Roman soldiers spilled into the square. Sarai tried to take a few steps, but the ache in her middle and the weakness in her legs made movement nearly impossible. She looked pitiful enough that the soldiers who approached her didn't yell or grab hold of her arms or even threaten her. That didn't matter, because she was under arrest just as surely as Laila, who wept and drooled and cursed, cradled in the Nubian's arms.

~~~~~

Sarai had far too much time to think, when they reached the sprawling complex of the Roman garrison, attached to the governor's palace. Her experience the last time she had been here and imprisoned had taught her it was wisest not to speak. The moment she and Laila and the soldiers crossed into the courtyard, they were separated, and that only seemed to make the demons more furious. The arresting officer treated Sarai kindly, compared to how Laila was bound and gagged, and carried when she refused to walk. On his orders, a soldier led Sarai down multiple long, torchlit hallways. He put her in a quiet room lit by two lamps, and stayed in the hall, in front of the door. She trembled a little as she settled on the bench on one side of a long table that occupied most of the plain room.

The silence made her thoughts seem like shrieks in the solitude of her mind. She suspected the two men who came to learn from her were part of a nasty plan. Menahem hadn't come upon her by accident. He had intended to accuse her of daring to teach men. Had Laila found them there just in time to cause a ruckus and humiliate her as part of the plan, or just an unlucky accident?

Why couldn't her father's enemies be satisfied with the harm they had already done?

Or had Simon earned enemies so early in his career among the Sanhedrin, and they were using her to hurt him? Or perhaps just teach him a lesson, to stay in his place?

However, what could she call the arrival of the soldiers in time to stop the Nubian from carrying her away? An accident? Could it be the hand of God, rescuing her yet again, as He had rescued her through Simon? Or was that arrogance, to think El Shaddai truly kept watch over one small woman? Far more easy to believe, now, that Lucifer was amusing himself by striking her just when her life was pleasant. And yet, why would the Evil One focus on *her*? What good did it do him?

Considering the why of her situation would do her no good. Sarai knew she would be questioned about the ruckus in the marketplace. She needed to prepare herself. She thought back over the steps she had followed, the portions of the story that needed to be told so no one would need to ask her questions.

Two men walked into the room, startling her out of her churning thoughts, and Sarai was grateful. The clerk who accompanied the returning arresting officer looked younger than her. He didn't explain himself, just spread out papyrus sheets and an ink pot and four reed pens, then sat on the bench on the other side of the table. He wrote quickly and neatly, recording the conversation between her and the soldier, who now told her his name was Marcus and sat at the end of the table. Sarai on his right. The clerk on his left. Under his questions, she related her reasons for being in the square and what happened when Laila joined them.

"Why did she claim she owned you?" he asked, after a few moments of silence once she finished speaking.

"I was ..." Sarai swallowed hard and wanted to ask for water. She wished she didn't have to explain the *why* behind the encounter. "My brother was arrested and killed for crimes against Rome. Our home and all our belongings were confiscated, and I was sent ..." She interlaced her fingers and found she could no longer meet his open, interested gaze.

Perhaps his kindness made it harder to tell the ugly parts of her past.

"Procurator Decianius sent me to the Decapolis as a gift to the Rose of Sharon. I am a healer and midwife. The intent was that I would tend the women in the brothel." She forced herself to meet his gaze. "She suffered from the demons and ..." Sarai shrugged. "I went to the auction block in the slave market instead. Simon, one of my father's former students, found me and bought me." She spread her hands flat, palms up on the table. "He married me."

"We will need to investigate." Marcus' lips twitched. He looked over at the clerk, who looked up, alerted by the pause. A small wiping gesture of his hand prompted the clerk to put down his pen.

Sarai caught her breath, understanding that the soldier was about to reveal something that was not to be part of the record.

"Normally, we would investigate thoroughly, checking the sales records in the slave market. However, the involvement of Procurator Decianius ..." He shook his head. "His patronage of the Rose of Sharon has contributed to his many problems. Records here will confirm the order to send you, and the execution of your brother. I am inclined to let you go home, before investigating today's events."

"That would be very kind of you," she said, her voice several notes higher than normal. That earned another twitch of a smile from him.

He gestured for the clerk to resume writing, and asked more questions of her: her name, Simon's full name, where they lived, his occupation. Then he and the clerk left her alone again. A slave girl brought Sarai wine and honey cakes, and the guard remained standing by the door. She dared to take the food as a good sign.

There were no windows, no light coming from outside, so Sarai could only guess the passage of time. She thought about Hannah and Deborah preparing the evening meal and wondering why she hadn't returned. She thought about Simon coming home and wondering why she didn't come to greet him. Then a shudder went through her, as she imagined Simon not noticing whether she or Hannah performed the duty.

Sarai wished she had her flute, to play a psalm for comfort. Then she thought of the guard standing out in the hall, beyond her sight. Would she earn punishment for doing anything other than sitting quietly and waiting for judgment to pass?

A servant boy came, spoke quietly with the soldier, then beckoned for Sarai to follow. He led her, and the soldier followed, down more long, torchlit hallways. Sarai nearly cried out in relief when they stepped out into an open space, where daylight and a warm afternoon breeze touched her. From the angle of the light, she supposed she had been inside, waiting, maybe two hours. Not nearly as long a time as she had feared.

The open space was an inner garden, with vines climbing the walls, benches, and a fountain in a far corner. A tall man in Roman dress, rich robes and gold chains and the white stola of men of high rank, paced slowly along the pavement in front of the fountain. He walked with his shoulders slightly bent, hands clasped behind his back, until the servant boy brought Sara to stand on the edge of the pavement. Then he gave her a brief, sideways glance, nodded, and the soldier and servant left them.

"I am Governor Pilate," he said after looking Sarai over, head to foot just once. He waved his hand, gesturing for her to stop, when Sara began to go down to her knees. "No need to fear me. You have actually done me a small service. More than enough payment for the … inconvenience and time taken in …" He shook his head. "The former procurator has made many foolish decisions in his career, and serving as patron to that madwoman, bringing her to Jerusalem, has only condemned him. Today's messy incident helped make my judgment easier. A respectable woman does not deserve such embarrassment. I thought it best, in the interest of keeping the peace in Jerusalem, if I explain to you personally, and to your esteemed husband, and assure you that the records state you are innocent."

"Thank you, sir, you are most kind." Sarai bowed her head, when she wanted to look around, feeling a little sick with mixed terror and relief. If he mentioned Simon, was it possible he was there? Where?

That sick feeling increased, as she understood Pilate cared more about irritating the Sanhedrin by arresting the wife of one of its members. Even if just a very junior member. They were just small, helpless markers in a massive game being played by authorities and powers.

Pilate continued speaking, but she could make no sense of his words. Then it didn't matter, because Simon stepped up next to her and caught hold of her hand, and he responded to Pilate. Where had he been when she came into the garden? The governor's words were for him, not her, so what did it matter? She focused on the gentleness of Simon's hand. She pulled herself from her thoughts enough to know when to bow again and gladly leave the garden at a brisk walk when he made farewells for both of them.

They walked in silence, leaving the noise and traffic of the

Roman precincts behind. The tightness in her shoulders seeped away as smells and sounds and sights became familiar again. Yet not familiar enough. She realized after another twenty minutes that Simon took her in a long curving path around the marketplace and the neighborhoods that she normally went through in her daily errands. Meaning, she realized with a sinking feeling and renewed tension, they were going down streets and past homes and shops where no one would recognize them.

Simon walked briskly, but not too quickly for her to keep up. His hand stayed gentle, gripping hers. No angry squeezes. Yet he didn't speak to her, even when their surroundings became safe enough to allow it. His profile was calm, and Sarai hated the growing certainty that his calmness should worry her. She needed to break the silence between them.

"It is a good thing, then, that the new governor values the good opinion of all members of the Sanhedrin?" she ventured, after they had passed through yet another square.

"Is that all you took away from this afternoon?" Simon's hand tightened on hers, just for a moment.

"Then you wish I had submitted quietly and allowed them to snatch me away to a life of harlotry? You think I was wrong to resist them? You would prefer that I had vanished, and you never knew what happened? Oh, but Caiaphas would know, and he would rejoice, and he would laugh at you if you ever mourned publicly for me. If you ever mourned." She ended on a squeak when Simon turned and grabbed hold of her shoulders and shook her, just once.

"What are you babbling about?" He looked to the right and left, seemed to be satisfied no one noticed, then caught hold of her hand again and resumed walking.

"The Rose of Sharon --"

"I know that part of the story. What does Caiaphas have to do with it?" Simon shook his head. "I know you hate him because of how he attacked your father, but seriously, Sarai? What makes you think Caiaphas had anything to do with what happened today?"

"His man, Menahem, raised a ruckus in the marketplace and caught Laila's attention."

Simon's steps slowed and he glanced once at her. She nearly lost her breath in the cool relief seeing the doubt in his eyes. Simon didn't like some of Caiaphas' followers. He could believe they would cause trouble, even if, apparently, he refused to believe it of Caiaphas. With a sigh, he led her around another corner and then asked her to start from the beginning. Why was she there in the marketplace at all? His hand tightened again when she explained that she had been asked to teach some women to make the healing salve, and three times as many people as she expected showed up.

"Why did they ask you?"

Simon's expression darkened when Sarai backed up to explain. Manasseh and the tax collector, Nabel. Phoebe's uncle and the threat of having their home declared leprous. How she taught Phoebe to make the salve, to satisfy her uncle's miserly ways.

"Well, we might have enough evidence and testimony to have that filthy priest removed from authority at last. Those other stories about his threats and false testimony, for the sake of profit, those are also true? You know all those people's names?"

Sarai assured him she did.

"Manasseh is a blight. Caiaphas will be pleased that we can finally depose him and send him to one of the priestly towns, where he can't do any harm. Others will keep an eye on him and away from innocent folk. And that tax collector … it won't do any good to bring a thousand people with complaints against him. Rome doesn't care how wealthy his kind become, as long as they get their due share." He shook his head. "Some good came of today's mess, I suppose." A sigh. "But what did I tell you, Sarai? What did I ask you to do for me? Not to attract attention."

"I was *asked* to help. I don't walk about the city with a herald shouting the news that I am a healer. Isn't it a sin in Adonai's eyes to *refuse* to help those in need?"

"Yes, but … "

Yes, but, she echoed in the silence of her mind. Something throbbed deep in her soul.

"Why do you think Menahem targeted you? Why would he make sure that foul woman found you?"

"Because Caiaphas asked the procurator to send me to her in the first place."

Simon stopped short, turning to stare down at her. His hand tightened painfully on hers. Quickly, Sarai told him what she had heard the jailer say.

"No. That's ridiculous. No matter how much he disapproved

of your father's teachings, Caiaphas wouldn't strike at you like that. And certainly not ask favors of the Romans like that. How would he even know that woman existed?" He shook his head and resumed walking.

This time Sarai was nearly yanked off her feet before she could move again. Simon reasoned aloud through the conundrum as they finished the journey home. The increasing pounding of her heart in her ears made it difficult to hear. She wished she hadn't heard anything, as Simon convinced himself that another priest had struck at her.

Why was he so desperate to stay on Caiaphas' good side that he would automatically judge *her* mistaken?

Caiaphas' approval was obviously of higher value to him than his wife's feelings. Simon had yet to ask how she was feeling, if she was frightened, if all the rapid, strange events of this afternoon had harmed her. Sarai supposed he wouldn't ask now. He had far more important thoughts to chew on, and questions and doubts to reason away.

~~~~~

Ruth was in good humor and full of all the gossip Sarai could want to hear about the procurator, the Rose of Sharon and Governor Pilate after the incident in the marketplace. Sarai tried not to feel anything when she heard the Rose of Sharon had been cast off and Decianius had been sent back to Rome in some disgrace. Norah's quiet support and the amused, exasperated expressions they shared behind Ruth's back helped ease her frayed feelings in the days that followed. For Simon's sake, Sarai avoided the places where people could usually find her when they needed her help. When she had to leave the shelter of her home, she took Saul with her to carry purchases and act as a guard. Sometimes, she needed to relax and chatter and escape her concerns. Then she went to Ruth's cloth stall. She could always be depended on to have more gossip about Jesus.

The three friends were together the day Jesus returned to Jerusalem after a long teaching journey through Galilee. Sarai had come seeking a bolt of fine cloth for a dress for Hannah. Norah showed up while Sarai was still deciding between three different shades of blue. When Saul headed home with the cloth, to give to Deborah to hide from Hannah, Sarai lingered to talk.

For years afterward, Sarai thought about those rare occasions she was in the market when Jesus appeared. Something always seemed different about the light, the taste and feel of the air, the way the crowds sounded and moved. More intense, purer, cleaner. When she came to recognize that change, it always filled her with excitement, because she loved to hear Jesus speak, despite the risk.

She needed to hear something to soothe her troubled mind. Just two days ago, Simon had snarled at her as soon as he walked through the door in the evening. He had immediately apologized, but his explanation worried her.

Reuben had commented on how undignified it was for the wife of a religious leader to serve the poor as a midwife and healer. He expressed his opinion, at some length, that such activities were detrimental to the career of the husband of such a woman.

Caiaphas, however, had rebuked Reuben. That was unusual. He usually pleased Caiaphas when no one else could. In this rare disagreement, Caiaphas approved of such charitable works. Then he accused Reuben of speaking against Sarai, specifically, because he was jealous of Simon's advancement in the Sanhedrin. Simon, however, couldn't be sure Caiaphas would continue to approve of Sarai's activities. Reuben had been arguing with Caiaphas over something. No one was sure what. Later, Caiaphas had favorably compared Sarai to several wives of members of the opposition in the Sanhedrin. These women were reputed to spend much time and money on currying friendship with wives of Roman officials. Once Reuben and Caiaphas had reconciled and the other women had been adequately humbled, Simon feared Sarai would be criticized once again.

Simon hadn't specifically said she should stop helping the poor, or acting as a midwife, but that could change any day. When Caiaphas criticized and condemned, Simon complied. Sarai prayed to El Shaddai, fervently believing He had given her such skills to help others. How could the Creator allow such petty things as dignity get in the way of doing good works?

That day, as she sat with her friends, several people walking past the stall spoke Jesus' name. Norah stepped forward to look out and down the winding market street past the square.

"There's Jesus. Wouldn't it be wonderful if He is the Messiah? He's done so much good for people."

"The Sanhedrin hate him," Ruth said with a snort. She reached for the platter of honey cakes.

"What has Jesus done wrong?" Norah asked with a slight roll of her eyes. Sarai muffled a chuckle.

"Sarai, Simon is part of the Sanhedrin." Her eyes took on that gleam that meant Ruth thought she knew something no one else did. When they were children, that had been an amusing trait. Nowadays, it did nothing but irritate. "He can tell you what they say about Jesus." She wriggled a little on the stool. A sure sign she wanted to make some mischief.

"Don't you have any sense, Ruth?" Norah snapped with unusual asperity. "Sarai doesn't want to hear about another man claiming to be the Messiah, after what happened to her father." She flinched. Her eyes were wide, stricken when she turned to Sarai. "I'm sorry. I didn't mean to bring that up."

"It's all right." At times like these, Sarai felt she was the wiser, the more experienced and older of the three. "I'm not worried. Simon has too much sense to be fooled. When the Messiah comes, He will work miracles and wonders, and no one will have any reason to doubt who He is."

"Rabbi! Have mercy on us!" a young woman called, from the crowd gathering to the right of the cloth stall.

The knot of people grew and spread around the bend where the market street turned away from the square, out of the sight of the three women. Ruth always complained about that bend, the obstruction to clear sight of everything that went on in the market.

Chapter Twelve

Ruth stomped to the front of the stall, planted her plump elbows in a pile of cloth, and leaned out so far to see she nearly lost her balance and fell over the counter. "It's just one of the beggars and his daughter." She snorted, disappointed. "They're trying to get to Jesus through the crowd."

"What do you think they want?" Sarai joined her at the counter.

Norah took two steps out into the street, to see around the crowd. "That's old Blind Ebenezer. Remember him? We used to give him cherries, when we went through the Potters Gate."

"Now, that's a clever idea." Ruth reached for the bowl of figs sitting on a board under the counter.

"What is?" Sarai didn't like that sparkle of anticipation in her eyes.

"If Jesus is from God, then He will heal Ebenezer. I'm surprised someone didn't think of this test months ago." She popped a tiny fig into her mouth and chewed. She managed to grin as she chewed, without being disgusting.

"It's cruel," Sarai spat, "to play games with a man and promise to heal him!"

"Jesus didn't promise them anything," Norah said.

"What did I say?" Ruth's eyes went wide with confusion. She sighed loudly, when Sarai wrapped her veil around her head and scurried out of the stall. "It's the truth, isn't it?"

"Sometimes, it's kinder to whisper the truth instead of shouting it in the marketplace." Norah hurried to follow Sarai.

"I'm being childish, aren't I?" Sarai muttered, when Norah caught up with her. She continued down the winding street, out of the market. All she could think about was reaching the safety and shelter of the cool shadows in her own house.

Every few months, she dreamed she walked through her home, pillaged and shattered by Romans. She couldn't understand the dream, because Simon was too cautious to do anything that would anger the authorities.

"No, you're not being childish," Norah said, her voice a

soothing murmur that penetrated the babble of the people streaming past them in the other direction.

"Do you think --" She shook her head. She refused to speak the words.

It was bad enough she had thought the question, dared to hope for the sake of the old blind man she had pitied in her childhood. Too many people claimed God only punished people who deserved it. However, she had her doubts that God would be so vindictively righteous. Why would He destroy her home, her family, humiliate her and force Simon to sacrifice to rescue her, simply because she had been vain and thoughtless?

So why were people cursed with leprosy and blindness and tormented by demons, if they had done nothing bad enough to deserve their fates?

"Perhaps things like this happen so people like Jesus can heal them, and prove God's power moves through them," Norah said.

Sarai stopped short. Had she spoken her thoughts aloud? Yes, it seemed she had.

"I thought you were the smart one among us," her friend said with a crooked smile. She hooked her arm through Sarai's and gently got her moving again.

"There is the knowledge that comes through much study of the scrolls … and then there is wisdom. I think I am slowly gaining wisdom, and it shoves all my scroll knowledge out of my head."

"Ah, then you truly are becoming wise. Now, tell me about this dress you're making for Hannah. Does she know about it?"

~~~~~

Simon sent word that he would not be home at sunset for the evening meal, and when he came, he would bring Rabbi Nicodemus. His messenger didn't explain, and Sarai didn't ask. Something momentous had happened to keep the religious leaders, the teachers of the law, and the scribes busy with discussions and meetings. Something had happened in Jerusalem that day, or some disturbing news had come from elsewhere in Judea. The three women said nothing about the interruption in the smooth routine of their household.

They ate outside in the courtyard, to enjoy the cool evening air. They sewed while they ate and chattered happily. The evening meal, the only time Simon ate with them, usually centered around him, whatever news of the day he cared to share with his wives.

Hannah had already retired to bed and Deborah was busy in the kitchen, banking the cooking fire, when Simon and Nicodemus came into the house. Sarai smoothed her hair and checked her clothes for dirt from her day's work. Then she hurried to the receiving room to greet her husband and their guest.

"Someone should investigate whether old Ebenezer was ever really blind," Simon said, as she approached the doorway. "Suppose he has been a fake all these years, living off charity?"

"Why didn't you make that suggestion earlier?" A hint of laughter rumbled in Nicodemus' low voice.

Sarai smiled. She knew the wise old man admired her husband. Even when he criticized or reprimanded Simon, he did it with kindness. Rabbi Nicodemus was another blessing from El Shaddai, for what other master would have applauded Simon's risky actions, and welcomed him back with open arms?

"When wiser men didn't think of it?" Weary, exasperated laughter tinged Simon's voice. "I may be ambitious, Master, but there are some risks I know better than to take."

"Israel needs leaders willing to take foolish risks."

"What do you mean by that?"

Rabbi Nicodemus' words seemed to linger in the air.

Sarai wondered the same thing. It was rude, thoughtless to stand there in the doorway and listen. She should have already welcomed their guest, but this conversation fascinated her and she wanted to hear more. They would change the subject as soon as she walked into the room.

Father was rightly scolded for indulging my curiosity. What sort of creature have I become, to spy and listen where I have no business?

Yet Sarai paused, wanting to know more. Just a little longer.

"If Ebenezer has been lying about his blindness all these years, why does he say Jesus healed him?" Nicodemus countered, after pausing for only a few heartbeats.

"Maybe it was a plot to make Jesus look better?"

"And lose the only income the poor man has?"

"Jesus never thought of the consequences to that poor beggar."

Sarai flinched at the harsh note in her husband's voice. How could he think to criticize Jesus, who spoke with God's wisdom and with kindness and compassion? How could anyone be angry that a blind man had been given back his sight?

"Perhaps he did. And the consequences to all of us."

"Master?" A chair squeaked as one of them settled into it.

"What happens," Nicodemus said slowly, his voice softening, "when people realize what the healing of a blind man means in prophecy?"

Rabbi Eliakim had taught that a sure sign of the Messiah's arrival was the healing of the blind. None of the prophets and priests had ever been able to heal the blind. Sarai caught her breath, startled at the implications of today's event in the market.

Then she realized her gasp had been loud enough for the men to hear. Sarai prayed her face wasn't as hot as it felt. She hurried into the room, arms spread, hands up in greeting.

"My husband, welcome home. Forgive me for not coming to greet you at the door. Rabbi Nicodemus, welcome. You will stay for dinner?"

"Looking at the two of you, I can't help remembering the proverb that warns against being too frequent a visitor. You don't need an old man as a dinner guest." He smiled, reminding her so poignantly of her father, Sarai wanted to cry.

"No! You are most welcome. You have always been like a father to us. I shall certainly make sure you have a wonderful dinner." She gestured at the low table set up in the next room, and the two dining couches on either side of it. "Please, come and make yourself comfortable. Saul is coming to wash your feet."

She led the two men into the next room.

"You are a most blessed man," Nicodemus said with a chuckle that ended with a weary sigh. "Giving up everything to find and redeem Sarai was the wisest thing you have ever done, Simon."

"I hope I am always so wise." Simon caught Sarai's hand momentarily and squeezed it as he settled onto the dining couch. "Remember when I first came to Jerusalem to study?"

"You wanted to learn everything and see everything."

"I thought if I could become as great a scholar as Rabbi Nicodemus and marry the beautiful daughter of Rabbi Eliakim ben Levi, I would be a happy man."

Saul hurried into the room with a basin and towels and proceeded to help Simon and their guest wash their hands, then washed their feet for them as they continued speaking.

"And?" Nicodemus tipped his head in query. "Are you happy?"

"I will never be as great a scholar as you, my teacher, but I am happy. Surely God has blessed me for my good deeds." His gaze followed Sarai as she brought cups and wine to the table and poured for him and their guest.

"I prefer rather to believe God smiles on your love, which prompted your good deeds."

"Yes, of course. And do you know what I have learned? God has done the same for Israel all through our history. He redeems us from slavery. Just as I saved Sarai."

A tiny shiver ran through Sarai's middle as she turned back to the serving table to fetch bowls of cheese and olives to place before the men. She had thought she would never tire of hearing Simon speak of his sacrifice for her sake, but tonight, the pride in his voice sounded ... *too* prideful, perhaps?

There was good pride that rejoiced in doing right and in doing the best one could. The pride in pleasing others. Then there was the pride that puffed up a man and destroyed his soul.

Or did it merely frighten her to hear Simon compare his actions with El Shaddai's wise leading of Israel?

"Yes," Nicodemus said, nodding, "but Sarai was innocent. Israel chooses constantly to disobey God, and we have brought our punishment on ourselves by our actions. Or lack of action," he added on a sigh. He turned his head to watch Saul leave the room.

"And that brings us back to this Jesus of Nazareth. *Could* this Jesus be an instrument of God? How can Yahweh turn a carpenter into the mighty war leader Israel needs to be free of Rome?"

"Who said God would free Israel? We have sinned and earned our punishment. All people have sinned by choosing their own will over His plan for our lives. Imagine the arrogance of Man, to defy the will of the Creator. That is true sin. We have destroyed our fellowship with God for the sake of our self-will. Adonai is not required to do anything to save us from the punishment we earned.

"He should let all humanity rot in our sickness and filth. Yet God loves us all so much, someday He will send the Messiah to cleanse us of our sins and bring us back into fellowship with Him. And if He chooses, He can even use an uneducated carpenter."

"Not if Caiaphas has anything to say about it," Simon said with a snort. He scooped up a few olives and popped one into his mouth.

"He does what he believes is best for Israel -- even if all Israel disagrees with him."

"Caiaphas seems to care more about what would please Caesar than what would please God."

"True." The older man nodded.

Sarai wished Nicodemus were an uncle, or the father that he had made himself to them. Then she would be free to offer to rub his temples and try to soothe away some of the weary ache that visibly plagued him.

"Sometimes," he continued after only a few breaths, "a man's fears become his god. But do not underestimate Caiaphas. He knows how to make the people believe what he has decided is best for them to believe. Neither should Caiaphas underestimate Jesus."

"Then you believe Jesus is the Messiah?" Simon put down the last olive he had begun to lift to his mouth.

Sarai froze in the doorway of the room, watching them, terrified by the danger Jesus faced if He dared to make such a claim. Curiously, an aching hunger grew inside her; a longing for Jesus to be more than just a good man full of compassion and wisdom. And now, apparently, filled with the power of Adonai to heal the blind.

"I don't know," Nicodemus said, shaking his head. "I need more than a few moments listening to him teach. More than the reports from Caiaphas' servants."

"Let me go with you, when you speak with Him."

"No." He smiled at Simon. Then a moment later he lifted his gaze to include Sarai in the benediction of his affection. "When you confront someone who might be sent by God, you must go for yourself, not following in another's footsteps."

Sarai wondered about those words, long after the men finished eating and she went to her room. She sat on her bed and rolled the little apple box Simon had carved for her between her hands. He had taken the time to stain the wood, so from across the room it looked like a real apple. Part of her wished sometimes that Simon had accepted the woodworker's offer and stayed in that small village. Life would be so much simpler, and safer, if Simon had chosen to use the skill Yahweh had put into his hands, rather than pursue his studies. Yet she wouldn't be here, now, catching bits and pieces of Jesus' teachings, hearing about His actions and miracles.

At times like this, those bits and pieces were not enough. She wished, not for the first time, she were a man and could walk about Jerusalem at night without fear.

Would she be without fear? After all that had happened to her father and brother, would she be brave enough to seek out Jesus and ask questions of Him? Sarai thought silent prayers for Nicodemus and imagined him going to see Jesus in the safety of the darkness. She hoped that whatever he learned, eventually either he or Simon would tell her what had happened.

~~~~~

A month later, Sarai saw Laila in the marketplace of Jerusalem. She wasn't surprised, because she had heard plenty of rumors from Ruth about how the Rose of Sharon had raged when Decianius went to Rome without her. The demons inhabiting her had taken over, so she laughed and wept and screamed and cursed until the air darkened and smelled foul, touched by the poison in her soul. Rumors said while Laila had been in Jerusalem, Roman officials had raided her brothel in the Decapolis and taken all her wealth. Her stable of harlots had been turned out into the streets, to survive as best they could.

Laila had nowhere to go, nowhere to find refuge when she lost everything. She had stayed in Jerusalem because she didn't have any funds to go to another city, and no reason to do so.

That morning had started off with shadows of worry. Hannah had slept late, and that was enough to alarm Sarai and Deborah, because she was always an early riser. When they checked on her, she said she felt uneasy in her stomach and her head hurt. They made her stay in bed and didn't leave for the market until they were sure she wouldn't need them. Their first stop was at Ruth's stall to choose cloth for a coat for Simon. Sarai and Deborah lingered when Norah arrived with a basket of apricot-studded rolls, Ruth's provisions for the day. Sarai looked across the crowded street and saw a face that looked familiar, but she couldn't place it right away. Recognition came slowly, with disbelief

Laila's face had smears of dirt instead of carefully applied cosmetics. She wore a thin, ragged veil that barely covered her head, instead of the gold-trimmed, transparent gauze she had worn when Sarai met her. Dirt and bruises, not henna, decorated her arms and legs. She had no jewelry, went barefoot, and had no Nubian guard watching her steps. Her dress of undyed rough-spun, instead of silken scarlet, revealed just as much of her body as before.

"What are you staring at?" Ruth rested her elbows on the counter, nearly nudging Sarai aside, and looked. "Oh. Her."

"Her?" Sarai's voice squeaked. "You've seen her before?" She bit her tongue to keep from asking what Laila had done or said when Ruth saw her. She didn't want to stir up questions by asking if Laila had asked about her.

"She doesn't come to this part of the market very often." She shrugged and stepped back to her stool and the bowl of figs she had been picking through when Sarai and Deborah first arrived. "If she's wandered this far, either she can't find a customer or her demons are especially nasty today."

"Yes," Sarai murmured. "Her demons."

"Do you know her?" Norah asked.

"That's the Rose of Sharon."

She wrapped her arms tight around herself and silently thought a prayer of thanks, mixed with guilt. If Laila hadn't been attacked by demons that first day Sarai met her, she would have gone to work in the brothel. There was no knowing what would have happened to Sarai in the wake of Laila's downfall.

How had she fallen so low, so quickly? Didn't the Zealots she worked with owe her some kind of help? As far as Sarai knew from listening to Simon and his friends, Barabbas and his Zealots were just as active as ever. Just as irritating to the Romans, and just as elusive as always.

"She's the Rose of Sharon? But she's ..." Norah turned back to the bolt of cloth she had been examining. "From the condition of her, I'd be surprised if she could buy bread to eat tonight."

"Once, she wore gold and scarlet. She owned many harlots," Sarai said, her voice soft. "She sold women to Roman officers and officials, to spy on them and give information to Barabbas."

"I hear she is sometimes out of her mind for days," Ruth said. "How did she ever stay sane long enough to become rich?"

"Perhaps her demons were merciful, when she still had the patronage of the procurator," Deborah offered.

"Perhaps." Sarai nodded and turned to smile at the woman. "I'm sorry, Deborah. You were going home, and my mind has wandered so much ... I honestly can't think of anything else we need." She held out her hand for one of the baskets the woman carried. "Leave something here, and I'll bring it home with me. It's too hot today for you to carry everything."

"I'm not that old and feeble. Yet," the woman added after a noticeable pause. She smiled and straightened her shoulders, then left the stall.

Three Roman soldiers walked down the market street just a short while after Deborah left. Sarai watched, cringing, as Laila approached them. Before, she had simply wandered down the market street, looking at anything and everything, her stride as loose as a child's. Then she saw the soldiers, and from one step to another, became a different creature.

Her hips undulated with every step, so she didn't need the tinkling of her missing jewelry, her scarlet and gold clothing, to capture the attention of the men. Her hands smoothed down the sides of her ragged dress, displaying her curves. They had diminished since Sarai last saw her, but she still had a figure to make men stop and watch her pass.

Laila tipped her head to one side, watching the soldiers through the veil of her hair. She walked a wide circle around them, and the three men grinned and nudged each other. One said something that made the others laugh. Laila stopped her circling. He stepped forward to meet her.

The merchants whose stalls the soldiers blocked glared at the four, but no one said anything. Sarai wondered who they feared more, the soldiers, or the demon-possessed woman.

Sarai wished things had somehow turned out differently, better for both of them, in that first encounter. She remembered the effect that a simple psalm had had on the demons. What if the Nubian hadn't interfered and carried Laila away? Yet what could Sarai have done, other than play another song? Was it her responsibility to do anything about Laila, the Rose of Sharon, harlot and spy?

Yes, something whispered inside her. She was responsible. Everyone was responsible. No one ever slid into sin, into bad choices, without someone helping them, nudging them, forcing them, taunting them, or frightening them in some way.

"That's disgusting," Ruth said with a snort.

Laila rested her hands on a soldier's shoulders and tilted her hips so close, she almost brushed against his thighs.

"Why does she have to do that in front of my stall? She'll frighten away my customers. Doesn't she have any respect for anyone else?"

Sarai sighed. Knowing Ruth, her friend wouldn't care if Laila let all three Romans use her, one after another, in the middle of the street. Just as long as their activities didn't interfere with customers reaching the cloth stall.

"Why does she do that?" Sarai murmured. Surely Laila could have left Jerusalem and sought shelter with Barabbas. Perhaps the demons wouldn't let her?

"For goodness' sake, Sarai. You're a married woman now. Can't you guess?" Ruth said with an exasperated sigh. She rolled her eyes dramatically for good measure.

"You're not a married woman." Sarai balled her fists to keep from slapping Ruth. "How would *you* know what she's doing? Does your father know that you understand such things?"

Ruth turned red. Norah met Sarai's gaze and winked. They kept silent. Better to ignore Ruth's embarrassment until she recovered from it. Otherwise, she would make them both miserable for days. She always found justification to punish everyone else for the embarrassments and missteps in her life.

"She's looking right at us," Norah whispered.

Sarai turned without thinking and looked at Laila. For two heartbeats, their gazes met and held. Blushing, she continued turning, as if surveying the street. Then she turned back to Norah. Her friend's eyes widened. Sarai was afraid to turn and see what happened in the street behind her. She could guess, however.

"Little dove?" Laila's voice rang out honey sweet and loud enough to penetrate the drone of people buying and selling and trying to ignore the scene on the street.

Sarai turned around to face her. If she didn't act politely, would the demons wake?

"There you are. I have been looking all over for you. Have you been hiding from me?" Laila tipped her head to one side. Her giggle sounded like tinkling bells.

"Go away, you filthy whore!" Ruth growled.

"Filthy?" She slapped at her ragged dress. Particles of dust rose into the air. "Yes, I suppose I am. Now you, I could have gotten rich just off you. Men like lots of softness under them."

"I like lots of softness," one of the soldiers called. He sauntered across the market street, and his two companions followed. "How much for one night? The whole night, not just for a few hours."

Ruth, for the first time in her life, was speechless. Her eyes watered and her face alternated between flushed red and terrified white, and her mouth gaped open and closed like a dying fish.

"If you take her for one night, you have to take her for the rest of your life," Norah snapped. "We're all three respectable women. For the sake of that feast your commander expects in three days, you'll leave us alone right now, Marcellus Lucanous."

"Jupiter save me from respectable women," the soldier said with a chuckle. But he gave a nod of respect to Norah and Sarai, and his grin sobered quickly enough.

"What a relief." Laila rested her elbows on the counter and gently swayed her rear end from side to side as she talked. All three soldiers watched her movements. "I'm glad we're not rivals. What kind of payment would that have been for my kindness?"

"What kindness?" Two bright spots of color lit Norah's cheeks. "You would make us all whores if it would profit you."

Sarai knew no one had shown Laila any kindness in a long time. Where was Barabbas? Shouldn't he have taken care of her, given her shelter, instead of leaving her to wander in rags and offer herself to soldiers in the marketplace?

She kept silent. One mention of Laila's association with Barabbas and those soldiers wouldn't smile and ogle her, but take her into custody. Sarai refused to endanger anyone, no matter how irritating -- or frightening.

A commotion just beyond the bend in the street caught her attention. She looked past Laila and the soldiers, with some gratitude for the interruption. The sound of children laughing and chattering made her wonder.

"Son of David!" a man called clearly through the rising babble of voices.

"It's Jesus," Norah said with a sigh and a smile.

The soldiers looked at each other, their smiles fading. Muttering words that might have been curses, they turned away and waded into the growing crowd. They didn't move away from the approaching teacher, but toward Him.

"What has Jesus done that the Romans are interested in Him now?" Ruth's voice squeaked and rasped, still recovering from the shock of the soldier's proposition.

"Power calls to power." Laila's voice cracked and deepened.

A chill raced up Sarai's back and wrapped stifling hands around her throat. Not here. Not now.

Laila's eyes rolled back in her head. She stumbled backwards from the counter of the cloth stall. The street had begun to clear as people hurried to gather around Jesus. The harlot took three stiff-legged steps before losing her balance and falling to the street like a bundle of sticks.

"She's only getting what she deserves," Ruth sneered. "Disobey God's laws and see what happens. She's demon-possessed, and it serves her right. The filthy whore."

Laila screamed, the sound shattering like an amphora dropped from a roof onto sharp stones. Her back arched so that for a few heartbeats, she rested only on her head and heels. The background rumbling of the crowd stilled at the same time she fell silent and collapsed like a pile of rags. Sarai let out a breath she hadn't known she was holding.

Another scream tore through the air. Laila arched again. Men shouted and part of the crowd raced to see the source of the incredible, inhuman sound.

Chapter Thirteen

"Oh, no," Ruth moaned. "Why here? People will remember for months what happened here."

Sarai fought not to slap her. She knew better than to expect pity from Ruth. She only worried about what the ruckus would do to her business, not the abuse Laila suffered from the demons.

The crowd parted and Jesus stepped into the cleared circle around Laila. Her scream stopped, breaking like a taut rope sliced with a sword. She rolled onto her side and curled into a shivering ball. Jesus walked around Laila until He stood by her head.

"Child," Jesus said.

The warmth and compassion in His voice brought a tight pressure to Sarai's throat. Her pity for Laila was like mist compared to the concern she sensed Jesus felt for her. No one else could, or would help her, but He could do anything. Sarai knew it, believed it, heart and soul.

"Go away!" the demon snarled, shredding Laila's voice. "I don't want You here! I don't need You."

"Be silent!" His voice echoed off the stones of the street.

Despite the crowd clogging the street, in the resulting quiet the sounds of voices in the next quarter of the market came clearly through the air.

"Caiaphas!" Norah whispered, and pointed down the street.

"Where there are corpses, vultures gather," Sarai murmured, remembering one of her father's favorite quotes, when it came to the religious leaders and the suffering of sinners.

Caiaphas and his entourage strode down the market street. If they had heard Jesus was here, or were merely wandering through, Sarai didn't care. What mattered was that Rabbi Nicodemus and Simon walked behind the richly robed band.

Her heart sank. Then she wondered if she were being foolish. Simon and Nicodemus had both expressed interest in Jesus and what people said about Him. She had never heard the outcome of Nicodemus' intended visit with Jesus. Perhaps this was the opportunity to prove to both doubting men the power Jesus held in

Yahweh's name.

"Laila, speak to me." Jesus went to one knee on the cobblestones by her head.

"How does He know the name of a harlot?" Ruth whispered. "You can be sure Caiaphas will pounce on that slip. He'll say Jesus was a customer."

"Shut your vicious mouth," Sarai whispered back. She gripped the edge of the counter to keep from slapping Ruth.

"The demons of anger and fear and lust will not hold you silent," Jesus continued. "Would you like to be free of them?"

"Free?" Laila spoke in her own voice. It sounded so weary that tears burned Sarai's eyes. "How? I welcomed them into my life."

"Ask Me, and you will be free."

"Don't waste your time, Nazarene," Caiaphas sneered.

Sarai jumped. She had concentrated so hard on Jesus and Laila, she hadn't noticed Caiaphas and the others encircling them.

"She has brought her punishment on herself," he continued. "It is God's justice and only He can free her."

"Laila, ask Me, and you will be free." Jesus smiled with all the warmth of a father, willing to carry his disobedient child home and tend her wounds. "You will be clean. Your soul will be your own again. But be warned. The demons will return. If you do not armor your heart and mind and soul, you will become their prisoner once more. You must serve either God or Satan. You must choose. No one can go through life without choosing. Do you understand?"

"No," Laila whimpered, "but help me understand!" She struggled to her knees.

The movement turned her so she looked straight at the stall, and Sarai. Laila's face crumpled into tears. She pointed to Sarai.

"Teacher, make me clean and innocent like her!"

Sarai couldn't breathe. Half the crowd seemed to turn to stare at her. This was worse than the day she stood on the auction block.

"Come out of her," Jesus said.

He spoke calmly. No angry shouts, no wild hand gestures, threats or incense, like the self-proclaimed prophets and seers who made a living by casting out demons. His voice rang with authority, with the assurance that He would be obeyed.

For a moment -- silence.

Laila shrieked, caught halfway to her feet. Her back arched.

Her legs stiffened and straightened, propelling her upward. Then she fell with all the grace of a bundle of logs.

Sarai swallowed a sob. She wrapped her arms around herself and stared at Laila, so limp and pale, lying at Jesus' feet. She prayed. It didn't matter that Simon's Pharisee friends claimed Adonai didn't listen to women's prayers, she knew God *did* listen. El Shaddai had saved her, answering her prayers. Almighty God would listen when she prayed for Laila, too.

Caiaphas stepped forward, holding up the hem of his robes as if Laila made the ground unclean. He leaned over her, studied her pale, still face, then looked at Jesus. His frown turned into a sneer. He stepped back among his followers. Sickness caught in Sarai's throat. Was Caiaphas *pleased* with what had happened to Laila?

"You've killed her, Teacher."

The crowd's murmuring increased.

Sarai saw a flicker of movement. Laila's dirty, bare foot. A few fingers on one hand. She gasped and happy tears filled her eyes.

"Everyone, see what happens when a man falsely claims to come from God." Caiaphas gestured first at Laila, then at Jesus. "You did indeed free her from the demons, Teacher. You freed her into death. Now the demons will carry her soul into eternal damnation."

"Tell me, when did you try to help her?" Jesus used almost the same calm, commanding tone he had used on the demons.

Sarai wished she could appreciate the irony more, but she was too busy watching Laila, willing her to sit up, to prove Caiaphas wrong and Jesus right.

"She is a harlot." Caiaphas' voice almost broke with incredulity at Jesus' suggestion. "A filthy sinner. Condemned by God! I will not soil myself with anyone like her."

"That's not what I heard," Ruth muttered.

Norah slapped her arm. Sarai bit her lip to keep from telling her yet again to be quiet.

Still, she ached with the need to shout that Caiaphas had indeed soiled himself with Laila. How else would he have known about her, to ask Decianius to send Sarai to her?

"Laila." Jesus smiled and knelt next to her.

He took hold of her hand. The crowd gasped, a few people cheered softly, when she sighed and opened her eyes. Jesus helped her sit up, then He stood, reached down, and helped her stand.

"You are clean and free now, Laila. Go and sin no more."

Laila laughed, spreading her arms as if she were a bird. She spun on her toes. Several in the crowd jerked, flinching backwards as if afraid she would touch them.

She turned to Jesus, dropping gracefully to her knees to press her face against His feet. Then she leaped up again. Laughing, her face gleaming with joy, she spread her arms again and ran down the street. The sound of her voice was like bells chiming, echoing off the shops and stalls and the cobblestones.

A collective sigh escaped the crowd. A few scurried away, muttering, some smiling and others scowling. The big fisherman among Jesus' disciples stepped forward. He grinned and let out a guffaw. The crowd shifted, some moving away from Caiaphas toward Jesus, others stepping back as if they didn't want to be near either man. Simon ended up nearest to the fisherman. Gesturing at the spot where Laila had lain just moments before, the big man turned to Simon.

"Maybe Jesus really is from God. What do you think, Pharisee?

"God works through Caiaphas," Simon said with impressive calm. "If it had been His will, Caiaphas would have sent one of us to free that woman."

Caiaphas turned to Simon and nodded. His small smile of approval made Sarai cringe. She didn't want Simon to value Caiaphas' approval. Respect, yes. Approval, no.

"Another lame excuse." The big fisherman snorted, then turned his back on Simon to return to Jesus' side.

The crowd shifted more. Caiaphas and his entourage moved up the street, closer to the cloth stall. Sarai instinctively drew back into the shadows. Ruth stayed perched on the edge of the counter, of course. Norah stepped back and rested a hand on Sarai's arm. Most of the crowd drifted away. Jesus gestured for His disciples to follow and started down the street again.

"Isn't that Sarai over there?" Nicodemus said, gesturing with a nod toward the cloth stall.

"Sarai?" Simon's voice cracked. "No. Why would she be here, instead of at home?" He glanced into the stall and for a moment his gaze met hers. Sarai tugged her veil closer and turned her head away. A cold spot settled hard and sharp in her chest.

"A woman can't stay in the house all day," Nicodemus said with a chuckle. That cold spot softened. "A palace turns into a prison, otherwise. She needs to be with her friends."

"Who are you speaking of?" Caiaphas stepped closer.

"Forgive me, sir. It is nothing." Simon stepped away from the stall, as if he could lead the entire group away.

"I believe they were speaking of that pretty young woman who was watching Jesus so intently. The harlot seemed to know her quite well. Enough to want to be like her." Reuben bent his head to look into the stall. His smile wasn't pleasant. "Isn't that your wife?"

"Your wife is a follower of Jesus, Simon?" Caiaphas' voice darkened, took on the chill of winter rains.

"No, sir." Simon's shoulders straightened. "She is here to purchase cloth for our household. She is an industrious housekeeper, as commanded in the Proverbs. She knows better than to listen to false Messiahs."

Reuben stepped closer, ignoring Ruth, who looked at him with sparkling eyes and flushed face. "She learned that lesson from her father's downfall, after all. You remember her, Caiaphas? The daughter of Eliakim ben Levi. Yet how can she be here? I thought you confirmed she was sold into slavery."

Sarai flushed hot. Was this proof? If the leaders of her people worked hand-in-hand with Rome, they were not loyal to Adonai.

"I have forbidden her to listen to Jesus, and she obeys me," Simon insisted.

"A man who cannot rule in his own home cannot rule Israel. Do you understand?" Caiaphas said.

"I do, and I vow my wife is obedient." He looked once into the stall, his eyes stern.

Sarai's knees trembled. She tugged her veil closer and bowed her head. She wanted to be ill. She wanted to weep. She refused to do so before these men. Even Simon. Maybe especially Simon.

It felt like an eternity before they moved down the street again, muttering among themselves, occasionally speaking loudly enough for her to hear. They condemned Jesus for saving Laila.

"That was a foolish thing to do," Ruth said, when it was finally safe to speak again. "Jesus should have at least asked Caiaphas' permission before He healed that woman."

"If Jesus is the Messiah, He doesn't need anyone's permission or approval," Norah said with a snort. "They need to ask *His*." Turning in a swirl of skirts, she stomped out of the stall.

"What did I say?"

Sarai shook her head, picked up her full basket and followed Norah. The two women said nothing, but linked arms and walked down the winding marketplace streets together. Before they quite knew it, they were among a slowly moving knot of people. Sarai shook off her twisting, tumbling thoughts before her lack of awareness got her into more trouble.

"My friends." Jesus' voice reached her through the crowd. The turmoil inside her calmed at the sound of His voice. "You are amazed as if I have done something wonderful, yet with God, nothing is impossible. Everything I do and say comes from God. I can do nothing unless He gives me the authority."

Sarai knew that was true. How could Jesus have cast out the demons unless God gave Him the power? That meant He had God's approval and support. What right did Caiaphas have to criticize and condemn Him?

"Are You the Messiah?" a man called, just a few people away from where Sarai and Norah had stopped. "Have You come to deliver Israel?"

"The deliverance Israel needs is not the deliverance she wants. Until you know what you need, until you know how to ask, I cannot heal you."

"We will go wherever You lead and do whatever You ask," a woman said, her voice muffled, coming from the other side of the small crowd.

"Today you say you will follow Me, when you see the power of God with your own eyes. But there is a day coming when everyone will turn away from Me."

Sarai choked on a sob, hearing the sadness throb in Jesus' voice. How could that be? Norah tightened her hold on Sarai's arm.

"Never!" a man cried. Others echoed his words, almost blocking out what Jesus said next.

"Consider the words of Isaiah, the prophet: 'He was despised and rejected by men, a man of sorrows, and familiar with suffering. Like one from whom men hide their faces, he was despised, and we esteemed him not. Surely he took up our infirmities and carried our sorrows, yet we considered him stricken by God, smitten by him, and afflicted. But he was pierced for our transgressions, he was crushed for our iniquities; the punishment that brought us peace was upon him, and by his wounds we are healed.'"

Sarai recoiled from the thought: Could Jesus be predicting His own death?

Long after Jesus and His disciples moved on and the crowd trickled away, Norah and Sarai stayed together. Silently, they walked, taking the roundabout way to Sarai's home. Neither could speak; neither looked at the other.

Finally, they reached the long street leading to her door. She invited Norah inside, to sit in the shady courtyard and have something to eat, to drink. To rest and think. Norah declined with a smile. She had to prepare a betrothal feast today.

"I've never heard," Norah said softly, "anyone claiming to be the Messiah who spoke about His death. All the false Messiahs we've ever had speak of crushing the Romans, not paying for the sins of others."

"What kind of teacher is this?" Sarai responded, just as quietly.

When they reached her door, Norah hugged her, then turned and continued down the street. Weary, Sarai opened the door and went inside.

She washed and changed her clothes and went to speak with Deborah. Saul sat in the kitchen, talking with her.

"Barabbas is in Jerusalem." His eyes gleamed and his knobby old knees trembled, banging against the leg of the table where he sat.

Sarai immediately thought of Laila. Had the Zealot leader finally come looking for her?

"The soldiers are already patrolling in larger numbers, and more often," Saul continued. "Soon, we won't even be able to talk in our own homes without some Roman ear listening in." He snickered. "It ought to make Passover very interesting, with ten times as many people as usual in Jerusalem and the Romans nervous and the Sanhedrin trying to keep the peace so they don't lose their easy living."

"We will not talk of such things," Sarai said. "At least, not while Simon is here. It is hard enough for him, dealing with such worries all day. We won't remind him of his problems when he is home."

"Indeed not," Deborah said. "This should be our master's

haven, his refuge." She sighed. "If only Hannah weren't so ill, everything would be wonderful. He does love to listen to her sing over her harp."

"She's still not feeling well?"

"She's feeling better, but she didn't sleep last night because of her stomach. I made her eat a little bread and milk and honey, and told her to rest in the courtyard."

"I have some ideas for a tisane or a poultice that would purify her blood ... If I had my scrolls, I would be sure of the ingredients, the steps to make each one. If only ..."

Her heart skipped a beat. Sarai wished she could ask Jesus to heal Hannah. That would not be wise after that little exchange between Caiaphas, Reuben and Simon. The worst thing she could do would be to bring Jesus into her home. Even for Hannah.

~~~~~

Sarai went to the courtyard to sit in the quiet and enjoy the fading day. Hannah was in her room, washing before the evening meal. Sunset painted the courtyard with shadows edged in purple, when Simon came home. He stepped out into the courtyard, his sandals clattering hard on the paving tiles. He slammed the door shut, making Sarai drop her sewing.

She stared at him, heartbeat racing. Simon's lips pressed together, almost bloodless. His fists gripped the sides of his coat.

"What is wrong?" Sarai prayed that bad news about Barabbas' presence near Jerusalem had distracted the entire council.

"You were in the marketplace today."

"Yes. I was looking for cloth for your new robes."

Had he forgotten what he had said to Caiaphas to justify her presence there? Hadn't she sworn she would never do anything to make Simon angry? Yet, none of what happened today was her fault. She had certainly not chosen to see either Laila or Jesus. Despite the certainty that she had done nothing wrong, Sarai still trembled.

"Then you didn't chase this teacher from Nazareth through the city? It was a chance meeting?"

"I went to the market for cloth, and hoped to meet with Norah, no one else." She thought of Laila, and suddenly couldn't meet his eyes.

"Sarai? What are you hiding from me?" He gripped her

150

shoulder, making her flinch.

He didn't hurt her, but suddenly she feared being beaten as other wives were, with no one to protect them.

"I spoke with no one but Norah and Ruth," she said in a soft voice, to hide the trembling deep inside. "And a chance acquaintance whom I thought I would never see again."

"Who?"

"Laila." She waited, but Simon just frowned at her. "She was once called the Rose of Sharon."

"My wife will not socialize with harlots or false messiahs. It is not proper!" He jerked his hand away as if scorched.

"She approached me. I couldn't escape, with the crowd gathering around. And then the demons attacked her. Then Jesus healed her. Did you see, Simon? It was the most amazing thing I've ever seen!" She smiled up at him, begging him to understand, to feel some gladness for Laila with her.

"He cast out those demons because He is a servant of Satan."

"Why would a servant of Satan help anyone? He told her to stop sinning." Sarai felt breathless. How could Simon make such accusations? Those were Caiaphas' thoughts, not something she expected of her husband. Surely Nicodemus wouldn't agree?

"Jesus *must* be in league with Satan. The alternative is unthinkable."

"What if He is truly from God?"

"He is not from God. Sarai, I forbid you to have anything to do with Jesus. If I must, I will forbid you to leave this house. Am I clear?"

"Yes. But -- how have I displeased you?" Tears cracked in her voice.

"Sweet Sarai." Simon sank down to the bench next to her. "I'm only doing this to protect you."

"I would never disobey or dishonor you."

"Your safety means the world to me. So when I say not to listen to this Jesus of Nazareth, you must obey me."

"Jesus has only done good for people. How can He be evil?"

"It's complicated." He sighed and closed his eyes, and Sarai knew in that moment how he would look twenty years in the future, worn out with stressful decisions and discussions and the weight of the Sanhedrin's responsibilities. "Sometimes, I don't fully understand, myself. I know Caiaphas is the leader chosen by Yahweh, and anyone he disapproves should be examined very carefully, no matter what miracles He performs."

Sarai wished Simon had found a job working with his hands, far from Jerusalem. They could have been happy, a simple farmer or woodworker and his healer wife, living in a small village.

~~~~~

That Sabbath, Sarai stayed home with Hannah, who still felt ill, but swore she was getting stronger. She wasn't there when Jesus healed Asa, a former stonemason, but Simon told them all about it. He also gave them a clear picture of Caiaphas' fury.

"He healed him on the Sabbath!" Simon spat for the fifth time, as he paced the courtyard where he had found his wives when he came home from the Temple. "Again and again, despite the rebuke from many authorities, Jesus continues to heal on the Sabbath. What is wrong with Him?"

Sarai thought of Asa, who had been a strong, rather short man with a hearty laugh. She remembered him from her childhood. He always carried sweets for the children who came to watch when houses or shops were being built. He had been injured while working on an extension of the Roman garrison. One man came to work drunk and bungled his portion of the wall. It toppled and Asa's arm had been trapped for hours before they could free him.

He had lost the use of that arm, scarred and twisted and always in pain. He had been reduced to charity and teaching boys and slaves the rudiments of stonework. The laughing, healthy, strong man had vanished behind a wall of pain and growing bitterness.

How, Sarai wondered, could anyone be angry that a good man had regained the use of his arm? Yes, the Sabbath was sacred, to honor El Shaddai. But surely El Shaddai would be happy a man had found freedom from pain?

"Caiaphas challenged Him, didn't he?" Hannah asked.

"Oh, yes. He reminded Jesus the Sabbath was holy, meant for rest and somber contemplation." Simon raked his hands through his hair and flung himself down onto a bench facing the women. "Do you know what Jesus said? He said 'God made the Sabbath for man, not man for the Sabbath. The truth is, the Lord of the Sabbath is among you and you know Him not.' Then He told Asa to stretch out his arm. Everyone there knew Asa could barely move his arm enough to get dressed, let alone lift it."

"But Asa did lift his arm," Sarai guessed. "He lifted it high, and everyone could see his arm was healed."

"Everyone celebrated." Wistfulness thinned Simon's voice and sadness gleamed in his eyes, like a child forced to watch other children play while he did chores. "I hear Asa's family has invited half the city to come celebrate with them."

"You didn't go."

"No one who wants to keep Caiaphas' approval would go." He shook his head. "Caiaphas says Jesus is a heretic and must be stopped before He destroys us all."

"Doesn't he care that Asa was healed or how long he has been in pain?" Sarai stood. She kept her hands clenched at her sides, when she wanted to grab Simon by his shoulders and shake him until he started thinking sensibly.

"Couldn't Jesus have waited one more day? After five years of suffering, couldn't Asa have waited one more day?"

Sarai couldn't believe those words had come out of his mouth. What had happened to the man who gave away their only loaf of bread to a beggar woman and her three children?

"Could I have waited one more day for you to rescue me from the slave market?" she whispered.

He stared at her, his face going white. His silence, his inability to answer her with an instant denial, hurt more than she could explain, even to herself. Sarai left the courtyard. She refused to cry in front of him.

~~~~~

The evening meal was nearly silent. Sarai wanted to claim a headache and stay in her room, but she knew better. Later, Deborah followed her when she retreated to the roof for some solitude. She told Sarai in whispers what she had seen and heard at the Temple.

"Jesus told Caiaphas, when a donkey falls into a pit, even on the Sabbath, its owners do everything they can to get it out of the pit and treat its wounds. He asked everyone there, isn't a man, made in God's image, far more important, far more valuable, than a donkey?" Deborah chuckled softly. "Caiaphas, of course, couldn't say anything in response to that. He wouldn't dirty his robes to save a donkey, but he shouts if his donkey isn't brushed and saddled properly on the Sabbath." She shook her head. "What is wrong with those men, that they can't see what is perfect sense?"

"I don't know. Can it be fear? Can it be they listen to Satan?" Sarai responded just as softly. Her mouth seemed to burn when the words left her lips.

"Don't say such things about the religious leaders." Deborah shuddered.

"I only know what my heart tells me. What my father would say if he were alive to see all this. God's Spirit must be in Jesus. I know Caiaphas is furious and he says Jesus is from Satan. Yet Jesus is right. Yahweh created the Sabbath to benefit us, His children. God created so many things for our good, and yet we have made them heavy burdens. How could a man do so much good, in the Temple, on the Sabbath, unless He received His power from Adonai?"

Chapter Fourteen

For the next three days, Sarai stayed home. She didn't want to listen to Norah and Ruth arguing about what had really happened in the Temple. Hannah felt better, so she took care of the day's errands with Deborah. When Sarai did leave the house, Saul went with her. He refused to let her go out alone, and she suspected Simon had ordered him to do so. She wanted to claim she felt ill when Simon came to share her bed, but it was easier, safer, to comply in silence, rather than risk having another argument with him. What justification could she give for her anger when he would only say again that he was protecting her? She feared his anger, or worse, agreement, when she said he didn't trust her to obey him.

The next time Sarai went out on errands, she avoided Ruth's portion of the market. The day's errands took only half the usual time. She didn't have the heart to chat with the merchants or haggle more than necessary over the prices. Later, Sarai sometimes wondered what would have happened if she hadn't changed her routine, if she hadn't turned to go home sooner than normal.

Laila strolled through the lower end of the market as Sarai began to retrace her steps homeward. She now wore a decent veil over her head and carried a basket hooked over her elbow. She smiled at everyone, just as she had before, and didn't seem to notice that people scowled at her. Just as they had before. Yet even from the other side of the market square, her smile clearly came from happiness, not the arrogance Sarai had once seen. Laila wore a dress only a little better than the rags she had worn when Jesus freed her from the demons, but it was clean and covered her modestly. Someone had taken pity and helped her.

Sarai stopped short, so Saul nearly ran into her. She closed her eyes, feeling sick in the pit of her stomach. Her face burned.

She should have taken pity on Laila. She should have sought her out and given her clothes and food and money. After all, hadn't she sworn to act from her gratitude for being saved, and see those in need and help them? Instead, she had been carried away by the wonder of Jesus' healing and the frustration of Caiaphas' reaction.

She had forgotten Laila. Yes, she had followed through on her resolve to help others, once she became able to do so. Using her skills in healing was easy, a joy, as natural as breathing. Something told her Yahweh would be happier if she did something difficult. Something she had to think about and consciously choose to do it.

Laila wandered over to a stall that sold fruit. She waited, head bowed, until the merchant finished dickering with a Roman slave. When the buyer left, Laila stepped up to the stall. The merchant smiled at her and gestured behind the stall. Laila bowed and hurried out of sight.

"What is she doing?" Sarai asked no one in particular.

"Probably taking what's bruised or too old and bad for anyone to buy," Saul said. "Why did she waste her time asking? It's there for the taking."

Sarai understood why. Laila had fallen too far to take anything for granted. Where others who were as destitute as her might take the merchant's leavings as their due, Laila chose to ask. Sarai suspected she wouldn't have had the courage or the gratitude, in similar circumstances.

"Laila?" Sarai called when the woman re-emerged. She nearly laughed at Saul 's startled gasp.

"Little dove." Laila smiled, as if lit from within.

"How are you?" Sarai asked, when the woman hurried across the half-empty street to join her.

"Jesus freed me from the demons. I am no longer a harlot or a spy."

"Yes, I know that. I was there when Jesus healed you."

"If only you could know how different I have become. But no, I wouldn't wish such pain and fear on anyone." She laughed, joyous as an innocent child. "My heart is clean now, and I am glad."

"No, really." She fought a surge of impatience. "How are you?"

"I told you. I am free and clean, and my heart has peace for the first time in years."

"But your clothes -- you look hungry -- where do you sleep?"

"Adonai provides for me. Some people see that I am changed, and they are kind enough to help me. One was kind enough to give me this." She reached inside her robe and brought out a simple clay flute. "I used to love music, before the demons came. They stole that from me. When you played ... I think that started something changing within me. The demons punished me, destroyed everything, because I regretted my choices. Well, now I have my music back. Jesus has given me my soul back. I can play again. Sometimes I earn a few coins, and that eases my way."

"Is there nothing you need?" Sarai heard Saul gasp and she frowned, wanting to slap the man. Who did he think he was, to criticize her actions or words? He was her servant.

"I need very little. If only ..." Laila sighed and looked away, and for a moment that happy glow faded. "I have heard Barabbas is in Jerusalem, but I haven't seen him."

"He should have come looking for you, to help you long ago."

"Perhaps. I once thought he cared for me." She shrugged. "Yes, I was angry he left me to live in rags. I was foolish to expect help from him. But I let that anger go when Jesus freed me."

"Would Barabbas make you play the harlot again, to spy on the Romans?" She glanced up and down the winding aisle of stalls.

While they had been speaking, the traffic had increased as the day grew older. A murmuring of voices strengthened in the distance, as if a crowd walked up the market street toward them.

"He could never make me do anything when I was owned by the demons. Barabbas can't make me do anything now, that I don't want to." Laila sniffed, a sparkle of mischief in her eyes. "No, I don't fear that. But I do fear *for* Barabbas. He is full of such anger. Such hunger to destroy. If only he would find Jesus, listen to Him, talk to Him, he would be freed and cleansed, like I was."

The crowd spilled around the bend in the street. Sarai's heart skipped a beat, even before she saw the man with a child perched on His shoulders.

Jesus laughed and talked with the child, a boy, perhaps five years old. Sarai had heard He highly valued children and had commanded His followers to be like them. She wished she could go back to her days of childish faith, easily trusting, and seeing only beauty and good in everything. Those days would never return.

Laila saw Jesus, and cried softly, "Master!" She sounded like Sarai had, when she had been a child visiting her grandparents.

"Wait." Sarai caught hold of Laila's sleeve before she ran to Jesus, and dug into the side sash of her dress with the other hand. She had a few coins left. Quickly, she pulled them out and slipped them into Laila's hand.

Saul grumbled. Sarai closed Laila's hand around the coins, afraid he would snatch them away.

"Little dove." Laila's smile dimmed. "I wasn't asking for help. You of all people owe me nothing."

"I of all people know what you have gone through. If Simon hadn't redeemed me, I would be living in a brothel now."

"And when the demons destroyed me, I might have sold you to someone far worse, to save myself."

"Adonai saved me, and I vowed to always be grateful and to help others."

"May Adonai bless you." She took a step backwards. That glowing joy returned to her face. Turning, Laila ran to Jesus.

Laila dropped to her knees before Him, and pressed her face to His dusty sandals. Jesus swung the boy down off His shoulders, set him on the ground, and bent to grasp Laila's shoulders and lift her to her feet again. A hot ache shot through Sarai when Jesus spoke to Laila, such tenderness in His eyes.

Then Jesus turned and looked directly at Sarai. Somehow, she was certain, Jesus knew what she had done and why. He nodded to her and it was a gesture of blessing that washed away the lingering residue of the hurt feelings of the last few days.

"Let me tell you a story," Jesus called, gesturing for the crowd to settle down around Him. He stepped over to the fountain and perched on the thick stone rim of the basin.

"In the end times, the King will divide all the world into two peoples. To those on the right, the King will say, 'Come, you who are blessed by my Father; take your inheritance, the kingdom prepared for you since the creation of the world. For I was hungry and you gave me something to eat, I was thirsty and you gave me something to drink, I was a stranger, and you invited me in. I needed clothes and you clothed me. I was sick and you looked after me. I was in prison and you came to visit me.'

"Then the righteous will answer him, 'Lord, when did we see you hungry and feed you, or thirsty and give you something to drink? When did we see you a stranger and invite you in, or needing clothes and clothe you? When did we see you sick or in prison and go to visit you?' The King will reply, 'I tell you the truth, whatever you did for one of the least of these brothers of mine, you did for me.'" Jesus again looked to Sarai and met her gaze.

"But what does it mean, Rabbi?" a woman called from the edge of the crowd.

"Mistress." Saul tugged on Sarai's sleeve. "The master will be angry, if he finds out you are chasing after that teacher again."

"I'm not chasing Jesus. I was standing still and He came here." Sarai scowled, wishing the man would be quiet so she could listen.

"I am to protect you." Saul tried to look stubborn, but he cringed when she glared at him.

"Protect me from what?"

She clenched her fists, resisting the anger that shredded her sense of peace. She knew in that moment what she had to do. As her father had often said, it was far more important to gain the approval of Yahweh than all the praise of mere men.

"Stay here," she snapped.

Before Saul could protest, Sarai gathered up her skirts and moved through the seated crowd. She knelt next to Laila and waited until Jesus finished speaking of the blessing on those who helped the smallest, the weakest, the least worthy. She barely heard through the thudding of her heart. When Jesus stood to leave, Sarai caught hold of Laila's sleeve and kept her sitting with her.

"Come home with me, Laila. Until I can find a place for you to stay, and care for yourself."

"But what about your husband?"

"Simon is a good, kind man who wants to serve God." She was certain he had merely forgotten that serving God meant mercy as well as careful scrutiny of the Law. "He will help find you a new home."

"Yes, if only to get me out of his house as quickly as possible!" Her laughter held no bitterness.

Sarai smiled, feeling somewhat breathless. The two women helped each other to stand. They walked against the current of the departing people as they made their way to where Saul waited and scowled. The manservant grumbled all the long walk home, but Sarai ignored him. She knew she had done right. She would make Simon see this was true justice and mercy and pleasing to Yahweh.

~~~~~

Midway through the afternoon, Sarai needed Saul to carry a water jar up to the roof. When she went looking for him, he was missing. Before she could ask Deborah if she knew where he had gone, Simon stomped through the door with Saul close on his heels.

She looked at the older man's face for two painful heartbeats. It was no comfort when Saul 's smug expression faded and he looked away, bowed his head and scurried out of the house.

"Sarai, how could you do this to me?" Simon caught hold of her arm and led her to the courtyard.

"What have I done?" She knew Saul had told Simon about Laila, but she wanted to know what sort of crime her husband thought she had committed.

"You brought that woman home with you." He slammed shut the door into the courtyard. The sound echoed off the walls. Sarai wondered what good he thought he did, bringing her out here. The bustle of the day was fading, and if Simon yelled, their nearest neighbors would likely hear every word he said. "Bad enough she's a harlot, she's demon-possessed."

"She is neither! Jesus drove away the demons, and she is a beggar, not a harlot." Sarai's throat hurt from the effort not to shout back at him. "Laila has no one to help her."

"God has condemned her. She earned her suffering. Why should we stand against God's judgment and help her?"

"Simon, God has forgiven her and cleansed her."

"No, *Jesus* has forgiven her. With authority that is not His."

"You don't believe He is from God." Sarai wondered if she had been a fool to hope he would see what seemed right to her.

"How could He be, when He spends time with harlots and the demon-possessed, the sick and insane, the tax collectors and thieves? And now you have brought one of them into my home!"

"I thought it was my home too, Simon," she murmured, the words catching in her throat.

"I redeemed you, Sarai," he hurried on. "You could be like Laila right now if I hadn't sold everything to buy your freedom. I turned my back on the Sanhedrin, on years of hard work, to find you."

"Yes, and I am grateful."

"You should be."

"But is gratitude all we have between us?"

Simon turned, his hand swinging up and cracking down, with a slap to her face that seemed to shatter the air.

Sarai stumbled backwards three steps before she caught herself. She couldn't raise her hand to her stinging face as she stared at him.

Simon stared back at her, his face deathly pale, his mouth falling open in a pale ring of shock. He closed his eyes and reached blindly for her. Sarai couldn't move, though everything inside her recoiled at his touch. She let him gather her close, pressing her face against the sweaty, dusty thickness of his robes.

"Sarai -- my darling -- I don't know why I did that! Forgive me."

She opened her mouth, tears spilling from her eyes. She struggled to speak her forgiveness, but his next words froze hers in her throat.

"You have no idea how the world operates. You don't understand. Your heart is too soft."

Is this all my fault, then? Sarai knew every man she asked would tell her, yes, it was her fault her husband struck her. Every man, she decided, but Jesus. He would know she had been speaking for truth, for honesty, for true love and mercy. He would have touched her stinging cheek and tears would have filled His eyes. He would have shared the frightened, lost aching in her heart.

"Yours is too hard, Simon," she whispered, and gently, insistently slipped free of his arms. Her tears stopped when Simon didn't resist, didn't fight to keep holding her. "Like the hard-packed ground that would not let the seed grow in it."

"What are you talking about?" He frowned and stepped back.

"Jesus told us a story, about good seed planted in many different types of soil. Good soil that nourished the seed, and stony soil where the seed could not grow roots, and thorny soil where the life was strangled from the young plants. And hard ground, that would not let the seed even come to life."

"Jesus can only lead you into trouble." He took another step back from her.

"What if you are wrong, Simon?"

"I am not wrong. I am a member of the Sanhedrin. I am your husband. You will listen to me, and you will obey!"

"Better to obey God than the laws men make for us. Every day, the priests find new sins to avoid. They don't know God's love, so they will not let anyone know His love."

"You learned that from Jesus, didn't you?"

"From my father's teachings, which you have forgotten."

"I warn you, Sarai, have nothing more to do with Jesus."

"What will you do? Take me back to the slave market? I should spend more time with Laila, so I know how to survive when you cast me out."

Sarai turned and fled before Simon could do more than gape at her. He didn't speak her name, didn't make a sound, before she reached the door, yanked it open and hurried into the house.

She intended to go to her room, but feared Simon following her. He might order her never to leave the house.

A burst of laughter caught Sarai's attention. She went to the kitchen and found Deborah and Laila working on the evening meal. Laila rolled out dough to fill with a mixture of chopped fruit and honey while Deborah finished cleaning a duck for roasting. The two women stopped when she paused in the doorway.

"Your husband wants me out already?" Laila smiled and stood, wiping her hands on a cloth. "I truly didn't expect to stay the night. My new clothes and my bath were wonderful. May Adonai bless you for that alone."

"You should have more than a bath and new clothes." Sarai choked on mixed anger, tears and shame.

"I have your friendship and your forgiveness for the harm I tried to do you. That is more precious than all the gold and jewels I earned with my body, and all the secrets I ever stole from the Romans." She nodded to Deborah, who nodded back. With a sigh, she wrapped her arms around Sarai for a hard, brief hug. Then she fled the room.

"Saul betrayed you to Simon?" Deborah sighed when Sarai could only nod. "Just see if that one enjoys his food for the next moon. I like that Laila. She's clever. Clear-sighted."

Sarai wanted to sink down onto the bench just inside the doorway and weep away the hurt churning inside her. "What a self-pitying fool I am!"

It was a matter of moments to find another change of clothes, a cloak, a blanket, a basket to put them all in. Last of all, she stopped in Simon's study room and searched for the little chest holding the coins he kept handy for day-to-day expenses. She scooped up a handful, not caring how much she took. Then Sarai ran out the door and down the street.

Laila was nowhere to be seen, even on the long, straight sections of street. Sarai ran, and prayed she had guessed correctly, and Laila had gone back to the market quarter. Otherwise, how would she find her in bustling Jerusalem? She slowed when her side ached, but kept moving, staring into the deepening shadows as afternoon faded into sunset. Sarai wondered if she could find Laila, give her what she had brought, and then manage to return home before full night had fallen.

It would not do for the wife of a member of the Sanhedrin to be out alone in Jerusalem after dark. If Caiaphas heard about it, he would scold Simon and shame him before all the scribes and priests and teachers of the law.

Sarai stopped short at that thought and laughed. Did she really care if Simon received Caiaphas' scorn?

"Oh, forgive me, blessed Adonai," she whispered, and moved on. "I swore to You I would honor and obey Simon and always work to protect his standing in the community. Even if he so hurts me that I never wish to see him again, I will not break my vows to You. Please, help me find Laila. Protect her. Protect me."

Ahead, the street widened to circle around a massive, square fountain. It was Roman, simply because a statue of a man stood in the center. No good Jew would ever carve a statue of a person and erect it where everyone who passed by or who thirsted would have to gaze on it. She shook her head and slowed as she caught a glimpse of movement at the base of the fountain pool.

"Laila?" Sarai called, even before the figure straightened from dipping up water in her hands to drink.

"What are you doing out here all alone?" Laila settled down on the rim of the fountain and dried her hands on the new veil she had been wearing around her shoulders when she left the house.

"You will need this. I wish I could give you more, but if I took longer, Simon would have stopped me." She held out the basket and wished she had thought to put some food in it. "This should help you find a safe place to stay and some kind of work."

"And what kind of respectable work is there for a woman among the Jews, other than to be a wife and mother, or a handmaiden? It's not vain to say I'm still beautiful, and no smart woman would allow me into her house. Even if I didn't have to carry the stain of my past as the Rose of Sharon." Laila sighed as she said it, but she still smiled. She took the basket Sarai held out to her and nodded her thanks.

"You know how to make even plain women beautiful, don't you?" Sarai asked, thinking aloud.

"Yes. Harlots still need to earn a living even after they've grown wrinkled and fat."

"Why couldn't you earn a living by helping women be beautiful? You could decorate brides on their wedding days, and help women who have gone through childbed and ... oh, I don't know. There must be many occasions when a woman wants to shine, and not just for her husband, but to earn him approval from his peers." Sarai thought of Simon showing her off to some of his peers. He hadn't been obvious, but she had heard him boasting to some of his friends who weren't so strict as others among the Pharisees. Why had she been so proud of his boasting?

"Any other woman but the Rose of Sharon could do that easily. Can't you just hear the mothers of Judea, shrieking in fear that I would teach their virgin daughters to act as harlots?" Laila chuckled softly. "It is a lovely idea, a dream, but no one would let me do such a thing. Not anywhere that I am known."

"Why can't you travel to places you've never been, where people don't know you? My friend's father is thinking of going to Damascus, to start over, build a new inn, away from the reach of the Sanhedrin. Why couldn't you?"

She knew what to do then. Norah's house was close enough, there was still plenty of daylight when Sarai and Laila reached the front door. Only after she knocked did Sarai feel a moment of uncertainty. Norah had showed sympathy for Laila, and was glad when Jesus healed her of her demons. She certainly didn't care about the criticism of the religious leaders, but how far could she resist them? Norah still relied on the good will of people who did listen and did care what the Sanhedrin said, even if only out of fear. What if the fear of losing respectable trade made her unwilling to help?

Malachi answered the door. He welcomed them in without asking about the woman with Sarai, and he didn't draw back in disgust or concern when he heard their story. Sarai thought she saw sympathy in his wrinkled face, more than any other emotion. He gestured for them to stay there in the entryway, and went further into the house, calling for a woman named Anna. He came back a few moments later with Anna, who reminded Sarai of her old nurse. Then he explained that Norah was away for three days, overseeing a wedding feast. He put Laila into Anna's care, then said he would walk Sarai home. It wouldn't do for her to be seen alone at dusk and after dark.

On the short walk home, he asked her enough questions, Sarai decided he had heard about Laila. To her relief, he seemed more than sympathetic. He promised that he and Norah would find a safe place for Laila, and respectable work for her to do. When Sarai mentioned her idea about starting over in Damascus, a broken chuckle escaped him.

"Hmm, yes, and I've been talking about starting over for several years now. I've been searching for the right place, between the outermost wall and the first inner wall -- that's the best place to set up an inn in a place like Damascus. Too far out, and we'd only serve caravans. Too far inside, and we'd just be a dark hole for drinking and whoring. I want an inn like I had, where travelers with families felt safe to stop for a few days, and where people could come for good food and fellowship."

They turned onto the street leading to Simon's door.

Sarai nearly stopped short when she realized the direction of her thoughts. *Simon's* house, but not *her* home. Malachi didn't seem to notice anything wrong, so the empty ache that shot through her didn't show on her face. She hoped.

"I would assume to be as successful as she was, your friend had a good head for business?"

"I suppose so." She choked a little, and barely kept from admitting that she really didn't know Laila well enough to call her a friend. Yet the woman had been kind to her, in that short meeting. She had given her hope and sympathy. Before the demons struck.

"In a new city, far enough away ... yes, I will send another message to the man who is supposed to be looking for a building for me." He gripped her shoulder a moment, as they stopped in front of the door. "You did many good things today, little Sarai. Be proud of that. May Adonai bless you."

She murmured her thanks, and watched him turn and walk away, into the darkness of the street. Sarai shivered, and didn't want to open the door and go inside. Yet she had to.

Simon was waiting when she went to the kitchen, watching Deborah work silently -- and far too slowly -- on their dinner.

"I took clothes and food to Laila, to help her on her journey," Sarai said before Simon could open his mouth.

"Sarai --"

"She is out of your house, Simon. Your reputation is preserved. The Rose of Sharon never slept under your roof. Your house is clean. And I am tired and my head hurts and I do not want supper. Good night, Simon."

"I didn't give you permission to leave." Simon followed her from the kitchen, across the common room.

"Forgive me, Master. I am just a stupid slave." Sarai blinked away tears as she reached to open the door in front of her.

"You are not my slave."

"I am your property, Simon. You bought me." A bitter chuckle escaped her. "History repeats itself. History always repeats itself, my father used to say, because we are foolish, sinful people. We never learn from our own mistakes, let alone the mistakes of our ancestors."

"What are you talking about?" He reached for her. His hand froze in mid-air when Sarai flinched and twisted out of his reach.

"As it was with Hagar and Sarah, Simon, so it will be with us. I know some of your friends already make scornful remarks, mocking you. You have two wives and neither has given you a son. That will change. Your son should come from the free woman, not the slave woman."

"You are not a slave!" he snapped.

"No, but neither am I pregnant. And I think Hannah is not ill, but she carries your child."

Sarai slipped through the door and gently closed it behind her while Simon stood in stunned, frozen silence.

Chapter Fifteen

Hannah seemed as stunned as Simon, when the women compared all the signs and concluded that yes, she was indeed with child.

Simon insisted that they consult a midwife, despite knowing all the training Sarai had done. Or perhaps, she wondered in dark, sad moments, he wanted another midwife's opinion because he didn't trust her? Sarai called in Naomi, a midwife who acknowledged her skills and wasn't silent about her opinion of Simon and his "pretentions to greatness." The little, white-haired woman with snapping black eyes confirmed the happy news. She supported Sarai's efforts to build Hannah's strength and protect the coming child. They made a list of forbidden foods and activities. The house required cleaning from roof to floor, and even the decorations and linens in Hannah's room were replaced.

Sarai gave Saul as much heavy, grueling, messy work as she could devise. Since everything was for Hannah's welfare, the grumbling manservant couldn't complain, though she did catch a few grudging looks shot her way. Every time he tried to accompany her when she went to the market, she refused calmly and decreed Deborah would go with her. If Saul ran to complain or tattle to Simon, her husband never countermanded her decisions or actions or rebuked her. Sarai did all the shopping now, so she met up with Norah nearly every time she left the house. Her friend reported that Malachi and Laila were becoming good friends, making plans for the inn in Damascus. It would be the wonder of the Roman Empire, if they had their way.

Those days of preparation were sweet. The two wives grew closer, and Sarai wept sometimes in secret, at how much Hannah depended on her and was grateful for her knowledge and support. There were a few sour notes, however. Mostly in the form of Simon's peers. She overheard several at different times congratulate Simon on the coming child. They made the usual remarks, prayers that El Shaddai would grant his firstborn was a son. Then each one, nearly with the same words, remarked that

Sarai's evident barrenness was a sign of God's displeasure. When she renounced her father's heretical teachings, then she would have the honor of giving Simon children as well.

Sarai tried to ignore and forget those hurtful, self-righteous comments. Carrying her husband's child should be a joy, not an honor. She feared Simon would throw his friend's critical words in her face the next time he grew angry with her. One time, she even remarked on the overheard conversations to Norah. Her friend laughed and reminded her of passages in her precious healing scrolls, reporting techniques to influence the sex of the child before conception.

"If you only had those scrolls again, you could become rich, selling potions to the wives of all the members of the Sanhedrin, to ensure they only gave those insufferable men daughters. That would bow their shoulders in shame, and maybe convince a few to change their attitudes," Norah had said.

Sarai laughed, but she prayed for Hannah to have a son. Not for Simon's sake, but for Hannah's. Perhaps then, her friend would feel safe.

~~~~~

Barabbas was active around Jerusalem. Sarai overheard Simon and his friends talking about the Zealot leader when the younger members of the Sanhedrin came to their home to talk long into the evening. They were irritated, not afraid, when the number of street patrols increased, and homes and shops, stables and warehouses were searched day and night. Sarai cringed when she heard Simon sneer over the inconvenience for the owners of those buildings. His peers agreed, those people likely deserved the mess the soldiers made, and to have possessions stolen during the searches. Even if no one knew what crimes they had committed, Yahweh knew, and He was punishing them. How could Simon, who had always protested that she was innocent, now agree that misfortune always equated Yahweh's anger and punishment?

Barabbas got into the city despite the increased guards at all the gates. He met with the malcontents and those who suffered injustice and were unable to achieve justice. He studied the mood of the city. Despite the veil and modest clothes Laila wore, and the lack of jewelry and cosmetics, he recognized her one day in the marketplace. He followed her back to Norah's house. He left when

Laila asked him to go away, for the sake of Malachi and Norah, but he came back. Several times. One day when she met with Sarai and Ruth in the market, Norah reported a conversation she overheard on her doorstep, early one morning.

"She was begging him to go talk to Jesus. Barabbas was so angry, I thought he would hit her. He actually said he liked her better when she was demon-possessed," Norah said with a gasp.

"He wanted her to play harlot and spy on the Romans again, didn't he?" Sarai guessed.

"The terrible part is, I think Laila is in love with him. Oh, how could any woman not fall in love with a big, strong man with convictions? Willing to risk his life for the safety of Israel. Barabbas isn't handsome, but there is something compelling about him."

"Don't fall in love with him yourself," she warned her friend.

Norah's mouth dropped open. They both burst out laughing, and quickly hushed the sound. Ruth was busy with a customer and had been in a foul mood when Sarai joined them. Reuben's wife was a sweet girl who wasn't clever enough to see the animosity behind the smiles. She thought Ruth was a good friend and included her in all the household news when she came to the stall to buy more cloth. Even when Ruth wasn't in a bad mood, she resented gaiety that didn't include her. Lately, any laughter that didn't include her, she assumed was mockery aimed at her.

"I truly hope," Norah said, when they were sure Ruth hadn't heard them, "Laila has finally made Barabbas so angry, he will wash his hands of her. He will finally realize that if she won't spy for him, he has no use for her. And he'll go away for good. She cried a little when he stormed away, but soon she was back to her peaceful self. She's making quite a name for herself with the lovely tunes she plays on her flute." She sniffed a little, and her eyes glistened. "She hopes to be used by Adonai, as your music was used to help her. Someday, she hopes her music can be used to ease the suffering of others who attacked by demons. Only Jesus could have brought about such a change in her."

~~~~~

Four days before Passover was set to begin, Simon brought a half-dozen friends home with him for the evening meal. Sarai and Deborah served them. Some of the new generation of Pharisees were offended by the sight of a pregnant woman, so Hannah, who tired easily, stayed in her room. Sarai tried not to listen to the men as she served them. Anything they said around Simon's table was just a continuation of whatever new irritation occupied the Sanhedrin.

Then there was always one who took the opportunity to console Simon, while she was in the room, for the sad thought that one of his wives was denied a child because of her rebellious spirit. Or as punishment for the heresy of her father. Sarai found her self-control strained to the limits. There was always something very hot or very messy in her hands, at such times. Something that would greatly embarrass the speaker if she slipped and accidentally dropped it on his head or his lap. She resorted to spending as much time as she could in the kitchen, where she couldn't hear their voices, much less make out their words.

"Sarai." Deborah hurried into the kitchen with the empty wine amphora. She set it down with a clunk and dropped onto her usual stool by the window. "Did you say Laila cared about that outlaw, Barabbas?"

"Yes. She's been trying to convince him to go see Jesus. She thinks Jesus can change him just as she was changed."

"Nobody can change him now. Oh, the poor girl." Deborah sniffed and rubbed at one eye. "The men were talking about Barabbas. He was captured yesterday. They'll crucify him for certain. Probably during Passover, to mock our holy days."

"How did they capture him?" Sarai sank down onto the bench by the door. Her head ached and sympathetic tears burned against the backs of her eyes.

"He was drunk. He tried to break into a wine merchant's warehouse and steal several skins. The whole time, he was shouting about Jesus. He didn't need Jesus' help. He didn't want Jesus to change him. He was tired of everybody talking about Jesus. He, Barabbas, was the one who would save Judea, not Jesus."

"And now who will save Barabbas?" Sarai whispered.

~~~~~

Sarai went out by herself the next morning, before the dawn shadows began to melt from the streets. She went to the well where Norah and her servant girls drew water. Sure enough, Norah was there, supervising. Ruth stood there with her empty water jar at her feet, leaning against the well rim, propped on her elbows, eyes bright with interest.

For a few heartbeats, fury toward Ruth scalded the back of Sarai's tongue. The merchant woman had servants to draw water, so she had only come to learn the latest gossip. Then again, hadn't Sarai herself come to find out what Norah knew? She had come to see if she could help or comfort Laila, of course, but curiosity had brought her just as much as compassion.

Adonai, she prayed, *are any of us pure?*

"The night before last, he tried to carry Laila away," Norah said as Sarai came close enough to hear. "She punched him in the eye. It was already turning black before he left," she added with a smirk that didn't last long. "Oh, he was furious. He needed her help, to find out something before he made his plans, and Laila refused. For such a brave man, so clever at leading the soldiers on a mad chase, he's rather stupid."

"Besides getting drunk and then caught making such a racket?" Ruth said with a snort.

Sarai wondered that she had never noticed how very pig-like Ruth was. Her tiny eyes, lost in increasing rolls of fat. The snorting sounds she made when she scorned someone. No wonder Reuben didn't want anything to do with her, no matter how she placed herself in his path or made calf's eyes at him -- or tried to bribe him with free cloth.

"Not that." Norah rolled her eyes in frustration. "He dared to stand there on the steps -- Laila had retreated to the roof to get away from him -- he stood there on the steps and told her that if she loved him, she'd do what he asked."

"Oh, now that was stupid," Sarai agreed.

"He should have told her he loved her, first," Ruth said.

"What man who really loved a woman would ask her to be a harlot?" Norah snapped. "Which is nearly what Laila told him. She said she loved him enough to say no, and to pray for him, and to beg him to go talk to Jesus. And then she told Barabbas she had been a fool, because he never loved her." She frowned. "She said even fools could learn from their mistakes, but the two of them had been worse than fools, and she refused to be one any longer. I really expected him to get even louder, but he seemed to ... I don't know. The life and spirit went out of him, like a wineskin with a hole in it. He left without another sound." She sighed. "And that's the last any of us will see of Barabbas."

~~~~~

Three days later, as preparations for Passover began in earnest, Sarai sent Deborah and Saul to the marketplace. She felt weak and even a little unsteady on her feet. Her usual morning infusion to calm her increasingly uneasy stomach didn't help until she had taken two cups. She busied herself with work she could do sitting down in the kitchen, and as the day grew older, she tried not to worry that Deborah and Saul were delayed in returning.

She was alone in the kitchen when Simon came storming into the house, hours earlier than his usual time to return. He shouted her name, and she heard the slapping of his sandals on the tiled floors as he dashed into the courtyard, then back to her room. The door thudded and he cursed her, at the same time she called out in response. Sarai put aside the mortar filled with the raisins and spices she had been grinding into a smooth paste. She wiped her hands as she got to her feet. Slowly. The floor had wavered under her feet several times that morning.

Simon shouted for Saul and threatened his "scrawny neck" if he was malingering somewhere. Sarai knew then something had happened in the city. Something relating to Jesus, which had earned more censure from Caiaphas, and which Simon had not wanted her to witness. A bubble of something that might have been laughter rose in her throat, when her husband snarled threats to have Saul sold to a Roman galley, despite his advanced years.

"He is not here," she said, raising her voice to be heard in that short pause after Simon slammed another door. "He and Deborah are in the marketplace."

"Were you in the marketplace?" Simon blurted, and dashed down the hallway to the kitchen so quickly his sandals slid over a few tiles when he tried to stop.

"No. I have been here all morning. There is twice as much work to do to prepare for Passover." Sarai flinched when she heard Hannah's door creak open. For a moment, she thought to scold Simon for waking her. As long as Hannah took several naps during the day and ate multiple small meals, she avoided the queasy spells and dizziness. Simon knew she needed peace and quiet to sleep, but Sarai knew better than to remind him. She refused to be a shrew like other wives who were treated far worse than Simon treated her.

Most of the time.

"You were here all day." Simon's shoulders heaved one last time as he caught his breath.

"Yes."

"You weren't chasing after Jesus? You weren't following Him up and down the streets of the city, proclaiming Him the Messiah like all the other fools? Waving palm branches, throwing their coats into the street before His donkey. The gall of Him! Trying to force scripture to support His arrogant claims."

Sarai silently recited the words of the prophet speaking of the deliverer, coming in humility, riding on the foal of a donkey.

"No, I have been here all morning, working," she said, when she wanted to snap back at him that she had never chased Jesus. Every time she saw Him, it had been a chance encounter. Mostly. If she heard He was near, she turned her path to hopefully hear Him. The only crime Simon could charge her with was staying to listen.

"Good." He nodded twice, took another deep breath, wiped the sweat off his face with both hands. "I am pleased to see you are finally learning to be obedient." Then he stomped away.

Sarai fought angry tears. She returned to the kitchen and worked without thought, the churning in her head and the churning in her belly battling each other for dominance. Then Hannah touched her hands, stopping her as she dug hard into the mortar, so the raisins and spices flew across the table. Her fellow wife smiled with tears in her eyes and settled down on the bench and wrapped both arms around Sarai. Hannah said nothing, while the two clung to each other and the world stopped spinning. Sarai was grateful.

They shared a few chuckles when they cleaned up the mess she had made. The heat in her face and the pounding behind her eyes faded eventually, so Deborah didn't notice anything amiss when she and Saul finally returned from the marketplace.

Before that, though, Sarai overheard Hannah approach Simon. With uncharacteristic strength in her voice, she scolded Simon for how he spoke to Sarai. Sarai nearly dropped the skin of wine she had just closed up, after filling a bowl to soak dried herbs.

"You are so full of your concerns about the dangers in the city, as it fills up with Passover visitors, you don't pay attention to Sarai," Hannah said. "She is ill every morning, but she hides it so she can take care of me."

"She is not." Simon had the same sullen tone Joseph had used when their mother scolded him for being rude or selfish, or fighting with other boys, and he didn't want to apologize.

"You wouldn't know because you don't pay attention to her in the morning."

"If Sarai were ill, why wouldn't she say anything?"

Sarai held her breath. She took two steps closer to the kitchen door, to hear better. Then she shook her head and returned to the table and the work waiting for her.

"No," Simon hurried on, most likely cutting off Hannah's answer, "she is not ill. She is a healer. Or so she claims. If Sarai seems ill, it is because she is jealous of you."

"Sarai? Jealous?" Hannah's voice cracked with what was likely incredulous laughter.

"I've heard of it happening. A man is jealous of another who is injured or ill, jealous of all the attention. So he falls ill, forcing others to attend to his needs. But the illness isn't real. Any more than Sarai's illness. She is jealous because you carry my child, so she imagines she is with child, and imagines she suffers as you do."

"My husband ..." Hannah's voice grew a little louder, and Sarai imagined she had moved closer to the hallway. "I could no more believe Sarai would be jealous of anyone than I could believe that you would listen to the foolish prattling of old, idle women in the marketplace. At least until now."

Hannah's soft, shuffling steps came down the hallway. Sarai bent back over her work at the table. Hannah didn't return to the kitchen, and in a minute or two, Sarai relaxed. She pressed her hands to her face, surprised that it wasn't hot with mortification again. Maybe Simon's low opinion of her character chilled her enough to fight that sensation.

Sarai focused on Hannah's words about her being ill. She thought she hid the queasiness well enough. A smile curved up one side of her mouth, pleased at this new strength in Hannah. Sarai had worried that her meek, hesitant nature might make childbirth difficult. This new strength was encouraging.

Even more encouraging was the way Simon left the house again, quietly, his footsteps slow. Hannah knew how to make him stop and think, apparently, and maybe regret his cruelty. Sarai wondered when she had lost that ability to touch his heart and mind. Maybe she had been fooling herself to think she had any kind of influence over him.

Just moments before Deborah and Saul returned, a new thought struck Sarai. Simon thought she was so weak, so self-centered, she would mimic Hannah's illness for attention? How he had changed, from the childhood days when he had gotten into a fist fight with the other students when one of them mocked her. Sarai couldn't even remember now what the other boy had said, or even who had said it. She only remembered that Simon had been quicker to defend her than her own brother. The boy he had once been would have noticed that she was unsteady on her feet every morning. The cool clamminess of her skin likely made her pale. Why didn't Simon notice that?

Then Saul stumbled into the kitchen and put down the sacks he carried, one over each shoulder. Deborah followed him, her shoulders bowed with the weight of the two baskets she carried. Sarai put aside her thoughts for later, and half-hoped she wouldn't remember what had just filled her mind.

"Jerusalem has gone mad," Saul announced.

Sarai looked to Deborah, who rolled her eyes heavenward. Hannah came into the kitchen then. Most likely she had been waiting nearby, listening for the two servants to return.

In short order, Saul and Deborah spilled the whole story, of how Jesus had ridden through the streets of Jerusalem, with the people shouting hosannas and waving palm branches. Speculation rippled through the city that He would proclaim Himself king and begin the revolution to drive the Romans out of Judea. Deborah was full of wonder, and sometimes biting remarks, about the people running to join the procession and the arguments that erupted in Jesus' wake. She had little respect for people who shouted glory to Adonai, and the next moment turned to snarl and slap at the people on either side of them, who didn't shout as loud or who remarked that High Priest Annas would be upset. Saul had work to do elsewhere in the house, but he lingered in the doorway of the kitchen, adding his own critical remarks to everything Deborah said.

"It's a good thing for you that you weren't anywhere around that mob." Saul smirked a little, when Sarai made the mistake of looking up and meeting his gaze.

"No, it's a good thing for you," she snapped, as the heat rose in her face. She didn't throw down the knife she used to chop garlic, and she barely refrained from pointing it at him. "When my husband returned in the middle of the day and found you weren't here, he threatened to sell you to a Roman galley by morning."

Saul's mouth flapped for a few moments. Then he snorted and pulled himself up to his full height. "We should be thankful then, that you're always sick. Keep you at home where you belong. Someone would think you're catching what that one had." He flicked his fingers at Hannah, then sniffed and shuffled back down the hallway.

"I swear his face went white," Deborah whispered, ending on a chuckle. "Serves him right. Nasty, self-righteous old fool. Making all sorts of critical remarks about the people around us. He entirely missed the glory of what was in front of us. It was a miracle the Romans didn't come down on us, thinking we were an invading army about to take Jerusalem by storm. People everywhere were calling Jesus the Son of David. Or proclaiming Him the Messiah. If Jesus had stopped His donkey in the middle of the street and told the people to rebel against Rome, they would have. Jerusalem would be free right this moment from Roman rule."

"For how long?" Sarai asked. "There are so many people crowded into Jerusalem on the eve of Passover, even three times as many Roman soldiers couldn't have controlled them if they rebelled. But how far would the rebellion have traveled before it failed?"

"If the people are proclaiming Jesus the Messiah and David's heir ... the Sanhedrin will not be happy when they hear about it," Hannah ventured.

"Simon will be late coming home tonight." She thought of Caiaphas' fury and how long he would rant and spew his venom into the ears of his followers. She shuddered.

"If he comes at all," Deborah said. "Most of the Sanhedrin saw the whole thing. The procession turned a corner and there they were. Caiaphas scolded Jesus for letting the people adore Him. As if He could have stopped us!" she added with a chuckle. "Do you know what Jesus said? He said if we were silent, the very stones in the streets would cry out. Caiaphas didn't like that at all."

"No, I imagine he didn't," Sarai murmured. She flinched when Hannah reached over and squeezed her hand.

She was glad Hannah was there. Simon had accused her of lying several days ago, when she said she was glad for Hannah's pregnancy. She would have argued with him, but it was as if she could see the words waiting to spill off his tongue -- the accusation that her loyalty to her father's heretical teachings had resulted in God making her barren, in punishment.

Sarai had wanted to hit him so hard that spots danced before his eyes. Instead, she bowed her head and hid her face in her veil and shuddered, hating the vicious feelings racing through her.

Now, with Hannah's hand gripping hers, Sarai was glad for her presence in their lives. Hannah's child gave the entire household hope, and the blessing of peace.

~~~~~

Nicodemus' wife had died five years before, and they had never had any children. Jude's parents were presently in Antioch and had chosen not to come to Jerusalem for the Passover. Simon invited both men to celebrate Passover with his household. Sarai wondered about the constant maneuvering for the sake of power in the Sanhedrin. Why wasn't Simon invited to another household for the feast? Was he just forgotten, or under censure, or was he high enough in prestige and approval now that he was expected to be a host and not a guest? Yet if that was so, why didn't he invite his peers to join their household for the feast? Perhaps he had invited them, but no one came? Could it be he chose discretion and silence, as the usual turmoil of Passover built up within the city, like a sealed pot threatening to explode? Surely he wasn't in some sort of disgrace with his superiors over her again, was he? Sarai felt sadly certain if that were the case, Simon would not be silent about her latest foolish transgression threatening his future hopes and secure position.

Hannah was much stronger and healthier that day. Perhaps knowing that familiar, welcome guests were coming to their household made her feel better. She, Sarai, and Deborah had a happy, busy day together in the kitchen, preparing the special Passover dishes, talking about anything and everything. They compared their childhood memories of Passover, the games and gifts and songs and traditions passed down through their families.

"Ah, but next Passover, we will start our own traditions," Deborah said, nodding at Hannah. "Your little one won't be old enough to remember, but that won't stop us from making merry, will it?"

"Perhaps you, too, will have a child by then," Hannah said. "It isn't right that you don't have a child. Simon loves you, Sarai. The wife of his heart should give him his firstborn."

"This is as Adonai wills it." Sarai blinked rapidly to fight an aching sense of tears.

She doubted Simon's love. As in the story Jesus had told of the many types of soil and the seeds that either flourished or died because of the soil, Simon's love for her had been planted partially in stony soil, and partially in soil filled with thorns. The roots of his love were shallow and there was much competition for his affections and loyalties. Adversity had come to scorch and choke, and Simon's love wasn't strong enough to endure.

Chapter Sixteen

Saul washed the feet of the guests, when Jude and Nicodemus arrived at the house. Hannah and Sarai waited while Simon greeted their guests, then stepped forward to give their own welcome. Sarai recalled Passover celebrations when her mother was alive. Many scholars and religious leaders had come as guests, with their wives and children. Sarai had played with the boys and girls, unaware of the politics behind the guest list.

After her mother died, Rabbi Eliakim only invited widowers, elderly men without families, or those who had traveled to Jerusalem without their wives and children. As her father's influence had waned in the Sanhedrin, the guests had dwindled to his students and the few loyal friends without families.

Tonight, Simon had decreed a family celebration. They would all sit at the table, rather than sequestering men from women. Sarai guided the guests to their dining couches at the long, low table. Because there were only the five of them tonight, they did not set up all the sections of the table. They could see each other and converse far more comfortably than those at large feasts, arranged around a squared horseshoe.

They settled down on their couches and Deborah and Saul brought in the amphora for the first cup of wine.

"Tell me, Simon," Jude said. "I've been away so often in the last few months, it's difficult to keep up with the rumors. I would like to hear your opinion. What do you think of Jesus now that you've had more chances to hear Him teach?"

"He has an interesting way with words." Simon's tone struck Sarai's ears as too uncaring. His words certainly didn't reflect his attitude toward Jesus. She considered him most unfair, because while he had had many chances to listen to Jesus, he hadn't taken advantage of many, if any. From what she had overheard, most of what Simon knew of Jesus' teaching had been repeated to him by other people, not heard first-hand.

"A wise man does not waste his words, but you are a miser!" Jude chuckled. "Haven't you made a decision yet about Him?"

"The Sanhedrin has condemned Him as a blasphemer and a servant of Beelzebub. That is enough for me."

"Do you agree, Rabbi Nicodemus?"

"I do not." Nicodemus still sat on the side of his dining couch, hands resting on his knees.

He didn't look at Simon as he spoke. Sarai wished Jude hadn't brought up the subject at all.

"What I have seen and heard," Nicodemus continued, "and have seen in all my study of the scriptures, leads me to believe Jesus *is* sent from Yahweh. His words come from our Creator. He has healed the blind, and that is a sign of the Messiah."

"You truly believe that?" Jude smiled. Could it be he wanted to believe in Jesus?

"Please, my friends," Simon said, "we are here to celebrate the Passover, not to discuss politics." He smiled, and for a moment Sarai could believe he wanted only a pleasant time with their guests, rather than avoiding a controversial subject.

As the eldest, Nicodemus had the privilege of making the Passover toasts. Each participant in the feast had four cups, and the Cup of Elijah sat all by itself in the center of the table. Sarai remembered how she had always watched the Cup of Elijah when she was a child, praying the ancient prophet would walk through the door of her father's house and proclaim that the Savior of Israel had indeed arrived. Looking at the elegantly simple cup of silver decorated with turquoise chips, Sarai felt only sadness now. What had happened to the hope of her childhood?

"The first cup of Passover, the Kiddush." Nicodemus raised his filled cup. The others followed suit. "May this holy day be sanctified in our hearts and minds, our actions and words."

Sarai barely tasted the wine. Hannah only sipped at hers, cautious even though her stomach was finally settling.

Deborah and Saul cleared the cups after the toast and brought in flat rounds of unleavened bread, fresh and warm from the oven, and cleaned, raw vegetables to dip in the saltwater in shallow bowls at each place. Sarai carried the platter of vegetables around the table to serve everyone.

"We dip our food into saltwater," Nicodemus said, "to remind us of the tears shed when our ancestors were slaves in Egypt. Passover is a time to remember our slavery and sorrow, and to look forward to our joy when the Messiah, our Deliverer comes to us." He dipped a radish into the little bowl, and the others followed suit.

Sarai nibbled on a few slices of carrot and ate only a mouthful of bread. She had been hungry all day, enticed by the aromas while she and Deborah and Hannah had cooked and baked. What had happened to her appetite? Was she merely tired?

Saul brought in the platter with the roasted lamb. Nicodemus stood to speak the blessing on the steaming meat. Hannah blanched when a wisp of steam touched her face. Though it was her turn to serve, Sarai touched her on the shoulder, gently keeping her on her dining couch, and stood to do that duty as well.

Simon watched her, his smile soft, the expression in his eyes warm. So different from the face he turned to her more often lately. Tears pressed at her eyes, and she was glad to retreat and take the platter back to the kitchen. Nicodemus stood to make the blessing and speak over the meat, when she returned to the table.

"The Torah specifies a lamb without any defect, pure and perfect. Its blood smeared on our doorposts reminds us that the blood of the lamb caused the Angel of Death to turn aside and not harm those inside the house. Someday, Yahweh will provide the perfect sacrifice, the Lamb of God, which takes away the sin of the world."

"John the Baptizer spoke those words." Jude looked at the portion of meat on his plate instead of the other diners. "I met him once, several years ago, during my travels. He spoke of the Lamb of God, who takes away the sins of the world. I had no idea what he meant. He might have explained if Herod hadn't taken his head."

Simon snorted and the conversation drifted for a time to the scandals of the royal household and the latest outrages perpetrated by the Roman government. Sarai didn't participate, content to listen and watch her guests. She noticed that Jude said little beyond affirming something the other men said. As if his thoughts were elsewhere, back to John the Baptizer and his words.

She wished she could speak privately to Jude, ask him what he thought, perhaps even learn more of what the Baptizer had said. Everyone acknowledged he was a prophet, this roughly dressed son of a priest. The Sanhedrin couldn't deny that Adonai's power had flowed through him.

It wasn't enough to save his life, though, Sarai thought. *What is the use of serving Adonai, living to speak His words, if service will not save you? Even the most perfect and blameless life is not safe. What is the good of all such sacrifice?*

Nicodemus stood again, yanking her from her thoughts. She was grateful. He raised the second cup of the feast.

"The second cup of Passover, the Cup of Plagues, to remind us of the power of God to avenge His people. It is also the Cup of Praise, for the deliverance that came from Yahweh's hand, and will come again from Yahweh's hand."

Hannah took only a sip of the wine from that cup, then quickly ate a small piece of bread, likely to settle her stomach.

"Stay still," Sarai whispered. "Let me do all the carrying tonight." Hannah's pitiful smile of thanks sent an ache through her.

Deborah brought the bowl of charoset paste and Saul carried the bowl of bitter herbs, for dipping their bread. Sarai took the bowls and served the occupants of the table while the servants took away the wine cups and dirty plates and brought more food to the table. The ceremonial aspect of the feast had nearly ended.

Carefully, Nicodemus tore a round of bread in half. He folded each piece in half and dipped one into the sweet charoset of apples, nuts, raisins and honey, and the other into the bitter herbs.

"We eat charoset and bitter herbs to remind us of our bitter labor in Egypt, and the sweetness of the Father's redemption. To give us hope through the bitter times ahead."

Hannah ate some charoset and the herbs. Simon must have been watching her, alert to her discomfort, because he smiled and renewed the conversation. The tightness in the atmosphere loosened and then faded. Sarai stayed quiet during the main part of the meal, attentive to the needs of the others.

She noticed Jude rarely looked at her unless she served him. His thanks were spoken softly, and his gaze flicked away quickly. Did his reticence stem from lingering feelings for her?

What if Jude had returned only half a moon earlier, and Joseph had given her to him as his wife before he was caught by the Romans? Would she be serving the Passover feast in their home tonight, or be a guest in another rich home? Would she and Jude have argued over Jesus?

Sarai nearly dropped a dirty platter when that question rang through her mind. She hurried to the kitchen.

Nicodemus stood to make the toast of the third cup when Sarai returned to the table.

"The third cup is the Cup of Redemption." He turned the cup in his hand, gazing into the dark red depths of the wine. "We look back to the redemption of the children of Israel from slavery. We look forward to the redemption of the Messiah. May it come soon!" he said, addressing Simon.

A chill curled through Sarai's belly.

Simon held Nicodemus' gaze, never blinking. Not a twitch of his lips or head betrayed what he felt. The silence stretched on for five heartbeats. Ten. Fifteen. Sarai counted, forgetting to breathe. Then Simon smiled and stood up from his couch and reached for the Cup of Elijah. As the host of the feast, that ritual fell to him.

Sarai and Simon had daydreamed about hosting Passover, during their long, dusty walk from the Decapolis to Jerusalem. She had planned the many dishes she would prepare for their guests and he had chosen the songs they would sing. They had chosen the names of their children, who would all sit in respectful, joyous silence when their father raised the Cup of Elijah, as Simon did now.

What sins have we committed, blessed El Shaddai, that our dreams will never come true?

"We fill a cup for the prophet Elijah, in anticipation of his coming," Simon said, with all the dignity of Rabbi Eliakim. Sarai wondered if he had learned such poise from her father, or through his own trials and testing. "Scripture says Elijah must come first to restore all things and prepare for the coming of the Messiah."

Simon walked across the room, out the open door, to the main door of the household. Everyone at the table sat up to watch him as he opened the door and stepped over the threshold, out into the street. Simon held out the cup, offering it to the prophet, who would bring the hope of the redemption of Israel with him when he returned.

"The servants of the Pharisees asked John the Baptizer if he was Elijah, when they found him at the Jordan," Jude murmured. "I wish he had said yes. Then I could be sure."

Sarai wanted to ask what he meant. She feared the disruption to their feast if she asked.

Simon returned to the table and set down the Cup of Elijah

where it had been before. "Elijah is not here. We must keep waiting for the Messiah."

Jude stood as Simon sat, and raised the remains of the third cup in a toast. It was not uncommon for a guest to salute someone in blessing after the cup of Elijah.

"My thanks, to the master and mistress of this house. Yahweh's blessing on us all this Passover." He lifted the cup high, then lowered it and drank. The others sipped, watching him. Jude set the cup down but did not sit. "Perhaps this will be the last Passover we celebrate." He looked directly at Simon.

"I'm sorry. I don't understand." The stiffness in Simon's voice told Sarai he understood exactly what Jude implied.

"When Messiah comes, there will be no need for Passover, no need to remember God's provision, for the Kingdom of God will be with us."

"When Messiah comes, yes, but that is far in the future. If ever."

"If ever?" Sarai was startled by her squeak of surprise. She had meant to stay silent, intended to give Simon no cause for anger with her tonight, of all nights.

"Be silent!" her husband snapped. "I forbid you to even speak of Jesus."

"Simon," Nicodemus said in a soft, gently rebuking tone that comforted Sarai. "How can you speak to your wife that way?"

"Please, my friends, it is Passover." Jude spread his arms in a placating gesture. "A time of celebration. A time of praise to our Creator. Let us pray that Messiah has indeed come --"

"He has *not* come." Simon stood. "And if you would be welcome in my home, you will not speak like a fool."

"Simon!" The gentleness fled Nicodemus' voice this time.

"I will not tolerate blasphemy in my home."

"Forgive me, Simon." Jude bowed to each person in turn. "Sarai. Hannah. Master Nicodemus. It is a graceless guest who brings strife to a house that has shared its bread with him, and on such a holy night. I should leave while the evening is still pleasant. God's blessing on this house."

Before Sarai could stand, to escort him to the door as a guest deserved, he left the room, snatching up his outer robe from its peg on the wall of the receiving room. A moment later the door creaked open and he was gone.

"It is the worst luck of all," Hannah whispered. "We did not drink from the fourth cup."

"El Shaddai understands and forgives us," Sarai whispered back. She caught up Hannah's hand and squeezed it, and prayed she gave her some comfort. She needed some badly, herself.

"Simon, you fear the Sanhedrin too much," Nicodemus said. "When will you learn your soul is far more important than status?"

"You have been my teacher and a good friend, Master Nicodemus," Simon said through gritted teeth. "Don't make me tell you what a fool you are becoming."

Sarai flinched as if Simon had slapped her again. She blinked rapidly, fighting tears. How had this pleasant, holy evening degenerated so quickly? Simon would blame her, if she did or said anything while this anger enabled him to speak so disrespectfully to Nicodemus.

Saul entered in those few seconds of silence as fragile as rare, Greek-made glass.

"Master, a messenger has come from the Sanhedrin. You are called to an emergency council."

"Of course." Simon released a deep, loud breath. "Immediately. Did you tell him Rabbi Nicodemus celebrates Passover with us?"

"I did." Saul's glance flicked to Nicodemus. "He was not summoned," the manservant admitted after a noticeable pause.

"Well." Nicodemus sat down on the foot of his dining couch. "That's … interesting."

"They would never gather without you." Simon sounded like his old self, concerned and respectful.

"Yet they have. What are you waiting for? If you want to advance in the Sanhedrin, you don't make Caiaphas wait." He smiled and made shooing motions toward the door.

Simon only hesitated briefly before giving a slight bow of farewell and departing. Nicodemus' smile faded into a weary frown before he had vanished through the doorway.

"What could be so important to interrupt the feast?" Sarai wondered. "Why would they exclude you, Master Nicodemus?"

"They have been gnashing their teeth over how to silence Jesus. Caiaphas knows I support Jesus, and I do not doubt they do their plotting when I am absent. To prevent the voice of reason speaking, rather than having to silence it." He sighed and shadows seemed to fall across his face, making him look a decade older. "If they could manage it, without starting a riot, they would arrest Jesus. I would not put it past Caiaphas to convene a court at night, even though it is against all tradition and our law. They would not invite me, because they know how I would vote."

"They can't put Jesus on trial. He's done nothing wrong."

"Hmm. When you grow to be as old as me, my dears, you realize the world no longer clamors for truth. Especially when truth becomes a mirror that reveals all the world's flaws and sins and diseases." He stood, moving like a man twenty years older as he went to the door. "I doubt being innocent will save Jesus, when He finally stands trial before them. I doubt it will save anyone who stands in the way of power and those who wish to possess it."

~~~~~

Even Saul seemed subdued by what had happened. Sarai regretted her harsh thoughts toward him. She had expected him to gloat and make snide comments while cleaning up after the meal. He didn't have to be told twice or even three times to move the table or the dining couches or sweep the floor.

Though the sounds of Passover celebration laughter and songs drifted through the warm night air from all directions, the household retired early to bed. Sarai couldn't sleep, however. It was simply easier to bear the waiting, the speculations, in the privacy of her own dark, silent room, rather than sitting in the kitchen or the courtyard, watching everyone else and wondering.

Wakeful, she heard Laila call. She leaped from her bed to run through the house and answer the door before Saul could stir.

"They've arrested Jesus." Laila gasped, drenched in sweat. She trembled, and Sarai feared she would faint. Even in the shadows, she looked too pale.

Saul appeared in the doorway of the kitchen, where Sarai took Laila. He had the tact not to even glare at her before he left them alone. Deborah joined them there. Hannah stayed in her room.

They settled down together by the light of an oil lamp and insisted she have some wine. After a few sips of the wine and nibbling on some bread spread with charoset, the color returned to Laila's cheeks and she stopped trembling. Her story was simple. After Norah's household had celebrated the Passover meal, Laila wanted to find Jesus. She didn't know where He and His disciples were going to have the meal, but she knew His habit of going to Gethsemane to pray, so she went there in hopes of finding Him. She found the disciples first, and debated waiting, or going deeper into the garden, to find Jesus while He prayed. Before she could slip past the few disciples who were awake, soldiers came to the garden, filling it with torchlight and noise.

"Why would Romans arrest Him?" Deborah asked.

"Temple soldiers. Caiaphas' personal guards." Laila shivered. "I hid in the shadows, while most of the disciples fled."

"Oh, Laila, what if you had been caught?" Sarai murmured.

"If only I could have found them earlier, if I had asked Him ... Jesus might not have been there." She hid her face in her hands.

Deborah stroked Laila's head, like she would comfort an ill child. "What did you want from Him?"

"Looking back ... it was foolish of me." Laila raised her head and knuckled tears out of her eyes. "I thought, Barabbas refused to go see Jesus -- maybe I could ask Jesus to go speak with Barabbas. He's in prison. He would have to listen to Jesus. He couldn't escape. But now?" She clutched Sarai's hands. "Iscariot led the soldiers. One of His own betrayed Him. What are they going to do with Him?"

"Put Him on trial. An illegal trial." Sarai sighed. "We weren't even finished with dinner with Caiaphas sent a messenger for Simon, but not for Rabbi Nicodemus." She waited until Laila reacted, meaning she understood the significance of that omission. "It is against Jewish law to hold a court under cover of darkness, but that doesn't matter to Caiaphas."

"That can only mean he intends to find Jesus guilty," Deborah said. "They want to kill Him."

"Nobody but the Romans are allowed to execute criminals," Laila said. "How will they convince Governor Pilate to put Jesus to death?"

"Let us pray they can't and won't," Sarai said.

~~~~~

Simon still hadn't returned when the first gloomy gray streaks of dawn touched the upper windows of the house. Was that a good sign? Perhaps Jesus' enemies couldn't gather enough witnesses and evidence to convict him. Knowing Caiaphas, the frustration alone could make him dangerous.

Still, Sarai needed to know what was happening. All she

intended to do was go to Caiaphas' house and speak to a servant, listen to the gossip in the courtyard. She had a vague plan of saying she had come to see if Simon wanted her to bring him a change of clothes. That subservience would make him look good in front of his Pharisee friends, at least.

Laila insisted on accompanying her, instead of returning to Norah's house. They crept down the too-quiet streets. The entire world seemed to hold its breath. The center of Jerusalem, entirely under Roman control, lay between them and the quarter where the priests lived. The two women had only walked down one street when the quiet dissolved into the muted rumbling of a mob in the distance. Their voices bounced off buildings and throbbed with the beat of an angry heart.

Sarai didn't want to go near that sound, but to try to go around it would use up time she could not spare. She and Laila linked arms and continued down the street.

The narrow streets widened, and the plain fronts of buildings vanished under Roman signs and statues and portraits carved in wood and stone; all the gods and generals and senators of the Roman Empire. People moved along at a brisk pace when Sarai and Laila stepped out onto the main thoroughfare. They looked at each other, and Sarai suspected her friend shared her thoughts: they couldn't cross that river of humanity. They would have to move with it, until they could escape on the other side.

"We're heading for the governor's palace," Laila called, raising her voice above the rumble of voices and feet.

The stench of unwashed bodies made Sarai grateful she hadn't eaten. She tightened her grip on Laila's arm as they tried to move at a shallow angle to the flow of moving people. She wanted to be on the edge of the crowd when they came into the plaza in front of the governor's palace. Otherwise, they could be trapped there.

Governor Pilate had been known to send his soldiers into the center of crowds to indiscriminately stab with spears, simply because the crowd irritated him.

The crowd spilled into the plaza in front of the governor's palace. The press of people around them loosened. Sarai and Laila had room to maneuver to the edge of the plaza, where the fountains forced the flow of traffic to turn. They aimed for a shadowed, open space, where several streets converged and offered escape. Just another dozen or so steps, and they would be safe and free of the crowd. Beyond that spot lay the main doors of the palace and the balcony where Governor Pilate stood to make proclamations.

"No." Laila pointed upward, then shuddered and crumpled to her knees.

Sarai helped her stand and managed to move them out of the current of people, but now they were trapped, blocked from moving any further, yet within sight of their goal. She seated Laila on the edge of the fountain, then looked around and saw what had struck her such a deep blow.

Caiaphas stood on the top step in front of the grand entryway to the palace, regally poised with his staff in hand, dressed in his priestly robes, looking up at the balcony where Governor Pilate had to appear. He would not enter the governor's palace because that would make him ceremonially unclean, barring him from celebrating the remainder of the Passover.

Behind Caiaphas, ranged in order of age and preeminence, stood most of the Sanhedrin. Nicodemus was not among them. Sarai knew enough of the religious leaders in Jerusalem to identify at least ten missing faces. Only ten, out of all those men charged with the spiritual leadership of Judea, disagreed with Annas and Caiaphas and their agenda?

Directly to Caiaphas' right, surrounded by Temple soldiers, stood Jesus. Sarai saw the bruises on His face, the stains on His robes and the tears in His clothing. Dark smears that she feared were blood streaked His chest and shoulders. His hair lay plastered to His head with sweat. His eyes were closed, and He held as still as death.

"He prays," Laila said. "I have watched Him pray, and I know He speaks with Adonai and hears Adonai. How can they kill a man who can hear Adonai speak?"

She no longer had to shout to be heard. The crowd had quieted. Sarai glanced upward and saw a man in the ubiquitous white robes of a Roman official striding out onto the balcony. A moment later, she recognized Governor Pilate. That brief meeting with him in the inner garden seemed like a lifetime ago.

"I was wondering when you were going to show up," Ruth said, startling Sarai.

"What are you doing here?" she whispered, as Ruth settled

down on the edge of the fountain.

"I'm here to watch the trial, of course."

"This is no trial. They can't put him on trial. Why are they doing this?" Laila stared at Jesus, ignoring everyone else in the plaza.

"It's simple," Ruth said with a shrug.

Around them, people murmured and pointed, and some laughed, while others cried out against what was being said. Sarai couldn't make herself understand anything, could barely focus on Ruth's words. All she could see was Jesus' battered face.

"Jesus was wrong," Ruth continued. "He said the wrong things, He did the wrong things, and no matter what miraculous powers He possesses, He lost the war with Caiaphas. The Sanhedrin won. If they have their way, Governor Pilate will crucify Him."

"No! They wouldn't be so cruel."

"Yes, they would." Sarai thought of how Simon had changed. "Oh, what can we do?"

"Nothing," Ruth said. "Do you want to go watch? I've never seen a crucifixion before."

Sarai slapped her with all the strength and fury burning inside her. Ruth squeaked and nearly lost her balance. For several long moments, she hung poised on the edge of the fountain. She regained her grip on the stone lip and pulled herself upright. Her face was white, except for the handprint on her cheek, redder than hot coals. Her little piggy eyes blazed.

"I'm facing reality, Sarai. Maybe you should, too, for a change. Or are you going to go home and hide your head and wait for another false Messiah to appear?"

Chapter Seventeen

Sarai turned and stumbled away from the fountain, with Laila holding onto her arm. They tried to go forward, aiming for that shadowed intersection of streets that promised escape. Governor Pilate spoke with Caiaphas, both men exchanging bitter-sounding words. Sarai could comprehend none of it, only the emotions, the scorn that sizzled through the air. The crowd surged, shouting and laughing and cursing in response, and the two women were nearly knocked off their feet, carried along until they were nearly on the steps of the governor's palace. They clutched at each other to stand upright. Any movement would attract attention, so they held still, until Sarai thought neither of them dared to breathe.

"Rome does not concern itself with your religion," Pilate said in bored tones. "He is one of your teachers. Deal with Him according to your laws."

"But we are under the power of Rome." Caiaphas' voice echoed off the stone fronts of the buildings. "We want justice, Governor Pilate. We want to protect Israel and remain obedient servants of Rome."

Yes, Sarai shrieked deep within her soul. *Whatever allows you to stay in power, you will do it.*

"You have already beaten Him. Isn't that enough?"

"We don't have the authority to put anyone to death," Reuben called.

"Why do you want Him dead? What has He done to you?"

"He claims He is Christ, the king."

"Anyone who makes himself a king is a rebel against Caesar!" Caiaphas raised his arms, his face a mask of horrified dismay.

Caesar demanded that his subjects address him as "King and God." Sarai wondered if Caiaphas would obey without a qualm, if he ever stood before Caesar.

"That doesn't make him a criminal," Pilate said, his voice sharp with laughing scorn. "I wouldn't want to be king to you Jews!"

"Sarai." Simon appeared as if out of the stone pavement. He grabbed her by both arms and shook her. She could only stare at him, the aching in her heart so deep nothing could startle her now. "Is this the man you thought was the Messiah?" He yanked her free of Laila's hold on her and turned her to face Jesus. "Look at Him!"

"I am looking."

Above them, Pilate questioned Jesus and continued to snap back at every one of Caiaphas' demands and accusations. She took a deep breath and let her heart speak.

"I don't understand, but if this is God's will --"

"This is not God's will! When Messiah comes, He will come in triumph, to destroy our enemies."

"Simon." Nicodemus stepped up and linked his arm with Laila's, supporting her. "Are you sure?" He watched Jesus as he spoke. "Scripture speaks of a suffering shepherd, a healer who takes our illnesses upon Himself. How can He be a destroyer?"

Simon shook Sarai and turned her so she couldn't look at Jesus, only at him. "Jesus of Nazareth is not the Messiah. He is going to die and there is nothing you can do about it."

"But you can." Somehow, she coerced her bitten lips into a smile. "Simon, please, if you ever loved me --"

"Enough! You are going home. Now!"

He shifted his hold to a bruising grip that threatened to crack the bones in her wrist and hurried her away. Pain kept her silent. She looked back once, to see Laila and Nicodemus struggling to catch up with them. Then they vanished into the crowd. A few more steps, and Simon had dragged her out of the plaza.

~~~~~

Sarai stayed in her room with the door closed. She alternately wept and stared into the darkness. Simon had said nothing to her the entire long, bruising walk to their home. He opened the door and stopped just short of shoving her through.

"You will be here when I return."

He gave her no threats, no ultimatum, but Sarai heard them in his rasping voice, read them in his angry, weary, shadowed eyes.

If she was not home when he returned, she would be wise never to return.

How had they come to this point? Her father had taught her to think, to choose what she knew to be right, to never listen to the anger and threats and fears of the mob. Even after her father had been ostracized, Sarai had held onto the conviction that El Shaddai blessed those who held fast to the truth and obeyed the laws of the Creator, rather than mere men.

She sat on her bed and thought, dozed, woke to think some more, and dissolved into tears. The tears grew fewer as the morning grew older. When she imagined Jesus walking the torturous, winding streets to the gate out of the city, to the execution hill, she could no longer cry. A haze filled her mind. Sarai had eaten nothing, drank no water, since the evening before. She didn't care.

Darkness covered the land in the middle of the day, plunging her room into darkness. Sarai dug her fingers into the blankets and prayed. When the earthquake struck, she waited for the roof to fall in on her. The shaking stopped. The storm faded. Silence reigned across the city.

The silence was the worst part of the waiting.

~~~~~

Deborah and Saul moved about the house, repairing what little damage there had been from the earthquake. Late in the afternoon, Deborah brought Sarai food and told her that Hannah was all right. She had been exhausted from worrying about Sarai and had slept through the quake. Sarai quietly thanked her for the food, then ignored it when the woman left the room.

The main door opened. Sarai moved stiffly, aching all over from spending the entire day sitting still, every muscle clenched, on her bed. Despite that, she reached the central room of the house before Simon finished closing the door behind himself. At the edge of her vision, Sarai saw Saul start to enter the room. The manservant's gaze met hers. He retreated.

Simon tried to smile, but weariness made his face stiff under the mask of sweat and smeared dirt. His clothes looked like he had been soaked, and then he had rolled through mud and over rocks. His fine clothes, made new for Passover, were torn. Sarai doubted he would ever wear them again. Simon was too careful of appearances nowadays, and too well off now to wear mended clothes. She found she missed the man who wore his clothes until they were nearly transparent.

"Sarai." He sighed, and the corners of his mouth managed to turn up a little more. "I'm glad you're safe."

Something cracked deep inside her, letting out the fears and anger and hurt, the longing for the sweetness they had shared in what felt like another lifetime. Sarai blinked against the tears that wanted to escape her eyes and her voice. If she let them come, she would fall down sobbing.

"There was an earthquake. I was worried."

"Nothing to be worried about. As you can see, I am unhurt." He spread his arms and looked down at himself. Simon frowned, as if he hadn't really seen the condition he was in until that moment.

"Is it over?"

"Thank Yahweh, yes, it's over. Jesus of Nazareth is dead. Now we can go on with our lives."

A silent wail filled Sarai's head. Anything else she could have taken, but the utter relief in Simon's voice hurt worse than if he had screamed fury, or laughed in triumph and venom. It reduced Jesus to a mere nuisance to be dismissed.

"How can you say that?" she whispered.

"Because it is the truth. He is dead. Gone. Life can go back to normal. You should be grateful that your foolishness has not harmed my future in the Sanhedrin."

"Foolishness? To believe that Adonai has fulfilled His promises to send the Messiah?"

"Jesus is dead. How can you still believe in Him?"

"I believe." Wellsprings of energy burst open inside her. "I will believe until my dying day. Nothing anyone can do will stop me from believing Jesus is the Messiah."

"I am your husband and you must obey me." The very reasonableness of Simon's voice chilled her. "You will renounce what you have said. Now."

"No, Simon."

"You will obey me!" His voice cracked, rising several steps in pitch.

"What is better, Simon?" Sarai heard echoes of her father, speaking to his students. "To obey God, or to obey mere men? Even if that man is my husband, whom I still love despite his blindness?"

"Sarai, I warn you. Say right now that Jesus is not the Messiah or --" He stopped, choking, and blanched for a moment before fury washed red over his face again.

Or what? She did not speak, but the air seemed to hum as if echoing the words.

"Or I will cast you out. You will not be my wife. Renounce your declaration. Renounce this ridiculous faith in Jesus."

Sarai looked at Simon and remembered that day in the slave market. She had believed then that Simon came to watch her humiliation, in revenge. Had she seen the true man that day, after all? Perhaps she had been the fool for believing his claims of love.

She didn't tremble, didn't feel cold with fear or hot with shame. Sarai nodded, accepting his decree. She had been warned, hadn't she? Her own words had warned her. The day Simon scolded her for bringing Laila into his house -- never hers -- Sarai had spoken of being cast out and forced to take up the life of a harlot after all.

Turning her back to Simon, she crossed the room. There was still a little daylight left. Enough to make her way to Norah's home. Her friend would take her in. Perhaps she would go with her to Damascus. Sarai thought she could be very good at helping to run an inn.

"Say it." Simon's voice cracked. "Sarai, say it right now!"

He crossed the room in three long strides, caught hold of her arm and slapped her hard across the face with the other hand. Sarai went to her knees. Her face ached, as if the bones had shattered, then went numb. She stayed on her knees, quietly wondering why her nose wasn't broken and bleeding. Why she didn't weep.

"A man must rule in his own home," Simon declared between gasps, "if he wants to rule in Israel. You will deny your belief in Jesus now, Sarai, or I will divorce you."

Then divorce me and set me free. I will never deny Jesus. I will never turn my back on what my father taught me. I will never turn my back on what is right.

She couldn't force her numb lips to say the words, but they rang in her heart. Sarai turned her face away from Simon, struggled to her feet, then continued out of the room.

"This is your last chance, Sarai. If you ever loved me, you will obey me!"

Those words stopped her. She turned in the doorway and saw that he had opened the door to his study room. It would be a matter of moments for Simon to find pen and ink and write her certificate of divorce.

"I will always love you, Simon, but I must love God more, no matter what it cost me." Sarai raised a hand and touched her swollen lips with one fingertip. "If Adonai loves the world enough to sacrifice His own Son, how can I love anyone more than Him?"

"Saul! Deborah! Hannah!"

Sarai turned and went to her room. Her first thought was to gather up the papyrus sheets where she had written down the things she had heard Jesus teach. Even if she left everything else behind, she could not leave those words.

She took no jewelry. Those gifts had not come from the man who had rescued her. She packed only her oldest clothes, her plainest veils, her sturdiest sandals. Everything else was still new enough they could be remade for Hannah. At least her flute was hers -- or was it? Simon had made it for her, back when he had been her father's student. Would he claim it, take it from her? She knew what the Law granted a woman when her husband cast her out. She would give Simon no opportunity to accuse her of thievery.

Her music had given her comfort the last time she had been reduced to nothing. Should she hide the flute inside her clothes and pray he wouldn't search her? Yet would she be able to play it again? How could she make music with such pain and all the memories tied to the flute?

Hand shaking, she put the flute back on the table beside her bed. Simon hadn't asked her to play the flute for him in months. She suspected that playing it in the days and months to come would be more painful than not having the flute. She could find another, have someone make one for her, if she could find music inside herself in the future.

The little apple-shaped box sat on the edge of the table. The stain had faded in spots, from much handling. Sarai held it in her hand one last time, wanting to take it with her, yet knowing that seeing it would churn up memories that would shred her heart. She put it down next to the flute. What had happened to the man who could create so skillfully and found beauty in simple things?

She had thought she wanted death, in those hot, dusty days before the slave market. Sarai knew there were worse torments than rape and enslavement, now. What Simon had done to himself, what he tried to do to her heart and soul, was far worse.

Hannah wept quietly, sitting in a chair to Simon's right, when Sarai returned to the main room. Saul and Deborah stood behind Simon. Deborah looked stunned, wringing her hands until Sarai thought she would wear off the skin. Saul stared at her when she stepped through the door, shock making his eyes huge.

"You are all witnesses." Simon held out a rolled sheet of papyrus.

His hand shook. Sarai's hand didn't shake when she took it from him.

"Sarai."

He swallowed hard, audibly. His eyes gleamed with the threat of tears and begged her to reconsider, to love him.

If she stayed, would Simon eventually change his mind and acknowledge Jesus was the Messiah?

Sarai held still, her thoughts spinning. Did she dare hope? While she hesitated, she glimpsed, just for a moment, the eager, idealistic, hard-working man she had adored.

Several heartbeats passed in silence. Simon's mouth flattened into a bitter line. Simply because she did not respond as quickly as he wanted? She shuddered at the conviction that if she turned back now, all her life would revolve around what Simon wanted, what made him happy. While that seemed to be obedient to the Law and to Yahweh, at the core of it such behavior, such a mindset, did not reflect what was right and true before Adonai.

Simon stepped back from her and turned his face away.

"I divorce you. I divorce you. I divorce you," he spat, following the required ritual. "Saul. Deborah. You are witnesses. Sarai, daughter of Eliakim, is no longer your mistress or my wife."

"But, Master --" Saul began.

"Obey me!" Simon gestured for them all to leave.

Hannah struggled up from her chair, head bowed. A few hiccupping sobs escaped her.

"No." The small woman flung her arms around Sarai, holding her so tightly all her trembling vanished. "Please, don't leave me. You must stay. How can I have this baby without you? You are my first, true friend."

"Hannah. My dear sister." The tears burned, pressing so hard at the backs of Sarai's eyes, her head ached.

She choked for a moment on the need to scream, to spill the aching that clawed upwards from her belly. The sorrow she felt for Hannah, the guilt and sense that she was betraying her stole her breath and gave her different words. She couldn't slash at Simon if Hannah would be hurt.

"You are Simon's wife, the mother of his heir. You are strong and you are wise, and you are a good wife, a good woman."

She hugged Hannah tightly, then gently grasped her shoulders and pushed her away to arm's length. "You will be a good mother, and you will need help from no one. I am not the kind of wife Simon needs if he is to rise to prominence in the Sanhedrin."

A choked sound escaped Simon.

"It is best for all that he has cast me out. Now, there will be peace in this household."

"Sarai…" Hannah sniffled a few times. Her lower lip trembled. Then with a wail, the tears returned. She bowed her head and fled the room.

"You could have poisoned her against me," Simon said.

"I don't hate Hannah. Why would I sow seeds of discord in this household, to hurt her?" Sarai tucked the scroll of her divorce into her belt and bent to pick up the two small sacks containing everything she had dared bring with her.

She was many times better off than the last time she had been torn from her home.

"You may take a few things for the sake of the happiness you gave me, for your kindness toward this house even now. What will you have?"

Sarai bit back her first response, scorning his offer. Did it make him feel righteous and charitable? Who was he to offer her a reward, a gift of any kind, after he had turned his back on the truth?

"I want the coat you wore when you bought me in the Decapolis," Sarai said, after a moment of thought.

"It is old and faded. I should have given it to the beggars long ago."

"No. It is beautiful. The coat of a man who had nothing, and yet was rich because he loved and believed and hoped. A man who didn't care what people thought of him, because he valued truth."

Simon said nothing and she didn't look back as she left the room. Sarai went to the baskets containing the old, discarded clothes of the household. When she found the coat, she left without speaking to anyone.

END

About the Author

On the road to publication, Michelle fell into fandom in college and has 40+ stories in various SF and fantasy universes. She has a bunch of useless degrees in theater, English, film/communication, and writing. Even worse, she has over 100 books and novellas with multiple small presses, in science fiction and fantasy, YA, suspense, women's fiction, and sub-genres of romance.

Her official launch into publishing came with winning first place in the Writers of the Future contest in 1990. She was a finalist in the EPIC Awards competition multiple times, winning with *Lorien* in 2006 and *The Meruk Episodes, I-V*, in 2010, and was a finalist in the Realm Award competition, in conjunction with the Realm Makers convention.

Her training includes the Institute for Children's Literature; proofreading at an advertising agency; and working at a community newspaper. She is a tea snob and freelance edits for a living (MichelleLevigne@gmail.com for info/rates), but only enough to give her time to write. Her newest crime against the literary world is to be co-managing editor at Mt. Zion Ridge Press. Be afraid ... be very afraid.

www.Mlevigne.com
www.MichelleLevigne.blogspot.com
@MichelleLevigne

Also by Michelle L. Levigne

Guardians of the Time Stream: 4-book Steampunk series
The Match Girls: Humorous inspirational romance series starting in 2020 with **A Match (Not) Made in Heaven**

Tabor Heights: 20-book inspirational small-town romance series.

Quarry Hall: 11-book women's fiction/suspense series

For Sale: Wedding Dress. Never Used: inspirational romance

Crooked Creek: Fun Fables About Critters and Kids: Children's short stories.

Do Yourself a Favor: Tips and Quips on the Writing Life. A book of writing advice.

Killing His Alter-Ego: contemporary romance/suspense, taking place in fandom.

The Commonwealth Universe: SF series, 25 books and growing

The Hunt: 5-book YA fantasy series

Faxinor: Fantasy series, 4 books and growing

Wildvine: Fantasy series, 14 books when all released

Neighborlee: Humorous fantasy series; re-releasing in 2020; 8 books and growing.

Zygradon: 5-book Arthurian fantasy series